DELL BOOKS BY BELVA PLAIN

Crossroads
The Sight of the Stars
Her Father's House
Looking Back
After the Fire
Fortune's Hand
Legacy of Silence
Homecoming
Secrecy
Promises
The Carousel
Daybreak
Whispers
Treasures
Harvest
Blessings
Tapestry
The Golden Cup
Crescent City
Eden Burning
Random Winds
Evergreen

HEARTWOOD

BELVA PLAIN

HEARTWOOD

A Novel

DOUBLEDAY LARGE PRINT
HOME LIBRARY EDITION

DELACORTE PRESS | NEW YORK

Published in the United States by Delacorte Press, an imprint of
The Random House Publishing Group, a division of Random House, Inc., New York.

DELACORTE PRESS is a registered trademark of Random House, Inc., and the colophon is a trademark of Random House, Inc.

ISBN 978-1-61129-210-7

Printed in the United States of America

This Large Print Book carries the Seal of Approval of N.A.V.H.

HEARTWOOD

GATHERING

The family is the country of the heart.

GIUSEPPE MAZZINI
1805–1872

Chapter One

Iris Stern turned her car into the parking lot in front of the supermarket and sighed; there wasn't an empty place to be found. Of course not. It was three days before Thanksgiving! What was worse, she was going to be back here all over again tomorrow when she came to pick up the fresh turkey the supermarket was holding for her. She'd have to get up at the crack of dawn to make it ahead of the crowd.

A more organized woman would not have found herself in this predicament. For instance, Iris's daughter, Laura, would have been shopping and cooking and freezing side dishes for weeks. "You make the holiday so hard for yourself," Laura told her once, "doing it all at the last minute."

Iris had tried to explain that she couldn't make herself think about sweet potato casseroles and cranberry sauce when her mind was still full of the classes she was teaching at her college. She was a professor with a full course load, and she wanted to have all the exams graded, all the lectures given, and all the office appointments cleared from her calendar; then she could focus on sweet potatoes.

"But you need to learn to compartmentalize," Laura said. "It's simple." And for Laura it was.

It certainly had been for Iris's mother, Anna. Even today seven years after Mama's death—she'd died in 1972—Iris could still remember the ease with which Anna had run her home and family while devoting hours to her charities, and somehow always managing to look as if she'd just stepped out of a bandbox. There had been a time when Iris had compared herself to her mother and had felt woefully inadequate. And if she was honest about it, she still did a little, but not nearly as much as she once had, because she'd finally gathered up her courage and gone to graduate school to earn her PhD. Her degree was in special education—she'd always been a gifted teacher—and now she trained young people who were planning to go into the field themselves. To her surprise and delight, she'd become one of the most popular professors on her campus, and this success had made it easier to remember her mother's formidable skills as a cook and hostess. Skills that Laura, who looked exactly like Anna, had inherited.

If it hadn't been for Laura, Iris would not be racing back to the supermarket tomorrow for that fresh turkey. "We can't serve one that's been frozen, Mom!" Laura had protested, making it sound as if Iris had proposed feeding the family fast food from a hamburger place. Since Laura would be flying in from her home in Southern California the following evening and doing most of the cooking for the holiday meal, Iris had bowed to the voice of authority and ordered the unfrozen bird. Today she was shopping for the rest of the items on a list that Laura had dictated to her over the phone.

If she could ever manage to find a parking space! She'd already reached the end of the first row of parked cars with no luck. She made a careful turn around a blue station wagon that was sticking out slightly in the line of traffic and started down the next row at a snail's pace. Thank goodness she had plenty of time today.

Thanksgiving was Iris's favorite holiday; there was something so . . . undemanding about it. There were no presents to be bought and wrapped and then opened with false exclamations that this was exactly what you had wanted. There were no tiny candles to be blown out as you tried to smile about the creeping passage of time. And there were none of the more complicated feelings Iris sometimes had during the traditional Jewish holidays. Holidays that Iris's husband, Theo, refused to hold in their home. Theo had been born into a prominent Jewish family in Austria in the 1900s, and he had lost everyone, including his young wife and child, in the Holocaust. It had been more than three decades since those horrors, but he still could not forgive the God who had allowed such things to happen.

So it was Iris's second son, Jimmy, who, with his wife, Janet, did the honors for the Sterns on Rosh Hashanah, Yom Kippur, Hannukah and Passover. Theo did go with Iris to Jimmy and Janet's home to celebrate these holidays, as he had gone to her parents' house before Anna and Joseph died, and Iris had always told herself she was content with that; marriage was a series of compromises after all. And Janet did the holidays efficiently and smoothly, as she did everything. But lately Iris had started to feel . . . a little . . . well, "cheated" was probably the right word.

She remembered her mother on the holidays. Anna had presided over tables that groaned with the food she had cooked; the pot roasts with rich dark gravy, and crisp potato pancakes, the stuffed fish in silky jelly, carrots sweet with prunes, and apple strudels wrapped in crisp buttery crusts and running with cinnamon-flavored juices. On the holidays Mama's table had gleamed with the fine china, sparkling silverware, and crystal that had been bought for just such occasions. The grandest of grand occasions, because they were for the family.

Of course Iris would never manage that level of splendor, she knew that. But there were times when she thought perhaps she would like to create her own traditions. And perhaps her grandchildren would remember them fondly. She was in her fifties, with sixty looming, a middle-aged woman, although that was a misnomer because how many people lived to be a hundred and twenty? She had two grandchildren already, and hopefully there would be more. Suddenly it seemed very important that they have fond memories of her. Funny, how you woke up one day and wanted immortality when you never had it before.

But her feelings went deeper than that. Her religion, and the holidays that were such an integral part of it, had always been precious to her. She was like her father in that way. She could still see how his eyes would shine when he watched Mama bless the holiday candles on the first night of Passover. That moment was the best time of the year for him. It had been that way even during the Depression when they had to scrimp to get by—although Papa had been happier when Mama presided over their Seder table wearing the huge diamond ring he'd bought for her. He'd had to pawn it when they were broke, but when his fortunes had finally turned, the first thing he'd done was redeem it. When Passover came that year and the ring was once again sparkling on Mama's hand as she served food and poured wine, Iris knew that had been the proudest day of her father's life.

That was what the holidays were truly made of, little scraps of memory like that one. Some of them were purely joyful, some were more somber if there had been pain and loss during the year, but when you put them all together, over time they became the story of a family.

And on the holy holidays your personal story was then added to the bigger one of your people that stretched back for four thousand years. It was a story that children absorbed without even knowing they were doing it, especially if it was told with humor and love over food cooked from old family recipes. Sometimes Iris felt that Janet's efficient gatherings, catered and served by professionals, were rather bloodless. Or maybe she was jealous.

And if you are, that's just plain foolish, she told herself sternly. *Theo has made his wishes clear and you won't go against him. That's the marriage you have. Stop wasting your time thinking about all of this.*

Besides, the holiday ahead of her was not Rosh Hashanah or Passover. It was Thanksgiving. Cozy Thanksgiving, when the weather was just cold enough and the days were just dark enough to make it a pleasure to be indoors. Thanksgiving, that most American—and neutral—of all holidays. Theo loved it even more than Iris did and happily celebrated it in his home each year. And this year they were going to be even happier than usual because all of their children would be together under their roof for the first time in years. Given how busy and scattered the kids were it was nothing short of a miracle.

Iris spotted a parking place at the far end of the lot, and headed toward it. But at the last second, a white van slipped into it ahead of her. She resisted the temptation to pound on her horn and continued her slow round of the parking lot.

Of course Janet and Jimmy were coming for Thanksgiving; they lived in Manhattan, which was a forty-five-minute car ride away from Iris and Theo's home in the suburbs, and they and their little daughter, Rebecca Ruth, always celebrated Thanksgiving with Nannie and Grampy. Iris shook her head. Could there be a worse nickname for regal, old-world Theo? When Jimmy's wife had first suggested that Rachel call him Grampy, he had actually winced. But Janet hadn't noticed. Janet was the salt of the earth; not only was she a successful doctor—an anesthesiologist—she was a fine mother and a conscientious daughter-in-law. But Iris couldn't help feeling that she was a little . . . stolid.

"What does Janet laugh at?" Iris had once asked Laura. She and her daughter talked on the phone every week, and Iris enjoyed the calls thoroughly. "I don't think she has much of a sense of humor. Otherwise she'd understand how funny it is to watch poor Theo trying to answer to 'Grampy.'"

"I know," Laura had said. "But Jimmy doesn't have a sense of humor either. So they're well matched."

"Do you really think so? Because sometimes I wonder, you know. Janet is so certain about everything, and Jimmy has never been a fighter . . ."

"What on earth would he have to fight about? He and Janet are practically the same person." In her mind's eye, Iris could see Laura on the other end of the phone ticking off her points on her fingers. "They're both doctors, and they love to talk shop. They both agree they only want one child. They both adore living in Manhattan, and they're both passionate about the opera. They're perfect for each other. Even you can't worry about them."

After that Iris hadn't—at least, she hadn't worried as much. Laura could always do that for her.

A large delivery truck cut in front of Iris, forcing her to stop. She looked in her rearview mirror and saw that she couldn't back up because the cars were lined behind her. There was nothing to do but wait for the men, sweating in the cold, to unload their cargo onto the loading dock of the supermarket.

Once again, Iris went back to her thoughts. *I wish just for a moment I could get inside my children's minds. So I'd be sure that they are all right. But do we ever know that about anyone we love? Especially our children. Those little creatures we held and rocked and fed, grow up to be full of surprises.*

That was certainly true of her oldest son, Steven, arguably the most brilliant of her children. Throughout his teens and early twenties, he had been a rebel, sullen, and bearded, with long hair that was seldom clean—the uniform of his time, although he would have been furious at anyone who suggested that. He had been passionately opposed to the Vietnam War, which Iris had thought was understandable and perhaps even laudable, although it had infuriated Theo.

But then Steven had taken his politics too far, even for Iris. He'd dropped out of college and joined a radical group that "protested" in ways that were downright terrifying. Iris shuddered, remembering the torment of those years when she'd been afraid to look at the evening news, because the young face suffused with rage and screaming obscenities as its owner was taken off to jail might be her son's. Eventually Steven had been arrested, nearly breaking his father's heart and causing a schism in his parents' marriage. Or, to be more honest, he had widened one that had already been there. This had led to an accident that had cost Theo, a plastic surgeon, the use of his hand, and his career, and . . . Iris stopped herself. She never let herself think about the days and months after Theo's accident.

It had been a dark, bleak time, but

they had weathered it. With an amazing effort of courage and will, Theo had re-trained himself in a new medical disci-pline, and become an oncologist. And she had become Professor Iris Stern. Together they had discovered the gift of forgiveness and their marriage had en-dured. Enough said.

And Steven? Iris felt a smile creep over her face. Her son, the rebel, who had once wanted to tear up the Consti-tution, was now . . . a lawyer. "We have to change the system from within," he'd told his bemused parents. He'd had this epiphany after the worst of his rebellion was ended and he was work-ing as a researcher for a liberal think tank in Washington, DC. Finding the ivory tower atmosphere too limiting, he'd gotten his law degree—in record time, Iris thought proudly—and he'd gone to work for a not-for-profit legal firm called People's Prosperity. They only represented clients who were des-perate and unable to pay for their ser-vices, so Steve still hadn't sold out to The Man, but—as his sister, Laura, pointed out—he *was* wearing a shirt and tie every day. And he seemed happy with his life at last.

"At least, I hope he's happy," Iris had said to Laura six months earlier during their weekly phone call.

"I think he's lonely," Laura had said.

"There's plenty of time for him to meet someone. There's no hurry about that."

There had been a pause on the other end of the line. "Actually he has met someone, Mom," Laura said. "Her name is Christina. He told me about her."

And not for the first time, Iris had been aware of how much everyone in the family confided in Laura. Laura never judged, and she never gave her opinion unless asked, but her advice was usually sound. Anna had been like that. In the worst of times she could get through to the Stern kids when their frantic parents couldn't. Lucky Mama, who had been not only beautiful and charming, but wise. Lucky Laura, who was so like her.

"Steve never said a word to us," Iris had said, trying not to sound hurt.

"I know. He asked me to smooth the way for him first. Bringing a girl home to meet his parents isn't easy for a son."

"He wants us to meet her? So soon?"

"It's been going on for a few months now, Mom. Just try to keep an open mind."

"I always do, you know that."

But she and Theo hadn't liked Christina. They'd tried, but they couldn't. The girl hadn't been in her home more than ten minutes before Iris realized it.

"From what I can tell she barely finished high school," Iris reported to Laura after the disastrous visit had ended. "You know I'm not a snob, I don't believe that everyone has to have a college education. Look at my own parents, Mama worked as a maid when she first came to this country and Papa was a housepainter ... But this girl Christina ... I don't think she's ever read a book or a newspaper. She certainly isn't interested in politics or the law or any of the causes that drive Steve. I can't imagine what they find to talk about!" Then Iris had blurted out, to her shame, "She's not even pretty!"

"Oh, Mom! I hope you didn't . . ."

"Don't worry, I was very nice to her. Although I doubt she would have noticed if I wasn't. She was too busy trying to figure out how much things in the house had cost."

"Maybe she was just nervous."

"She couldn't take her eyes off your Nana's silver candlesticks. And it was her opinion that I could get over twenty thousand dollars for that ring Papa gave Mama."

Even nonjudgmental Laura didn't have an answer for that. "Did Daddy behave himself?" she asked.

"Your father is a gentleman."

"In other words, he was aristocratic and Viennese. And icy."

"I'm sure she didn't pick up on it."

"I hope Steve didn't."

"He's too besotted with her to see anything else. What can he be thinking of ? He must know they have nothing in common. When I think of all the pretty, smart girls he could have had . . ."

"But that's not Steve. He wants a girl he can rescue. And Christina was one of his clients—wasn't she?"

"Oh yes, she told us all about it. She was overcharged by her landlord and she was evicted and Steve won her case for her. Of course, now she doesn't have to worry about where she's going to live because she's moving in with him."

"That is quick."

"Do you know what she told us when she was here? Steve makes her feel like Cinderella because no one has ever taken care of her before. Why would a grown woman want to feel like the heroine of a silly fairy tale? But Steve just sat there smiling and listening to her. I couldn't believe it."

"Mom, promise me that you won't say anything like that to him. He's in love with her."

"He can't be."

"He says he is. And he means it."

"She's using him. Someone has to make him see that."

"When has anyone ever been able to make Steve see anything—if he doesn't want to?" Laura paused. "And if you try to talk him out of this . . . you know what Steve is like."

Iris did know. She'd learned the hard way that when her brilliant, passionate son felt he had to do something that was foolhardy, or even dangerous, trying to reason with him just made it worse.

"After all we've been through with him . . . now this . . ."

"Don't start thinking that way, and don't let Daddy get started either. This is nothing in comparison to what Steve did during Vietnam—he's come a long way. Besides, what if Christina really is the right one for him?"

Iris had wanted to cry. "He deserves so much better."

"Maybe she's better than you think. Give her a second chance. I don't think you have any other choice."

Iris had tried. In the months since that phone call, she had not said one word of criticism against Steve's girlfriend. She had even invited Christina to come for Thanksgiving.

"But Steve says she can't make it," Iris reported to Laura. "And I'm not going to lie, I'm glad."

"I'm sorry this relationship of his is so hard for you."

"It's just . . ." Iris could hear her own voice cracking. "I thought I didn't have to worry about him anymore."

But even as she said the words she knew how ridiculous they were. You always had to worry about those you loved, because human beings couldn't stay safely in one place. They changed and they grew and they moved on, that was a part of life and you couldn't stop it. Even if you were convinced that they were headed in the wrong direction, like Steve. Or like her youngest son, Philip.

Up ahead, the sweating men having finally finished unloading the truck, they climbed back into the front seat and began inching forward. Iris followed them, her mind now switched over from her firstborn to the last of her children.

Philip wasn't making an overt mistake like Steven was with Christina. What was going on with him was more subtle than that. And more unexpected. That was what made it so hard; because when Philip was growing up, she'd never had a moment's anxiety over him.

He'd been her surprise baby who had come to her after she'd thought her childbearing days were finished, and from the beginning he'd been easygoing and affectionate. And talented. From the age of five, Philip had been something of a piano prodigy.

His grandfather Joseph had been especially thrilled by this. "You can't tell where genius will come from," he'd say when Philip had finished playing a Chopin étude for the family. "His grandmother and I aren't at all musical. Iris, you had talent, but forgive me if I say that even you were not in the same class as our little Philip." And Iris would agree that her son had surpassed her, and Joseph would go on to predict a great career for the boy. "Yes, yes, yes, I know what the odds are against making a success in classical music," he'd say as Theo and Iris tried to restrain him. "But someone has to play at Carnegie Hall, and why shouldn't it be my grandson?" And in spite of themselves, Iris and Theo would let themselves dream a little too.

They were careful to keep these

dreams from Philip, and not to push him in any way, but they might as well have saved themselves the effort. The boy knew what his family was hoping for. And even though Joseph had died by the time Philip entered the Juilliard School of Music, Iris knew that when he walked into his first class Philip was re-membering the old man who had had such faith in him. That was why it was so awful when two years later he said he was quitting. "I've seen real genius now," he told his parents. "I've heard it in other students. I know I'm not good enough to be one of the best, and I'm not humble enough to be content with second best."

And so he had left Juilliard and gone to business school. "After all, most mu-sicians are good at math," he'd told Iris with a sad little grin that broke her heart. Then he'd become a trader on Wall Street, working his charm and winning personality on his clients, and doing rather well.

"But look at the way he lives," Iris said to Laura. "Always running around. And all the money he makes, doesn't he have enough? He's never home . . . if he isn't working he's going out every night to restaurants and nightclubs with those so-called friends who drink too much . . . and do worse things. And he's with a new girl every week."

For once, Laura didn't try to soothe her. "He's still mourning for his music," she said. "He loved it so much, and I don't think he enjoys what he's doing now. But he's not ready to face that yet. We just have to wait until he can."

"I wish he'd come home for Thanksgiving instead of running off to some overpriced resort."

"Yes. That might be good for him," Laura had said thoughtfully.

Iris had thought that was the end of it. But a few days later Philip had called to say he was coming home for Thanksgiving. Iris had been sure Laura was behind it. It was the kind of thing she would do. It was the kind of thing Anna would have done.

It was shortly after Laura had engineered Philip's new Thanksgiving plans that something occurred to Iris.

"Every time I talk to you, I'm going on

about one of my other children," she said to Laura the next time she called. "You are all right, aren't you? I know money is tight for you and Robby." Laura's husband, Robby, was a graduate student working on his PhD in archaeology. He earned a small salary as assistant to his faculty advisor, teaching two of the man's undergraduate courses and doing research for him.

"Of course money is tight for us," Laura had answered cheerfully. "But we never expected to have much, with Robby in academia. You know that."

"But Katie's getting older, it can't be easy." Katie was Laura's nine-year-old daughter.

"Katie is fine. We all are. Don't forget we have a terrific deal on our rent, because Robby qualifies for faculty housing, and I bring in a little extra doing some baking for that caterer I've told you about. Please don't start fretting about me, Mom."

Iris felt herself sigh with relief. The truth was, she counted on Laura to be her carefree, happy child. "Your Nana always used to say about you, 'You'll

never have to worry about that one,'"
she said. "And she was right. You do
everything so beautifully . . . I just . . .
well, I admire you, Laura. I'm not sure
too many mothers can say that to their
daughters."

*Mine never could have said it about
me,* she added silently.

And Laura, who always seemed to
hear the things that weren't said, had reassured her. "We'll make this the best
Thanksgiving ever, Mom."

Her sons might have their problems,
but Laura truly seemed to have everything under control. Beautiful, loving
Laura.

Iris looked ahead. A red car was
pulling out directly in front of her. The
parking spot was hers! Triumphant, she
turned into it.

Chapter Two

✻❧❦✻

The springform cake pan was too bulky to fit into the overnight bag Laura had filled with cooking utensils. "Why do you have to lug that thing all the way across the country?" Robby had demanded when he saw her wrapping it up to keep it from getting dented. "Doesn't your mother have pots and pans of her own?"

Of course her mom did have pots and pans, and other basic tools for getting a meal on the table. But a gourmet cook like Laura required special equipment.

"She doesn't have a springform pan," Laurie said patiently. "I need one to make my chestnut torte." The torte, which was filled with Laura's special chocolate buttercream, was her most recent re-creation of a classic Viennese dessert. When Laura was a child she'd learned to bake old-fashioned European treats with Nana. A few years ago, when she and Robby had needed the extra cash, she'd begun baking her Americanized versions of the traditional baked goods for a local caterer. This season, her chestnut torte had become a fad with the caterer's clients; it seemed as if half the San Fernando Valley wanted to serve it for Thanksgiving and Laura had been baking around the clock.

Robby had complained about that. "You don't have time to cook dinner for Katie and me, you're so busy making those damn cakes," he'd said.

"It's going slowly because I have a regular stove, not a professional one. So I can only make one cake at a time," she'd said, and given him a quick smile. "Why don't you take Katie out to Martin's Drive Thru tonight?"

But Robby had stayed home, and he

and Katie had eaten cold cereal for dinner. Laura had felt guilty and it had been hard to keep herself from thinking that Robby wanted her to feel that way.

The truth was, she could have done her baking in the large professional stove in the kitchen at the catering company, because the woman who owned it had offered her a full-time job. But Laura's salary would have been higher than her husband's. She knew that there were many women who would say she was being ridiculous to let that stop her; this was 1979, not 1950 after all. She admitted to herself that a steady paycheck would be nice, and yes, sometimes she thought it might feel good to have an actual job instead of being treated like a little housewife who was earning her pin money with her cute baking hobby. But none of that would matter if Robby felt threatened.

Laura wanted a perfect marriage. She knew such a thing was possible because she'd watched one when she was young. It hadn't been her parents' marriage, that relationship had always had deep problems for all the love that was there. No, it was her grandparents Laura wanted to emulate. Specifically her grandmother. Even as a child, Laura had understood why Nana had such a happy home. Anna Friedman was smarter and stronger than her husband, but she had never let him know it. On the contrary, she had always made him feel like a king. In return, he had rewarded her with undying love and devotion.

Her grandmother's methods had seemed so simple, until Laura tried to use them in her own marriage. She had learned fast that there were dozens of ways to undermine a man's confidence without meaning to. Taking the well-paid job with the catering company would have done it, so that was out of the question.

Still, she was grateful for the money she earned from her baking. The extra income meant she could pay for things like the airplane tickets for the trip east to her parents' home for Thanksgiving without dipping into the small savings account she'd been putting aside for a rainy day. And she couldn't help being proud of the success of her torte. She really wanted to bake one for her family at Thanksgiving.

"I don't see why you're bothering," Robby said. "Your brothers will eat anything, your mother really doesn't appreciate food all that much, and the only sweet your father likes is apple strudel." It was his petulant tone that got to her. She'd looked at him, and it was as if she was really seeing him for the first time in quite a while.

Robby wasn't at his best these days. His jaw, which had once been so sharply etched, was beginning to blur, and the waistline he'd once been so proud of was starting to thicken. Perhaps he shouldn't spend quite so much time hanging out with his students at their favorite beer joint. But it was the sullen, closed-off expression in his eyes that really got her attention. She knew what that look meant; Robby was going to be difficult about taking this trip. He was going to find fault with everything she'd done: the way she'd packed their suitcases, the time of their departure, and the five dollars she was paying their neighbor's son to drive them to the airport the next day. She braced herself for a barrage of complaints that would last until they were finally on the plane, taking off.

But Robby had something else in mind. "I've been thinking," he said. "I'm not sure I'm going with you tomorrow." This wasn't his normal nagging. Was he really going to stay home? "It seems like such a waste of time," he went on. "We'll only have four days there and then we have to turn around and come home because I have to teach on Monday and Katie has to be back in school."

"But you've known this for a long time, Robby. The plans have been made for months."

"I told you, I've just been thinking about it for the last few days. I've had other things on my mind, things that are a little bit more important than holidays and vacations. Not that this will be a vacation for me. We'll be flying on one of the worst travel days of the year and you know how I feel about all those crowds and the craziness. I'll be beat when I come home and then I'll have to go right back to work."

This was serious; he'd already talked himself into feeling like a martyr. She'd have to handle him very carefully. "The tickets are already bought," she said.

"You and Katie can go. You can get a refund for me. You're always worrying about money anyway."

For a moment she let herself think about being back home without him. She could stand on her parents' porch and breathe in the winter air—she missed the change of seasons so much here in Southern California—without having to hear Robby complain that it was too cold. She could go into Manhattan to window-shop without Robby at her side demanding that they leave because he couldn't stand the noise and the dirt. Why not take him at his word and let him stay home?

But she couldn't do that. Her parents were looking forward to having a big dinner with the whole family. If Robby wasn't there, they'd wonder why and they'd worry. Laura didn't want anything to spoil the day for them.

"You know how my folks love having the whole family together. And Dad loves Thanksgiving . . ."

"It's a hyped-up commercial travesty, and you know it."

It was fashionable in their circle to say things like that, but suddenly, Laura realized that she didn't believe it. She pictured her parents on Thanksgiving Day after the meal was set out on the dining room table, and everyone was seated. Mom would be glowing, although there would be something tentative in her eyes, because Mom never could trust her happiness. But there would be no such shadow in Dad's smile. He would look around the table at his handsome children, their spouses and children, and his eyes would shine with the joy of a man who had built a life for himself on the ashes of despair. His love of this country that had taken him in was not a hyped-up travesty.

"I don't mean to be corny, but my dad knows in a way that you and I never will what it means to be an American. That's why he loves to celebrate Thanksgiving. It isn't just about the food or Macy's parade for him. He really does give thanks, you know?" The sullen, closed-off look left Robby's eyes. For a moment he was the Robby she had loved and married— the sensitive boy who knew what she was thinking before she did. "Please come with me," she went on. "Dad and Mom are looking forward to seeing you. You know the way they feel about you. Please don't disappoint them." She paused. "And me."

A strange look crossed his face. "You don't need me to have a good time, Laura," he said softly. "You'd actually have more fun without me."

It was what she'd been thinking— could there be a worse moment for him to become the sensitive boy again?— but there was no way she was going to let him even suspect that. She gave him a kiss on the cheek "Are you kidding? I'd be miserable without you!" Then she added lightly, "Besides, you can't let me down. Steve is coming home instead of heading off somewhere with Christina, and Phil is canceling some fancy plans for a ski trip so he can make it to Westchester. I'm the one who begged them both to do it and now Mom is acting like it was all their idea and they're the world's best sons. You don't want me to have to explain that I couldn't convince my own husband to come, do you?"

"I see. This is all about sibling rivalry." He'd decided to give in and now he was smiling at her.

"You bet. I intend to show off my family shamelessly."

"Well, in that case I guess I don't have any choice."

She'd won. She covered a sigh of relief. "And maybe on Saturday we could ask Mom and Dad to take care of Katie and we could go into the city for the night. Just the two of us. Like the old days."

If she was honest, she wasn't sure she really wanted to spend any of her precious visit that way, but she thought he might like it. But she watched his smile fade—just a little—and she realized he felt the same way she did.

"Why don't we see what's going on when we get to your parents' house? They'll probably want us to stay with them for the entire time." He looked down at the suitcases she'd been packing and the cake pan she was still holding. "I guess you're going to have to put that thing in with our clothes," he said. "Just make sure it doesn't catch on my Irish sweater—okay?" And he walked out of the bedroom.

Laura sat on the bed. Suddenly her neck and shoulders ached from the hours she'd spent in the last week whipping egg whites for the tortes and her back was sore from bending over to pull them out of the oven. Because clearly, she and Robby weren't even a little excited by . . . or even interested in . . . the prospect of spending a romantic night together. She rubbed her neck. When she'd talked on the phone to her mother earlier in the day, Iris had quoted what Nana had said about Laura; the words Laura had heard all her life. "You'll never have to worry about that one."

Well, Nana, you should see me now.

And then she wondered, *How did we get here? In a few short years how did Robby and I get from our wedding day to this?*

Chapter Three

Her wedding day. Laura and Robby had gotten married in 1970, that time of upheaval and rebellion for American kids, and they'd chosen to have a secular ceremony. It had been devastating to Iris, who was so religious, but Laura had been firm.

"It's been years since Robby set foot inside the Methodist Church, Mom, and you know I haven't been observant since I went away to college. I never really was, I'm more like Dad; I do the big holidays because it pleases you. It would be hypocritical for Robby and me to suddenly start with all the religious stuff now. Be happy that I'm getting married. Most of your friends' daughters are just living with their boyfriends."

Iris had accepted the inevitable but she hadn't been happy about it. Laura, on the other hand, had loved her wedding day. She'd been married in the spring and she'd insisted on an outdoor ceremony because she wanted to have the whole sky above her when she committed herself forever to Robby, and she wanted the solid earth under her feet. Besides, everyone in her crowd agreed that if you were bothering to get married, doing it outside, usually in a park or on a beach, was the way to go. Laura had chosen her grandmother's garden because it was the most beautiful place she knew. Nana was a fabulous gardener.

Robby had worn slacks and an open-necked shirt and Laura had felt dizzy with desire just looking at him. She had worn a white shift and she had braided her red hair and let it fall down her back. Robby had looked at her as if he couldn't wait to be alone with her, which was crazy because they had been sleeping together for over a year. But the magic of their wedding day had made it seem logical—or whatever logic meant when you couldn't see anyone in the world but a young man with soft brown eyes in an open-necked shirt. They had recited a poem by Emily Dickinson. It had been their favorite. They had shared favorite poems and books and songs back then.

So how did we get here? Laura asked herself as she sat on the bed she and Robby had been sharing for nine years of marriage. *How did we get to a place where Robby resents it when I bake cakes to make extra money, and I resent him for complaining, and neither one of us really wants to be alone with the other in a hotel room for a weekend? We never admit that anything's wrong, we don't get angry—at least not out loud. But sometimes I think that would be easier than this . . . battle that seems to go on without us ever fighting. In the beginning I could finish his sentences and he could read my mind. When did that start to change?* Laura laid back on the bed next to the partially packed suitcase and closed her eyes. *Sometimes I feel there were signs of . . . "trouble" is too big a word . . . I'll just say warning signs . . . from the very beginning, even before we were married. Has it been going on for that long? Sometimes I can't help thinking so.*

—

When Robby and Laura decided to get married, she still had not met his mother and father. Her parents, to say nothing of Nana, were disturbed by this, but Laura told herself it was just because they were mired in dated ideas about family and old-fashioned rituals that she and her friends had thrown off. Robby was his own man, and she was her own woman, they were not bound by the prejudices, feelings or beliefs of their families. Meeting the relatives was simply not necessary when you were free-thinking adults of nineteen and twenty-two. But Nana had finally managed to convince Laura that the old-fashioned rituals had a purpose, even if it was just to soothe the fears of loved ones, so the McAllisters were invited to come east from their home in Blair's Falls, Ohio, to meet the Sterns.

Robby had been sure his folks would refuse. "They never go anywhere," he'd told Laura. But to his surprise they had accepted the invitation. Laura thought Robby seemed upset by this, but he insisted that he wasn't.

Robby would be graduating the following spring, and he and Laura would be getting married three weeks after his graduation. Iris said it would be nice for the families to get together a few months before the wedding, so a weekend in late October was chosen for the visit. On the first night, Laura had cooked dinner, and after it was finished, Robby, Laura, Theo, Iris and Mr. and Mrs. McAllister—whose names were Frank and Emma Ann—retired to the Sterns' front porch to sip coffee and try to get to know one another.

Physically, the McAllisters were a married version of Mutt and Jeff. He was small and wiry, without an ounce of fat on him; she was large and well padded. Frank McAllister's face suggested a lifetime of bitterness, and

Laura knew from Robby that he had failed in several businesses. Emma Ann was not an attractive woman and she didn't do anything to help herself; her brown hair was pulled back in a bun, which made her full face look even fuller, and big round glasses hid the brown eyes that were so like her son's and were her best feature. She wore the perpetually angry expression of a woman who felt life had passed her by.

They were the kind of married people who referred to each other as Mother and Father, and after Laura and Robby were married they wanted her to address them as Mother and Father McAllister. Laura was deeply grateful that her parents had simply asked Robby to call them Theo and Iris. She was also grateful that Robby didn't have any brothers or sisters and that her brothers hadn't been invited. The evening had been difficult enough with just the two sets of parents and Robby and Laura.

When Robby's parents arrived, Laura was pretty sure that his father had been drinking. He wasn't drunk, but she could smell liquor on his breath and Robby had thrown a worried glance to his mother, who had responded with a little shrug. Laura thought it was likely that they had been through this before, although Robby hadn't ever said anything about his father drinking too much.

Dinner hadn't gone very well; Laura had made her new specialty, coq au vin, and Mr. McAllister had announced that he didn't have a stomach for foreign food. Given how many glasses of wine he had consumed during the meal, it couldn't have been the alcohol in the dish that had bothered him.

"Father is a meat-and-potatoes man," Mrs. McAllister had said with an apologetic little laugh. She seemed to be accustomed to apologizing for him.

Robby had told Laura that his mother's family, and especially her brother, were prominent people in their small town. Mrs. McAllister had already regaled them over dinner with stories about the family department store, which was now being run by her brother. "Four generations of Landons have owned it," she told her captive audience. "It's a landmark in Blair's Falls.

But it took my brother, Donald, to put it on the map. It's well known all the way to Cincinnati!"

At another point during dinner, she'd told them all that Robby was the apple of her eye. She'd actually said those very words in front of strangers. Laura had waited for Robby to try to stop her the way any of her three brothers would have done if her mother had been so gushy about them. But even though Robby had turned bright red, he hadn't protested or even turned away. It had been his father who had snapped impatiently, "Oh for God's sake, Mother, don't make a fool of the boy!"

———

Out on the porch, Robby's parents were making no effort to extend themselves to the parents of the girl who was going to be their daughter-in-law. They sat side by side silently. It was left to Iris and Theo to try to make conversation.

"You must be so very proud of Robby," Iris said. Her voice, which was usually lovely and well modulated, sounded edgy; she wasn't at her best in awkward social situations. Mrs. McAllister pulled herself up proudly and gave them all a smug little smile. Mr. McAllister stared sullenly at Iris.

"Robby's record, graduating third in his class, is certainly impressive," Theo tried to help his wife.

"Archaeology is fascinating," Iris said. In the fall Robby would begin studying for his doctorate in the field.

"I'm afraid it's not a subject I'm familiar with," Mrs. McAllister had suddenly decided to speak. "But my brother's wife . . . her brother went to Yale, you know, so I trust him . . . he says that being asked to work on this dig in New Mexico is a feather in Robby's cap."

"From what I understand it is quite an honor," Iris agreed eagerly. "Even I've heard of Professor Hawkins and his work, although like you, I'm not really knowledgeable about archaeology."

Professor Hawkins, who would be mentoring Robby through the doctoral process, conducted an excavation site on a dig in New Mexico and he had invited Robby to be a part of his team. It was a very big honor indeed for Robby to have been singled out in a such a way at this phase of his education.

"I've been very lucky," Robby started to say, but his father interrupted.

"He's not going to be paid a thin dime," he said. His speech was slightly slurred. "Making mud pies in the desert!"

Laura looked over at Robby. Any of her brothers would have defended himself if Theo had said something like that. But Robby's face was blank, as if he hadn't heard his father. Only his fists balled up in his lap gave him away.

"He says he's going to get all this knowledge and experience," Mr. McAllister went on. "Knowledge for what? That's what I'd like to know. He's going to go to school for another six years, he tells us. And then he'll go dig up pieces of old pots and paste them together. A grown man playing with pieces of pots. After all the money that was spent on his education, and—"

"But my brother, Donald, is very pleased about Robby's choice," his wife cut in. "He was the one who sent Robby to college. Donald and his wife—she's

the one I mentioned a moment ago—
don't have any children. Robby's like a
son to Donald, and Donald is so proud
of—"

"Donald! Donald! Donald!" her husband exploded. "No one gives a god-
damn about your brother Donald."

Under the porch lights, Laura saw
Mrs. McAllister's brown eyes fill with
tears. Her round face crumpled with
pain. It only took a second, then she regained control, blinked away the tears
and forced herself to smile. But in that
second Laura saw a history of humilia-
tion that had probably been going on for
years, and her heart ached for poor
Mother McAllister.

Iris and Theo, meanwhile, were trying
to cover the awkward moment with
cheery offers of more coffee and another helping of the cake Laura had
baked. The offers were rejected by
Robby and his mother, who managed to
end the evening quickly, and Robby
drove his parents back to the hotel
where they were staying.

After that, it had taken Laura a while
to reassure her parents about her up-

coming marriage. "You can't judge Robby by his parents," she said. "That's not fair. You both love him. That hasn't changed. Besides, maybe tomorrow night things will be better."

It did seem as if the second evening started out better. Mr. McAllister was completely sober, for one thing, and Mrs. McAllister was making more of an effort to be friendly. This time they had dinner in the dining room of the hotel where the McAllisters were staying, and everyone seemed to be getting along, until the coffee was served. Then Theo announced that he had a practical matter he wanted to discuss.

"Iris and I wish to pay for an apartment for Laura and Robby to live in, as well as Laura's tuition," he told his prospective in-laws. "Just until Laura graduates from college. Then she can get a job to carry expenses until Robby has his doctorate."

"After all, we'd be paying for her room at the dorm if she hadn't transferred to be with Robby," Iris had added.

Frank McAllister put down his coffee cup. "I believe if a man is ready to get married he should be ready to stand on his own two feet. I don't see any reason to coddle my son the way you're suggesting."

And besides, you couldn't afford it, Laura thought angrily. She saw that once again, Robby was looking off with a blank expression as if he hadn't heard his father.

"But Laura and Robby won't be in a position to support themselves for a while," Iris protested. "At least, they won't be able to do it without tremendous hardship."

"We want them to concentrate on their studies, not trying to pay their rent," Theo put in. "I don't call that coddling. We expect them to work hard and do well. We just want to ease the way for them a little."

"After all, they have a long haul ahead of them," Iris said eagerly. "Laura still has three more years until she graduates from college and I know myself how long it can take to get a doctorate."

"Then perhaps Laura could put her own ambitions on hold and support her husband," Mrs. McAllister put in.

"Plenty of women have done that—and without complaining about it."

For a second, Laura wasn't sure she'd heard the woman correctly. Then she looked at both of Robby's parents and realized with a shock that this was what they expected of her. And Robby had never told them differently.

"I plan to work while Robby's studying for his doctorate," she said angrily. "And I promise I won't complain."

And I can't imagine why I ever felt sorry for you, Mrs. McAllister. You deserve your horrid husband.

"With a college degree Laura can earn more money," Iris said, even though she and Theo never would have thought of education in terms of dollars and cents.

"Well, all I know is, I quit school and went to work as a file clerk when Father and I got married," Mrs. McAllister said. "It wasn't an exciting job, or intellectually stimulating, but we needed my paycheck, and it was the best I could do. I don't remember anyone ever saying I had to go to college or have someone pay my way while I did it."

"But Laura's mother and I *do* say she must go to college," Theo snapped. And Laura could tell how furious he was, because his slight accent had suddenly become more pronounced, and his aristocratic face had taken on the expression that Laura and her brothers used to call "snooty" when they were young. "Laura will have the same education we have given our sons. And the same assistance."

It was going to get ugly—even more than it had last night. Mr. McAllister was now glaring at Dad, and Mrs. McAllister was taking in deep, angry breaths, and Dad was looking at both of them like they were something disgusting he'd found on the bottom of his shoe. If either of them said anything else Dad was going to let them know exactly how stupid and ignorant they were. And in spite of how much Laura felt she'd enjoy that, she knew it would devastate Robby. Plus, she wanted both families to be on speaking terms for the wedding. She was going to have to do something.

"Mom and Dad, don't worry about

us," she said. "Robby and I will both get jobs. We won't need any help."

And no matter how hard her parents protested for the rest of the evening, and in the coming days, she was adamant. After all, she was helping Robby save face—she was sure Nana would have done the same thing for her husband.

—

If she had expected Robby to be grateful to her for giving up the financial assistance that, frankly, she'd been counting on, she was wrong. He didn't say a word about those two terrible nights until they were safely back on their campus and in bed in his room at the dorm. He stared up at the ceiling, not touching her.

"So now you know," he said. "My dad drinks, not all the time, but too much. I've never been sure if that was why all his businesses failed or if he started drinking because he was a failure."

"It doesn't matter, it has nothing to do with you," she said fiercely.

It seemed to be what he needed to

hear, because he put his arm around her. But he was still troubled. "Try not to judge my mom, okay?"

"It seemed to me that she was the one doing the judging."

He sighed. "You don't know what her life has been like."

"She seems to think it was ideal. Or, at least, she was ideal."

"No. She knows better. That's why she . . . oh, you'll never understand." He pulled his arm out from under her and stared at the ceiling again.

"Try me," she said more gently.

"You had it all when you were growing up. A home full of culture and class . . . and your mother had the same kind of life before you. You've told me her father treated her like a queen. No one felt that way about Mom. My Uncle Donald was good-looking and smart—and he was the boy. She was just the girl. I know she brags too much. It makes me cringe when she tries to find a way to quote my Aunt Margaret's brother because she wants everyone to know she's related to someone who went to Yale. It's so damn sad!

"Your father is proud of your mother for getting her doctorate. I can see it whenever he talks about the work she does. My father would never be proud of anything my mother did. I've never seen him be tender or gentle with her. Not once. I've never heard him thank her for all the years she spent at that lousy job supporting us while he was screwing up business after business, until my Uncle Donald finally took pity on her and gave her an allowance. And now my father resents her for that.

"When I was younger, I used to wonder why the hell they ever got married. Now I don't care, I just know that I want to make life better for her."

He said it so earnestly. Laura propped herself up on one elbow. "What do you mean? You can't do that—for anyone."

"All I have to do is be a success. That's all she needs." His eyes were shining in the half light now. "She used to read to me when I was a kid, Laura. She'd come home from working all day, clean the house, make dinner, put me to bed, and then she'd read to me—not kid stories, books like *Ivanhoe* and *A Tale of*

Two Cities. Sometimes she'd be so tired she'd nod off in the middle of a sentence, and I'm not sure she even liked what she was reading—she picked those books because my Aunt Margaret said they were intellectual.

"Mom bought the collected Shakespeare and one summer we tried to plow through it." He laughed softly into the darkness. "She's probably the only person in the world who ever tried to read *Timon of Athens* for the fun of it." He stopped chuckling. "And she did get something out of all those words. She loved stories about honor and nobility. That's why she likes it that I'm going to be an archaeologist. She read somewhere that archaeology is the occupation of aristocrats. To her, that means I'm like Ivanhoe." He turned to Laura. "She meant it when she said I was the apple of her eye. I'm the reason she gets out of bed every morning."

Cruel, selfish woman, to put such a burden on him! "That's a big load to be carrying."

"Oh she's never said that, she wouldn't."

Not in so many words, Laura thought. *But she's let you know all the same that you are supposed to make it up to her for every disappointment, every unhappiness she's had. And that is so unfair!*

Robby stroked her face. "Hey, stop looking so tragic! I'm not some driven Mama's boy. If I worked a little harder at a math problem when I was a kid, or if I studied a little harder for an exam because I didn't want to fail her, where's the harm?"

He did have a point. And she didn't want to argue. "There isn't any, I guess."

"I'll admit, I'd like to be famous. I'd like to discover a new dig site that's named after me and write bestselling books. But if all I ever do is add to the store of human knowledge, that'll be okay too. It'll be an honorable way to spend my life."

When Robby talked this way, he could quell every doubt. Especially when he was lying in bed next to her with his body pressed against hers and his fingers playing idly with her hair. "You and Ivanhoe," she breathed.

"Exactly," he whispered as he kissed

her. And then they didn't say anything more as they came together in the way that had always banished all thoughts except those of bliss for both of them.

Finally, when they lay next to each other spent and out of breath, Robby whispered, "Laura, we're going to have a great life! You'll see. I'm going to make you so happy."

At that moment she hadn't doubted it. And if, later, as he slept and she thought back over what he'd said, she did have a doubt or two, she told herself she was being foolish. Robby had a first-class mind—their professors all said so—so of course he was ambitious. And if his mother had nurtured that ambition, there wasn't anything wrong with that. Most people who achieved greatness had at least one parent who had pushed them.

It wasn't until years later that she realized that perhaps her first instinct had been right.

Chapter Four

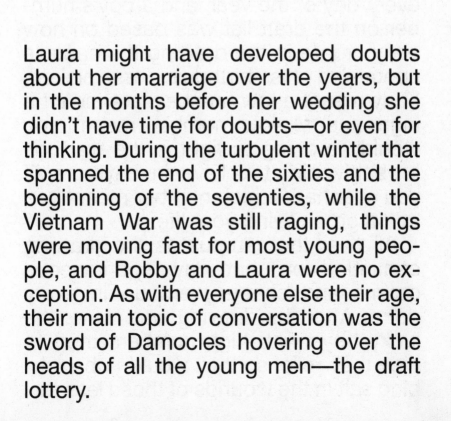

Laura might have developed doubts about her marriage over the years, but in the months before her wedding she didn't have time for doubts—or even for thinking. During the turbulent winter that spanned the end of the sixties and the beginning of the seventies, while the Vietnam War was still raging, things were moving fast for most young people, and Robby and Laura were no exception. As with everyone else their age, their main topic of conversation was the sword of Damocles hovering over the heads of all the young men—the draft lottery.

For the rest of her life, Laura would remember December 1, 1969, when she and Robby and most of the students on their college campus sat glued to the television watching as strangers they'd never met dipped into a big glass bowl and pulled out the little blue plastic capsules that would decide Robby's fate and that of every American male aged eighteen to twenty-six. Each of the capsules contained a birth date, one for every day of the year, and a boy's number on the draft list was based on how early or late in the drawing the capsule containing his birthday was picked. Early meant a low number, late meant a high one. A low number meant you would be going to fight in the war you probably didn't believe in anymore, if you ever had; a high number meant you could go on living your life.

All over the campus as the drawing continued on that day, spontaneous groans and cheers went up in every dorm. After the drawing was done, the lucky boys with high numbers tried to hide their relief so they wouldn't be rubbing salt in the wounds of those less fortunate. Many of those with low numbers cried openly in the hallways and the student lounges as hopes and dreams were replaced by fear and anger. Boys with numbers in the middle huddled in anxious groups and tried to calculate the odds of being called up or escaping. Girls like Laura held their boyfriends in their arms and searched for comforting words. By nighttime it seemed as if everyone knew what everyone else's number was, and most people were trying to get drunk or high as fast as they could. It didn't matter if they were celebrating or mourning.

Robby didn't cry or get drunk, he laid down on his bed, and stared at the ceiling with the closed-off look that Laura had come to dread almost as much as the draft itself. His number was in the first third of the drawing. This meant he probably wouldn't be drafted that spring, so he'd be able to graduate and he and Laura could get married. But Laura estimated that he'd be called up sometime during the summer. Unless they could find a way out.

"There must be something," she

cried. "Didn't you tell me your father knows some people who are high up in Veterans Affairs? Couldn't he pull some strings?" There was no sound from the bed. "Robby, you have some time. If your dad talks to his friends right now . . ."

Robby turned and sat up. "My dad pull strings so I can be a draft dodger?" he sneered. "You don't know what the hell you're talking about."

"A draft dodger? What are *you* talking about? You don't support this war . . ."

"Draft dodger is what my father will call it. The McAllister men go to war, Laura. They don't ask questions, they don't wonder if their country is right, they just fight. Get my dad to tell you sometime about how he saved his buddy on Omaha Beach during the invasion of Normandy. It was his finest hour. If you want to know the truth, he hasn't done anything better since."

"But that was different. That war was justified."

"It doesn't matter. 'America, love it or leave it.' That's what my father says."

"But when he stops and thinks about what we're really doing over there—"

"You don't understand!" he shouted. "Your parents think. My father doesn't."

"My father supported the war at first."

"But eventually he saw the light! Mine never will. He's never read the kind of books that make people question themselves or the things they believe. He's never traveled and tried to understand a different culture, or studied a religion other than the one he grew up with. He doesn't live near a big city with different people and ideas that aren't exactly like his own. He doesn't think, Laura."

"What about your mother?"

"When she hears about my number, she'll be scared to death. She won't care about patriotism or any of that crap, she'll beg Uncle Donald to fix it, which he can't do."

"But your father could."

"Maybe. But it doesn't matter, because he won't. Because Uncle Sam will make a man of me. I'll go into the army and get rid of all those crazy notions about making mud pies in the desert."

Laura finally accepted reality; even if

Robby's father could have helped, he wouldn't. And there certainly wasn't anything Iris and Theo could do except worry about their daughter and the young man they were so fond of. It didn't help matters any that the war that was probably going to take Robby away had nearly torn their own family apart and because of it their son Steve was still estranged from them. Laura did her best not to talk about Vietnam in front of them.

But it seemed to her as if that was all her contemporaries *were* talking about. In every dorm, coffeehouse, or hamburger joint where the college kids congregated, no matter how the conversation started, eventually it would turn to Vietnam and the draft. Or, more specifically, avoiding the draft. There were few supporters of the military on Laura's politically liberal campus, where most of the students and faculty had been taking part in protest marches long before the televised images of young Americans coming home in body bags, and Vietnamese children burned by American napalm, finally turned the rest of the

country against the war. In 1968 their
school had firmly supported the peace
candidate Eugene McCarthy. Robby
and Laura, and everyone they knew, attended rallies wearing black armbands
for the slaughtered Vietnamese and
bracelets for American soldiers missing
in action. But before the advent of the
lottery, those protests had been intellectual exercises engaged in for abstract
beliefs. The new policy brought the
war and fear of dying onto their lovely
campus and into their protected dorm
rooms.

Suddenly Robby had a new circle of
friends; all of them boys who had low-
or middle-range draft numbers and
would probably be inducted by the end
of the year. Before the lottery had gone
into effect, most of these boys had
planned to wait out the war safely
tucked away in graduate school, or in
jobs deemed vital to the national interest. But the government had declared
most of those deferments unfair and
ended them. Now the boys gathered in
Robby's dorm room every night to rant
and rave about the old bastards who

had started this mess. And to spend hours trying to figure out how to get out of it.

Robby was always the one who brought up the subject of leaving the country or going to jail. "It's the only honorable way," he said over and over again. And Laura would remember the night when he'd told her that he'd wanted to be Ivanhoe when he was a kid.

Sometimes Robby talked about Laura's brother Steve, who was now deeply into the underground movement. Steve was doing it the right way, Robby declared. Laura was torn when Robby started saying things like that. She was proud of Steve's courage, but she knew what her brother was doing was illegal and dangerous, and although he had never hurt anyone, members of his movement had, and that was as wrong as the war itself. And Steve had caused such pain and suffering at home. No, she didn't want Robby to follow in Steve's footsteps.

But she knew that Robby and his friends never would. The smart boys who gathered in Robby's dorm room were opposed to the war but they weren't fighters like her brother. They just wanted to get on with the future, which had once seemed so bright for them, and they were furious because they couldn't. Furious and scared out of their minds. That was the worst part: underneath all the shouting and self-pity— fueled by what seemed like endless amounts of alcohol and other substances—was a horrible truth. These boys were right to be terrified, because thousands just like them had already died.

———

But then there was the night when the group had assembled in Robby's room and the usual ranting and raving was well under way, and all of a sudden everyone was silent. Laura's attention had been wandering but she looked up to see that a guy named George who lived at the other end of the hall had just rushed in. All eyes were on him.

"Well?" One of Robby's friends demanded as the others sat forward eagerly. "Is it true?"

George laughed. "Oh yeah! Larry got himself his little deferment. He and Nancy are off getting married right now, then they're going to drive up north to tell her folks. They'll probably be mad because their little girl is knocked up, but Larry's going to be sitting out LBJ's war."

There was an explosion of hooting and cheering from the boys and someone raised a bottle of beer in a bleary toast. "Let's hear it for Nancy!" he shouted.

"Let's hear it for the Daddy Deferment," someone else added. "And for Larry, the lucky S.O.B.!"

That was when Laura remembered that Larry Whatever-His-Last-Name-Was, had talked about having a baby as the one foolproof way to get out of the draft. "I call it getting a Daddy Deferment," he'd said. "Not only do you skip jail and hang on to your citizenship, you can have a good time while you're working on it."

Everyone had laughed except Laura.

She couldn't imagine having a baby unless she knew she and Robby were ready to love, support, and care for it—draft or no draft. Anything else was unthinkable, even as a joke.

But now, as the boys continued to cheer for the father-to-be, she heard Robby's voice at her side. "I never thought Larry would actually go through with it," he said softly.

She glanced up and saw that he was staring at her. He turned away quickly; the look only lasted for a second. She told herself it didn't mean anything.

But after everyone had finally straggled off to their own rooms, and she and Robby were alone, he didn't take her in his arms and begin the long, slow process of kissing and undressing each other, which had always been their prelude to a night of lovemaking. Nor did he yawn and flop down on his bed the way he did when he was tired and wanted her to know that there wouldn't be any sex that night. Instead, he avoided looking at her, and began cleaning up the debris from the evening. Laura watched as he lined up empty beer bottles neatly in a corner of the room, and folded the pizza boxes so they'd fit in the incinerator at the end of the hall. Normally Robby was a slob—his clothes stayed on the floor where he'd dropped them, and it could take him days to clean up after an all-nighter. Usually it was Laura who got rid of the garbage and washed his dirty laundry. But now he was cleaning up. And not looking at her. He was building up to say something. Suddenly she knew she didn't want to hear it.

"I think I should go to my dorm tonight," she said. "I have that test in Poli Sci on Wednesday, and I need to hit the books."

"You're not going to study tonight, it's too late," he said.

"No, but first thing in the morning."

"Stay here now. And you can leave early. I'll set the clock radio."

She still didn't want to stay with him, but she couldn't think of any good excuse not to. "All right." She sat on the edge of the bed and began taking off her shoes.

Robby continued clearing up. His

back was turned to her. "Wasn't that something? About Larry and Nancy?"

She drew in a deep breath. "I think it's wrong," she said.

He turned to her. "That's a little judgmental, isn't it?"

"I just don't think it's right to have a baby for any reason except that you want one."

"Perhaps they do."

"He doesn't have a job. They don't have a place to live. They aren't even married . . ."

"Wow. You really are being judgmental—we both know people who slipped up and she got pregnant before they were married . . . and you never said a word."

"Yes. Because it was an accident."

"That makes it okay?"

"It's better than a cold-blooded decision."

"How do you know it was cold-blooded? What if Nancy and Larry were planning to have children someday anyway, what if they just hurried it up a little bit?"

"You know what I mean."

"What I know is, Larry's draft number was 77. If it weren't for this baby he'd be fighting a war he hates. He might have gotten killed. For nothing."

"I know that."

"Nancy loved him enough to save him. What's wrong about that?"

She wanted to say that Larry shouldn't have let Nancy do it for him even if she had begged him to. But then she looked at Robby. His face was pale; he knew what she was thinking and he probably agreed with her. But she also knew that at that moment, if she said she'd have his Daddy Deferment, he'd jump at the chance. She watched him look down at his hands, which were clenched into fists, and she could tell he was ashamed of himself. A part of Robby would always want to be Ivanhoe, and that part wanted to go to jail for his principles, or cross the border into Canada and live as an exile. Those were the honorable choices—that was what he'd said.

But everyone had heard horror stories about what happened to conscientious objectors in prison, and giving up your

American citizenship was a huge price to pay for someone else's mistake. Because that's what it was—this war that no one could explain, no one could end, and no smart person thought America could still win. It was a horrible, bloody mistake made by men who were too old to fight and too proud to admit they were wrong. How could anyone expect a boy like Robby to be strong and self-less when he knew his own country was willing to get him killed so that those evil old men wouldn't have to look bad? How could anyone be honorable when every week there were more pictures in *Life* magazine of dead soldiers and Vietnamese children being burned in their rice paddies? When you thought about all of that, having a baby to get out of the draft didn't seem that terrible.

Laura reached out to take Robby's fists in her hands. "I'm so sorry," she said softly. "This shouldn't be happening to you."

There were tears in his eyes. "I just don't want to die," he whispered.

"And I don't want you to."

And so, in spite of everything she believed, the seed of an idea was planted in her.

———

Robby never actually asked Laura to have a baby to keep him out of the draft, and she never said she would. But over the next few weeks whenever she saw Robby smile, or heard him laugh, or watched him study, biting his lower lip and puckering his forehead in concentration, Laura knew that seed was growing in her. And when at night he lay next to her in his narrow bed and together they began the sweet journey that melded them into one, she knew that she was like Nancy and so many other girls in that terrible winter of 1970. She could not let the boy she loved die.

She didn't want to be a pregnant bride, she was her mother's daughter and Nana's granddaughter after all. But after the wedding, without really admitting what they were doing, she and Robby started taking chances. Laura had never gone on the pill like some girls, Robby had always been the one who took "the precautions," as he called it. But now he was less careful than he had been. And she didn't stop him. That was all it took. One month after they'd moved out to the archaeological dig in New Mexico, Laura and Robby knew that he wouldn't be going into the army after all. There was a baby on the way.

Chapter Five

Laura got up, and carried the overnight bag full of cooking utensils, along with the bulky springform pan, into the kitchen. She was going to have to repack the bag, and find a way to fit in the pan, or she'd have to leave something else home—maybe her whisks or her copper bowl—even though she knew her mother didn't have either. As she dumped everything out onto the countertop she went back to her thoughts.

If Theo and Iris had suspected that Robby's draft status had anything to do with Laura's "accidental" pregnancy they'd kept it to themselves. They had simply sent a loving note of congratulations to the young couple in New Mexico, and renewed their offer of financial assistance—and Laura had rejected it again. But Robby's father had come to his own conclusions and he sent his son a four-page letter in which he called Robby a gutless traitor, half a man and a coward hiding behind a woman's skirts. To Laura's amazement the vitriol from his father devastated Robby. She couldn't believe the man had that much influence over her husband. But when she looked back on it later she would realize that letter had seriously damaged Robby's spirit. It had torn at his self-esteem. Maybe it was because Robby feared his father was right. Or maybe it was just that children are never immune to attacks from their parents.

Laura had tried to comfort her husband as much as she could, but the truth was, she was struggling too. In all of her charmed, happy-go-lucky life she had never been as miserable as she was during that summer in New Mexico.

She and Robby had rented an ancient

trailer near the dig where Robby would be working. They would live in the desert for three months, as would Professor Hawkins and the rest of his students and volunteers. Robby would be the professor's right-hand man, and Laura had signed on as a volunteer. At the end of the summer, the dig would close down until the following year, and the professor and his students would return to the San Fernando Valley and the small but prestigious school—Custis University—which sponsored the dig. This was where Hawkins taught and Robby would begin studying for his PhD.

When Robby and Laura had first made all these plans for the summer, it was right after their wedding, and Robby, who had volunteered on digs before, had warned Laura that conditions could get primitive.

"You know this is my first time working with Hawkins," he'd said. "But I've been told by some of the other guys that it's no picnic. Deserts always get boiling hot during the day and freezing cold at night, and this site is smack in the heart of the desert. There will be bugs and snakes and some really nasty critters."

"Critters?" she'd mimicked him. "Did you actually say 'critters'?"

"Wise guy! But you get the picture. And the trailer isn't going to be a luxury hotel."

"I can take it, don't worry about me."

But Laura had said that before she became pregnant. Before the morning sickness that lasted all day. Before her energy seemed to drain out of her, leaving her continually exhausted. She hadn't expected to feel like that. Her mother had always had an easy time with her pregnancies; she'd been one of those women who actually did glow. And even now, after all these years, there was a joyful shine in Iris's eyes when she reminisced about that part of her life. Of course Nana had not talked about being pregnant, she came from a generation that didn't share that kind of intimate detail. But Laura was sure that her grandmother had handled the whole thing gracefully and cheerfully—as she did everything.

Laura tried to do that too. She tried to

be cheerful as she nibbled on the soda crackers her doctor had suggested for her nausea. When Consuelo, the local woman who worked on the site as a cook, took pity on Laura and brewed a special chamomile tea for her, Laura drank it with a smile. And each morning she told herself that today she would feel better. Today she would go to the site to work with the other volunteers, and she wouldn't mind the blazing hot sun or the bug bites that gave her a rash. Today she wouldn't mind the fact that no amount of air-conditioning could cool the darn trailer and no amount of scrubbing could clean the pitted linoleum floor. But each day she minded it all a little more. And sometimes when even the soda crackers and the tea wouldn't stay down, Laura would wonder if in some awful way the baby she was carrying knew why she and Robby were bringing it into the world now instead of waiting until they were really ready for it, and it was protesting from the womb. She knew such fantasies were ridiculous, and she pushed them away. But she couldn't get the words "selfish" and "irresponsible" out of her head. She didn't tell Robby what she was thinking, she didn't want to hurt him. But the words kept coming back. Until they finally burst out of her.

It happened because of a dog who had wandered onto the site. Actually, it was a large puppy, a half-starved female, with huge feet, and ribs sticking out under her skin.

"The poor thing!" Laura cried. "Robby, we can keep her, can't we?" Any member of her family could have predicted she'd say that; Laura had been adopting strays since she was a child. "We'll name her Molly, I've always thought that would be a great name for a dog . . ."

But Robby was shaking his head.

"I'm sorry, honey, we can feed her and give her water while we're here, but what would we do with her in California? We're going to have a tiny one-bedroom apartment—there's not enough room in it for us. That dog would go crazy and so would we. Besides, we're not going to have time for a pet. Why don't you let her wander around the site for a while and see if someone else will take her?"

The word "selfish" was on the tip of her tongue, but she bit it back. Besides, she told herself that he was right, with all the people connected with the dig, surely someone would offer to give the shambling stray a home. But no one did. People fed the puppy scraps from their lunches and several of them left out plates of food for her at night. But no one was going to adopt her.

"How can people be so uncaring?" Laura wailed.

"I guess they're all like us. They don't have the time or space." Robby shrugged.

"But everyone is feeding her."

"She's hungry."

"And she's getting used to depending on us. What will she do after we leave?"

"I don't know."

"Doesn't that bother anyone?" Laura was yelling now. "What is going to happen to her? She's just a baby . . . she's helpless. Someone has to take care of her. Is anyone even thinking about that?"

"Laura—"

"How can people be so irresponsible! How can they be so damn selfish?"

And what she was really saying was, "*We* are going to have a helpless baby. How can *we* be so selfish and irresponsible?"

Robby knew that was what she meant. Of course he did. He sat at the table in their little galley kitchen and he buried his head in his hands. This time it wasn't his father who had torn at his self-esteem, and the guilt Laura felt was overwhelming.

She worked even harder at being a good sport. She tried not to think about the soon-to-be-abandoned puppy. She fought back the nausea and she forced herself to work at the dig. And she fought back a homesickness that got so intense that sometimes it was like a physical pain. She was stunned by this in herself. Unlike so many freshmen she hadn't missed her home when she went away to college, she'd been eager for whatever new experiences would come her way. But in New Mexico, it seemed she was a different person. She knew intellectually that there was great beauty around her, but she couldn't make herself see it. When everyone gathered at the end of the day to watch the famous desert sunset, Robby and the others would be awestruck by the glory of the colors that spread across the sky. Laura would look at that same sky and long for rain and the green lawns of the Northeast. She would miss New York City. That was the biggest surprise of all. Robby was an outdoors person and she had convinced herself that she was one too. But now she was beginning to realize that she really wanted to live near a big city. She wanted to be able to walk down city streets and have access to theaters and museums and shops full of beautiful, exotic things from faraway places. She didn't need to buy these things—at least, she never had—but she liked to believe that someday, if she wanted to, she might.

One hot evening, she'd left the site's communal campfire early so she could take her shower while there was still some hot water, and she found herself daydreaming about a little Mediterranean shop on Lexington Avenue that sold candles and soap that smelled of lemon and lavender. The water that came out of their showerhead in the trailer always had a brackish smell, and as it trickled down her face she thought of the sweet-smelling candles and soap, and she began to sob. She got out of the shower, and dried off the nasty water with a towel and put on a clean robe, but she couldn't stop crying. She cried because the cramped little trailer in which she lived smelled of it's former tenants instead of herbs and citrus oils. She cried because she was afraid she was too young and poor to be having a baby. She cried because she wanted to run home and beg her parents to take care of her again, but a grown-up didn't do that. And most of all, she cried because she was Laura Stern McAllister, the girl with the charmed life who wasn't supposed to cry.

There was a sound behind her and she turned to see that Robby had come back. He had opened the screen door, which squeaked but she'd been crying too loudly to hear it, and he had walked up behind her. He had heard her cry and now he was saying, "Laura?" in a scared voice.

She swallowed the sobs. "I'm sorry," she started to say, "I don't know why I'm doing this . . ." But the sobs erupted again and she couldn't go on.

Robby sat down on the little cot that served as their bed. He looked defeated, which made her feel even worse. "You hate it here," he said sadly.

She managed to get control. "No, no. I just need to get used to it . . ."

He shook his head. "You think I'm blind? You're sick and the heat gets to you." He looked around the little trailer. "And you're not used to living conditions like this. I should have thought it through. I should have known."

She rushed to him. "How could you have? I won't have you blaming yourself because I'm being a spoiled brat!"

He'd smiled at that. "I would have said a child of privilege."

"Call it whatever you want, it's not your fault and I am going to get over this. In a few weeks I'll start feeling better. Consuelo says the morning sickness will be gone." Actually the cook had warned Laura that certain women never got over it for their entire pregnancy.

"Consuelo isn't a doctor and your father is. He thinks living here on the dig is too much for you."

"You've talked to Daddy?"

"And your mother."

She should be angry at Robby for going to her parents behind her back. She should feel ashamed of herself for letting Robby see how miserable she was. But she was glad he'd seen it. She was happy that Iris and Theo knew what she'd been suffering and now they could fix it for her.

"Your parents want you to come home," Robby said.

The grass would be lush, there would be summer rainstorms, and New York City would be a train ride away. For a second she let herself imagine it all. Then she looked at Robby. He was sitting on the bed, and he was all hunched over, like he'd just lost a fight. If she went back to her mother's house it would be such a defeat for him.

Nana would never have done that to

her husband, she wouldn't have run away just because she was uncomfortable and scared and not sure she was ready to be an adult. Not Nana, who had crossed an ocean while she was still in her teens and made her way in a new country where she couldn't even speak the language.

"I won't go," she said. "You're my husband, I'll stay here with you."

The smile that broke over Robby's face was dazzling. He threw his arms around her. "I'll make this up to you," he said. "I promise!"

She told herself whatever she had to endure, the heat, the bugs or the nausea, it was worth it if she'd made him this happy.

———

The next morning she slept late, and Robby was gone when she finally awakened. At the dig they told her he had driven into town on an errand—no one seemed to know what it was—and he wouldn't be back for a couple of hours. She decided to take the day off herself and waited at the trailer for him to come back. It was noon by the time he finally showed up.

"Where have you been?" she demanded. "I was starting to get worried . . ." Then she stopped. Because in one hand Robby was carrying a white dog's bowl on which he had painted the name MOLLY in big red letters. And in the other hand he was holding a leash, which was attached to the collar that had been buckled around the puppy's shaggy brown neck.

"Here," he said, as he grabbed the dog by her new collar to prevent her from launching herself at Laura and smothering her with kisses. "I thought maybe she'd keep you from feeling so blue."

———

In her kitchen, Laura finished packing up her cooking utensils. Behind her a snuffling sound announced the presence of a shaggy brown dog whose muzzle was starting to gray.

"Hey, Molly," she said softly. She leaned down to stroke the dog's rough fur. *There was a time when Robby and I tried so hard to be good to each other. We wanted to make each other happy. Now there are days when I don't think we even notice if we're happy or not. I keep on trying to figure out why it's happened, but maybe there isn't any reason.*

"Maybe Robby and I aren't doing that badly," she said to the dog. "Maybe this is normal for people who have been married for a long time. I always think I can make things better, but maybe this is as good as it gets."

Oh, how she didn't want to believe that.

Chapter Six

❦✦❦

When the summer had finally ended and Laura and Robby left the dig—and the hated trailer—for the apartment they had rented near the university campus, Laura was sure that at last their troubles were over. And at first things did seem to be better. The apartment was across the street from a row of adorable little shops and restaurants. It had air-conditioning that worked. There were sweet-smelling gardenias planted outside the front door of the apartment building.

But they had chosen to live in an area that was popular with undergraduates.

They had known that and they'd thought it might be kind of fun—they weren't so far away from their own college days after all. But they hadn't thought about how noisy it would be to live on the same block with two fraternity houses. They hadn't thought about how distracting it would be for Robby to hear parties going full tilt every night with music blaring and people shouting from building to building while he tried to study for his doctorate and do research for his very demanding mentor. It had never occurred to them that it would drive them crazy to listen to all the cheerful mayhem outside their windows while they were lying awake at night worrying about paying the bills.

Robby and Laura were broke. Continually. Scarily. When they were newly married and planning their future, they hadn't had any idea of the expenses involved with having a baby, or that those expenses would start before the baby was even born. They hadn't added the cost of doctor's visits and prenatal vitamins and the seemingly endless amount of baby paraphernalia—all to be purchased in advance—to the budget they were writing up. Furthermore, they had counted on Laura bringing in a salary to augment the small paycheck Robby would earn from Professor Hawkins. There were so many little shops and restaurants on and around the university campus, they were sure she'd get a job in one of them. It hadn't occurred to them that the little restaurants and shops would not want to hire and train a girl who was pregnant and would be leaving her job when she gave birth in just a few months. Laura kept on with her job hunt until she was a month away from her due date, then she finally admitted defeat and gave up.

———

The baby was born. She was a little girl, and they named her Katie after Robby's grandmother. According to the baby's two grandmothers, both of her parents had been rosy, round infants. Katie was angular, and her complexion was a warm olive. She stared at the world with big dark eyes. It was Robby who finally realized who she looked like.

"Remember your mother's baby pictures, Laura?" he said one morning as
Laura was bathing Katie, "Katie could
be her double."

Laura looked down at her child's face
gazing up at her out of the soapsuds.
"You're right. She does look like Mom."

The baby not only looked like Iris, but
from the very beginning she seemed to
have Iris's temperament too.

"She takes things in the way your
mother does," said Theo when he and
Iris flew out to California to see Katie. "I
know she's only a baby, but it's as if
she's watching everything that's happening and she's going to understand
all of it or know the reason why."

Once again Laura had agreed that the
similarities between her mother and her
daughter were amazing. But later on,
when she and the baby were alone she
had whispered in Katie's ear, "But you'll
never be afraid or insecure like my
mother has been all of her life. You'll be
strong, Katie. I'll see to it."

Laura had fallen in love with her child.
The guilt and doubts that had haunted
her during her pregnancy seemed to

have belonged to a different person. She could hardly remember them. Not that life with Katie was always easy. Especially when she was awakened in the middle of the night because the boys in the fraternity house at the end of the block had decided to march down the street singing the university fight song. Or when some noise her parents made in the tiny apartment woke her. She cried on these occasions; loudly, and for a very long time.

"Will she ever stop?" Robby demanded after a siege that seemed to have gone on for hours.

"She's angry," Laura said. "She was sleeping and minding her own business, and those idiots woke her up with their noise and now she's going to make sure we know how she feels about it." And she added quietly in her daughter's ear, "It's okay, Katie. Don't you pretend to be happy when you're not. Not my little girl."

But Laura and Robby weren't getting much sleep, and Robby, particularly, was exhausted. To fill in their ever-widening financial gap, he'd begun tutoring a few private students in math and science. Now, in addition to the hours he spent doing research for Hawkins, he was preparing lessons and grading papers. On the weekends he'd taken a part-time job at a shoe store in the local mall. Naturally all of this cut into the time he had for his own studies, and being sleep-deprived wasn't helping him either. In the early mornings Laura watched him stagger through their apartment, which was now crammed with the baby's furnishings, to sit at the kitchen table, and fall asleep over his books, and she knew he was falling behind. At the same time he was becoming fixated on the idea that he needed to get his doctorate as quickly as possible.

"Then I can start making a decent salary and we can get ourselves out of this miserable little apartment. You have to go back to school and get your degree too. We don't talk about that anymore but that doesn't mean I've forgotten it," he said. "And the baby is growing out of her clothes every few months. We have to have more money."

Poor Robby. He wanted to take care of his own so badly. He wanted to prove his father wrong and he wanted to show Theo and Iris that Laura hadn't made a mistake when she married so young and had a child so soon. But Laura knew he was pushing himself too hard. Throughout that first year, she tried to convince him not to rush. He needed to study at his own pace, she said. To ease the financial pressure on him, she went out job-hunting again and finally landed work as a waitress. But she quit after a few weeks because it was costing more to pay for a babysitter than she was earning in tips.

At the end of their first winter, Robby summed up their situation. "We're living in an apartment that would have been small for one person, let alone two people and a baby. We don't have even a small backyard for Katie and Molly to play in. And you still aren't going back to college, Laura. Some success I am!"

And nothing she could say would change his mind. So when summer came around, and he said he wouldn't go back to Professor Hawkins's dig because he could make more money at the shoe store, she didn't argue with him, even though she knew he'd be losing a valuable credit on his résumé.

It was so frustrating, it seemed as if every time they turned around, the lack of money was stopping them from doing something. And in Robby's mind the only solution was for him to get his doctorate. Laura watched this obsession grow and she was afraid for him. But again, he wasn't listening to her. When he began his third semester at the university, he announced that he would be taking his oral exams that year. The orals, as they were called, were the all-important first step to his coveted PhD, and he felt he couldn't wait another minute.

It shouldn't have come as a surprise when he failed. The exam was essentially a verbal grilling of a doctoral candidate by a team of professors from his department, and under the best of circumstances it was a grueling ordeal. For Robby, who had made the stakes way too high for himself, the pressure was too great. And the truth was, as Laura had feared, he wasn't as well prepared as he should have been. When the first question came at him, he froze and he never recovered.

Robby was shell-shocked. He was used to being the brightest boy in his class. Now he felt he was the class's biggest failure. For days he refused to go out of the apartment for fear of running into one of his fellow grad students.

Laura tried to reassure him. "You'll have a second chance at the exam, everyone gets two tries."

"I don't want to talk about it."

"But next time will be different. You'll see . . ."

"Really? And exactly how is that going to happen?"

"You'll study until you feel completely confident . . ."

"How? I'm asking you, Laura. How am I going to do that when I have to have three jobs?"

"I'll get a job instead."

"We tried that, remember?"

"We'll find a way. We'll make sure that next time you take the exam you're rested and you're not pressured, and—"

"Will you stop it?" He was yelling now. He sounded exactly like his father. "Will you stop being such a stupid little girl? Nothing is going to change—do you get that? I'm trapped here in this hellhole of an apartment and I'll never get out from under as long as I have to carry two—" He stopped himself. She knew he'd been about to say that she and the baby were like rocks weighing him down, and if he had finished the sentence she wasn't sure what she would have done. But he had caught himself in time. "I'll never get out!" he said.

Years later she would realize that she should have fought him then. She'd wanted to say that having a baby had been his idea so he could save his precious skin. "Don't you dare blame me!" she'd wanted to scream. And perhaps if she had, he would have learned to take responsibility for his own mistakes. Or maybe he never could have learned that. In any case, she hadn't screamed at him because then she would have been saying that having Katie had been a mistake, and there was no way she would ever say or feel that. And besides, in those days she still wanted to be the perfect wife. So she had choked down her anger, and she'd gone to the one small window in the room, and raised the blinds he'd pulled down. A narrow shaft of sunshine pierced the gloom he'd created.

"It's a beautiful day outside, Robby," she said as calmly as she could. "Go out. You can't hide in the house forever."

"Leave me the hell alone."

After that he refused to talk to her. He did finally leave the apartment; he had two jobs after all. But when he was home he sat in a chair reading magazines and watching bad television shows in silence until it was time to go back to work.

One day Laura realized that the war in Vietnam had been over for months, and she'd been so preoccupied she'd only noticed it in passing.

Chapter Seven

Rescue came in the form of a meeting with Robby's mentor. Professor Hawkins had been aware of Robby's struggles, and he summoned him to lunch at the faculty dining room. Even in his state of despair Robby didn't dare refuse.

"I know you have great potential, Robby," Professor Hawkins said after the steak sandwiches had been ordered. "I still believe in you. But your attention is too scattered. I believe I have a solution for that."

What he was proposing was a position for Robby on the university faculty. There were two freshman courses in archaeology that Hawkins taught every year, or at least, that was the claim in the university's catalog. In reality, the professor turned this drudgery over to one of his graduate students. The young man who had been teaching the courses was leaving, and Hawkins had chosen Robby to be his replacement. The workload would be light, certainly lighter than the one Robby was now carrying, and when he took over the classes there would be an increase in the paycheck he was already receiving as Hawkins's assistant. Best of all, Robby would be eligible for faculty housing. For less than he was now paying, he would be able to rent an entire house.

Robby's gratitude to his mentor bordered on worship. Laura was wary. From what she'd seen, Professor Hawkins enjoyed having eager acolytes surrounding him, but he never seemed to do much to advance the careers of the young people who worked for him. And a surprisingly high number of them never seemed to finish their degree. Still, Robby was talking to her again.

"I'm sorry I've been such a jerk," he said. "I'd never regret getting married, or having Katie."

"I know," she'd said. And she told herself that whatever her reservations were about the professor, this was the fresh start they needed.

———

In the beginning it seemed as if that was the case. Robby enjoyed teaching and he was popular with the kids. Most of them were taking the course to fulfill the school's science requirement and couldn't have cared less about the subject, so the fact that Robby managed to engage their interest was a boost to his battered ego. Also, the job was not as big a drain on Robby's time and energy as tutoring individual students and selling shoes. He could study more.

And the new house was sheer heaven. It was on a quiet street overlooking a park where Molly and Katie could play. There was a spare bedroom, which Robby could use as an office. There was a backyard; it was minuscule, but it was theirs. Of course the house was small, and there had been a time in her life when Laura would have said it was stuffy. But not now. Now she thanked God that she didn't have up-stairs neighbors who played their music at midnight. She set about making it their home.

She planted a small flower bed and soon had vases full of her homegrown roses scattered through the place. Gar-dening came easily to Laura; she and her grandmother had spent hours every summer pruning Nana's espaliered pear trees and weeding her beds of mauve-and-cream-colored phlox. Laura had learned about soil and sun and water during those hours, and these days as she looked at her tiny garden bursting with blooms she wished she could bring Nana back just for two minutes to show her how well she'd learned her lessons.

———

The inside of her home presented other challenges. When she and Robby had rented it, they were told it was partially furnished, but they quickly discovered that "partially" was the operative word.

Laura began haunting thrift shops to supplement the few meager pieces that had come with the house. Soon she had a collection of treasures; battered tables and chairs and chests of drawers, which she began to restore with sandpaper and paint. She picked up an ancient sewing machine and made curtains out of fabric remnants; she borrowed books from the library and taught herself how to reupholster a sofa. Several faculty wives told her she should put out her shingle and set herself up as an interior decorator for those on a shoestring budget.

Laura actually thought about doing it. She'd been trying to figure out how to bring in some extra money; even though their financial situation had improved with their cheap housing and Robby's bigger paycheck, she and Robby could always use more. But in the end she'd had a better idea than going into home decorating; there was one caterer in town who seemed to provide the food for all the parties and charitable events that were held at the university. Laura had attended several of them and while the entrées were fine, she thought the sweets were awful. They came from a bakery in Los Angeles, she'd learned, and the owner of the catering business was aware that desserts were her company's weakness. Laura spent two days baking, then she went to see the woman in her cheerful office, which was located in a shopping center.

"I hope this doesn't offend you, but when I was twelve I could bake a better chocolate cake than the one you served at the Faculty Wives Lunch last week," she said. "If you don't believe me, taste this." She'd opened the basket she'd brought with her and served the caterer a slice of Black Forest cake made from Nana's recipe—with a twist of her own. "I use raspberries instead of cherries," she told the woman, who had just loaded up her fork. Laura walked out of the caterer's office that day with two orders for Black Forest cake—made with raspberries. She bought a pair of pink sneakers for Katie with her first check.

Robby was still their main breadwinner of course, but the money Laura earned provided for some welcome extras. They were even able to start a small savings account, which really felt good to Laura. They had started making friends and that felt good to her too. So if she was still homesick for the Northeast and New York from time to time, she told herself not to be self-indulgent, she was building a new life for her family. Robby needed to be in Southern California. This was where he was going to pass his orals and earn his doctorate and start the career that had been his dream since he was a boy. That dream was far more important than her silly homesickness.

Only it hadn't quite turned out that way: Robby had indeed passed his orals on his second try. But there hadn't been any celebrating or popping of champagne corks as Laura had expected. Something seemed to have happened to Robby, he hadn't regained his bright-eyed self-confidence. Instead, with a hangdog look that Laura found a little frightening, he told her that his showing at the exam had been poor, and in fact he might have failed a second time if Hawkins hadn't intervened with the other professors on his behalf. This information had come from the great man himself, which made Laura wish she could tell him what an insensitive dolt—and egomaniac—he was. But her husband believed what his mentor had told him, so it was a scared and diminished Robby who began writing the thesis that was the final step on his way to his doctorate.

———

In her kitchen Laura sighed and ran her fingers through Molly's tangled fur. Robby had begun his thesis seven years ago. He was still trying to write it. He had started and stopped more times than she could remember. He had rewritten chapters, and thrown them away and then gone back to his original draft and then discarded everything and started over once again.

It's because you've forgotten who you are, Laura had wanted to cry so often during those seven long years. *Remember how intelligent you are. Remember who you used to be, Robby.* But Robby was past hearing her.

Gradually Professor Hawkins stopped talking to Robby about his bright future. He thought nothing of loading Robby down with work on a weekend or a holiday. And Robby always said yes. Because, he told Laura, where else was he going to go? Until he finished his thesis and had his degree, the world of archaeology wasn't exactly going to be banging down his door with work. But Laura knew Robby was still trying to prove himself to Hawkins, who had been the supportive father figure he'd always wanted. What he couldn't see was, Hawkins wasn't supporting him anymore.

"He's exploiting you," Laura finally said.

"You don't understand the pecking order in a university. I'm not baking cakes for ladies' lunches, Laura. My life is a hell of a lot more complicated than that."

The jab about her baking wasn't totally unexpected; she'd been building a bit of a reputation—and earning quite a bit of money—for her new undertaking, and she'd had a feeling he was resent-

ing it. Now she knew he was. He also resented her for being "unrelentingly
perky," as he put it. He never seemed to
realize that sometimes being cheerful
took a lot of willpower.

—

Robby's only solace was his popularity
with the students he taught. And as his
confidence continued to plummet, he
seemed to forget that it was his knowledge and love of his subject that had
originally won them over. Now he
wanted to be their friend.

"I'm effective because the kids feel
that I'm like them," he told Laura. "They
know I'm not some dried-up academic
type."

But he wasn't supposed to be like the
kids. He was supposed to be the adult.
It was part of his job to maintain a line
between himself and his students, but
he'd been blurring that line out of his
own neediness. So finally, predictably,
there had been a disaster.

A female student—a sad-eyed girl
who had serious emotional problems—
later everyone would agree on that—

mistook Robby's friendliness for something more passionate and developed a desperate crush on him. When she finally realized her feelings were not reciprocated, she made a halfhearted attempt at suicide.

No one believed that Robby had actually had an affair with the girl, but her father accused him of encouraging her. Since the man was an alumnus of the school and a major fund-raiser, Professor Hawkins had been forced to defend Robby and endure some very unpleasant moments on his behalf. To his credit, he had never considered abandoning Robby, but after the girl was safely off campus, he had given him a blistering lecture on inappropriate behavior and lack of judgment. Instead of taking any of this to heart, Robby announced angrily that Laura had been right all along about Hawkins.

"He is a total egomaniac, just like you said," he fumed. "He was furious, just because he had to defend me to the dean! And now instead of being on my side, he told me to stop socializing with my students. Do you believe that? That girl was disturbed, and I'm being blamed for it. Why, there isn't a professor or an instructor on this campus who hasn't gone out with the kids for an occasional beer or pizza. That's all I ever did. You know that, Laura."

Yes, but I also know that you blurred the line.

———

After a few weeks, as always happens in such cases, the incident and the sad-eyed girl with the emotional problems had faded from most people's memories. But there was still a black mark against Robby's name. And Professor Hawkins had seen for the first time that the young man he counted on to do his dirty work and make his life easier could be a liability. So from that point on, it was essential that Robby be on his best behavior. And he had been very careful. He skipped his usual Friday night beer with the kids at their favorite bar, and he never dropped in on the pizza parlor or any of their other favorite haunts anymore. But Laura knew he was feeling abused, and she was worried. When

Robby was in that mood, there was no telling what he'd do.

———

Laura must have pulled too hard on Molly's tangles because the dog gave a little cry and moved away. Laura stood up and got a biscuit for her as an apology.

Was that one failed exam the cause of everything that followed? Laura wondered as Molly crunched contentedly at her feet. *Did that destroy his courage so much that he never got it back?*

But that was ridiculous. Because life was full of failures, and overcoming them was what made you grow. One single fall could never destroy your courage—or your self-confidence—unless they had been shaky all along. So there had to have been something in Robby from the start, a weakness she had missed in the smart, handsome, but untested young man she had loved and married. She still loved him, but now it was a love mixed with pity. And that was not a good thing for any spouse to feel.

"I'm glad Robby and Katie and I are going to my home for Thanksgiving," Laura told Molly. "It will be good for Robby and me to get away from here for a few days."

That was when the phone rang. And in an instant the world spun one hundred and eighty degrees. When it stopped, there was no ground beneath her feet.

"Laura, do you think you could get an earlier flight out here?" It was Jimmy on the phone, his voice too controlled, too calm. "Dad has had a heart attack."

Chapter Eight

The next few hours were a blur of activity punctuated by phone calls. There was a call to the airline to change her flight time, and more calls to cancel the tickets for Robby and Katie, who would be staying home now because Laura didn't know how long she'd be needed in New York. There were calls with Jimmy and Janet for updates on her father's condition—he was stable—and with Phil who reported that Iris was in shock and he was almost as worried about her as he was about their father. There was a call from Steven, who was on his way from Washington with

Christina. This had prompted a second phone call from Phil because Iris was upset about Christina coming.

"Mom doesn't like Christina, and she doesn't need this right now," Phil said. "What the hell is Steve thinking?"

"Maybe that he *does* need Christina right now?"

"Well, he shouldn't have done it, because Mom's in bad shape, and this is too much for her. I don't care if she is being unreasonable. When are you going to get here?"

It was the same question Steve asked when he called her twenty minutes later. Jimmy phoned to ask her again an hour after that.

And throughout it all, the terrible fear, the phone calls and the unpacking and repacking—no need for the springform pan now—Laura tried not to let herself think about the fact that Robby had gotten his way, after all; he wouldn't be spending Thanksgiving with her family.

———

Her plane left that evening. Laura sat upright in her seat, not even trying to sleep, because she knew it was out of the question. She'd called Janet for the last time from a telephone in the airport and learned that her father was "resting comfortably" and she clung to the words. She blocked all thoughts of a scarily sick Theo lying on a narrow white bed, with the smells and sounds of a hospital swirling around him, and instead she forced herself to imagine him "resting comfortably" in a sunny room with a pile of his favorite books on the bedside table and music by Verdi playing gently in the background. For the six hours that the flight lasted she hung on to this fairy tale, until the plane finally started circling for its descent at Kennedy Airport.

It was early morning when she landed. Assuming that everyone in the family would be at the hospital, she hadn't expected anyone to meet her. But as she walked out of the gate she heard someone call her name. She turned and saw a young woman with bright blond hair. Her small face was dominated by round hazel-colored eyes and a full mouth. A slight overbite kept her from being truly pretty, and the pantsuit that she was wearing was a shade of purple that could only be described as electric.

"I'm Christina," she said as she came to shake Laura's hand. So this was Steve's girl. "You're Laura. I've seen pictures of you all over your parents' house. Stevie and I just got here a few hours ago, and he thought you'd like to have someone pick you up."

"Thanks. That was very nice of you. And Steven," Laura said, thinking to herself that her brother, who was no fool, had probably seen how upset his mother was, and he'd grabbed this opportunity to keep his lady love out of her hair.

"Sure. Let's get over to baggage claim," said Christina and she led the way, walking amazingly fast on high-heeled shoes that looked like stilts.

Christina was an excellent driver, negotiating the mazelike exit from Kennedy Airport with ease. Laura suspected that she was probably equally good at most mundane tasks. Laura's brilliant brother, Steve, on the other hand, couldn't balance a checkbook and regularly locked himself out of his car and his house. Laura began reassessing Steve's disastrous choice.

When they were finally clear of the airport, Laura drew in a deep breath and asked the question that she'd been refusing to think about on the plane. "How did it . . . the heart attack happen? Do you know?"

"Like I said, Stevie and I just got here ourselves so we weren't around when he had it. But the way I understand it, your mother and father were putting groceries in the refrigerator when he felt the pain. She called your brother James, who told her what to do for him until the ambulance got there and they brought your father to the hospital out in Westchester until he wasn't in danger anymore. Then your brother and your sister-in-law—I think her name is Jane . . ."

"Janet."

"Right. They had your father moved to the hospital where they work in Manhattan."

"And Dad . . . is all right . . . ?"

There was a pause. Christina was trying to figure out what to say. A cold finger ran down Laura's spine. She wanted to cry, but if she started, she wouldn't stop and what good would that do?

"Before I got on the plane, Janet told me he was doing well . . . Did something happen during the night? Did he take a turn for the worse?"

"No, no, nothing like that. Your dad is going to make it."

"Thank God."

"But there was some damage. The doctor . . . the cardiologist told your mother and your brothers that this morning . . . he said there will have to be some big changes. Your father can't work anymore—it's too much for him. And there was a whole lot about his diet and he'll have medicine he has to take . . ."

"But he can live with this."

"If he takes good care of himself."

Laura leaned back, the tears wouldn't be stopped now. It wasn't a death sentence. Theo could live with this. "Thank you," she said. "How did Mom react?"

Again there was a pause.

"Christina?"

"Look, it's none of my business, but . . . your father has been asking . . . for details about what happened . . ."

"He would. I'm sure everyone knows that he'd want to have as much information as he could."

"But your mother . . . she said no one should tell him about . . . the damage."

"What?"

"She doesn't want your dad to find out. She's told everyone, including your father's doctors, that they can't say a word about it."

Her mother was giving crazy orders like that? She *was* in bad shape. Very bad shape.

"The thing is, your father really wants to know," Christina continued. "He keeps asking and asking. I think it would help him to know what he's facing."

"Of course it would! Mom isn't thinking . . ." Suddenly, Laura felt a need to explain this bizarre behavior to a person who was a stranger to the family. "She can't imagine life without Dad, so she's panicking."

"Oh, I understand. I'd be insane if it

was Stevie." Christina's hands tightened on the steering wheel at the thought. "My life started when I met him. That's how I feel—you know?"

"I guess."

But Laura didn't know. That was a guilty little secret she'd always kept to herself. Even when she was newly in love with Robby, she hadn't needed him the way her mother had always needed her father. And, it seemed, the way Christina needed Steve.

———

They were approaching the George Washington Bridge now; Laura looked out the window at the tangle of traffic as drivers tried to cut each other off to get to the entrance three seconds earlier than the person in the car next to them. Suddenly, Christina said, "When we met, your mother didn't like me."

Oh God. "I'm sure she—"

"It's okay. It was all my fault. I got off on the wrong foot with her. You see, I was scared. Stevie really didn't tell me much about your family before we went to visit them . . . well, you know how he is."

Laura nodded. She knew exactly how "Stevie" was and how little help he would have been in preparing his girl for the ordeal of meeting his parents.

"I knew your father was a doctor and your mother was a teacher at a university, and I'm not very well educated, so I was okay with them not thinking I'm smart enough for Stevie, which I'm not . . ."

"Most of us aren't."

"But when I saw those candlesticks and that ring your mother wears . . . I wanted her to know that I wasn't some hick who doesn't know the value of nice things. So I said the ring was probably worth about twenty thousand, and that was the wrong thing to do. Stevie told me so later. He said his mother didn't like to talk about money and what things cost." Christina chewed her lip. "That was the problem."

"What was?"

"You have to be really rich not to care about what something costs. Stevie never said his mother came from that kind of money."

"She didn't. You know that ring you admired? My grandfather had to pawn it during the Depression. My mother loves that story, get her to tell it sometime."

"Are you kidding? I'll never talk to your mother about that ring again. I learned my lesson." Christina chewed her lip again. It seemed to be a nervous habit. "I just wish I could convince her that I'm not after Stevie for a meal ticket. And please don't try to tell me she doesn't think that, because it's what I'd think if I were her. And it's true, I do love beautiful things—like her candlesticks, and all those pictures on the walls in her house . . . I wish I could afford things like that. But I know I won't, certainly not if everything works out with Stevie and me. Making money doesn't matter to him. He loves what he does and I'd never ever try to make him be any different."

"Really? Because I think he has lots of room for improvement," Laura joked.

Christina didn't laugh. "I don't. Not at

all. Stevie is a great man. What he does is . . . well, it's downright noble!"

Laura wished her mother could see Christina at that moment. Her small jaw was set and her big eyes looked fierce. Steve might have started out as her protector, but for as long as they were together she would protect him even more.

———

They had reached the city; Christina swung the car onto the West Side Highway. "By the way, if you can do it, you need to get your mother out of that hospital," she said as she deftly avoided a large station wagon that had crossed into her path without signaling. "She spent all last night there and she won't go home and she gets mad when anyone suggests it."

Chapter Nine

Iris sat in the hospital waiting room and braced herself. Soon, one or more of her children would come in and try once again to convince her to go home—her family and the doctors all wanted her to do that. "You have to sleep," they kept saying, as if sleep was a possibility. "Theo wouldn't want you exhausting yourself like this."

They walked into the room, and they pulled up chairs next to hers—heavy metal chairs that dragged noisily over the bare linoleum floor—and they leaned into her with their worried faces and they gave her all the reasonable arguments for leaving. But this thing that had happened was beyond reason. It was beyond thinking. This called for screaming and fists driven into walls with howls of pain. Theo had had a heart attack. Theo could die. He could die before she did. She'd always known that one of them would go before the other but she'd never considered the possibility that it might be him. Even though he was older than she was. Because she didn't know how to live without him. That was what she wanted to tell her sons and her daughter-in-law and the doctors in their white coats when they stuck their faces so close to hers and made all their reasonable arguments. *I don't know how to live without him, do you understand?*

He had come into her life when she was twenty-eight years old. When she thought she was too old to get married, and had resigned herself to it. And then the miracle had happened and he had fallen in love with her. He'd been wounded past endurance, but he had seen something to love in her. And if a part of that love was gratitude for a safe haven, and if she had loved him more than he had loved her, so be it. He had loved her. And he had given her the only life she'd ever wanted; he'd made her his wife. And even now, when she had so much—a career, and children, and grandchildren—she still needed to be his wife. She knew that because there had been times in the past when she'd thought she'd lost him. And she'd felt that she'd lost her reason for being.

My mother wasn't like that, she thought, as she stared at the hideous tan walls of the waiting room. *Mama loved Papa, she was a perfect wife. But there was always something she was holding back. Papa knew it too. He was like me, he finally accepted being the one who loved more.*

There was a sound behind her. The waiting room door was opening. Next, someone would sit next to her, leaning in and taking her hands, speaking gently. Would it be Steve, looking bewildered because he'd never known her to be so stubborn? Or Jimmy in his rumpled white doctor's coat offering a sedative to take the edge off? Janet would offer that too, only her white coat would be crisply starched. Or maybe it would be Philip, with his charming smile trying to coax her to take a nap like a little child. It didn't make any difference which one of them it was, they had nothing to say to her.

The person who entered the room did not sit next to her. She felt a presence standing over her and looked up. For a second she thought it was Anna who had come back. But her mother had been gone for years. She looked up again at the face that was so like Anna's. "Laura," she said.

"Mom, you've got to go home for a few hours." Laura didn't reach for Iris's hand and her voice was not gentle. "Everyone is spending too much time worrying about you. And it's not good for Dad to see how frightened you are."

I can't leave him!

"It doesn't matter what you want," her daughter went on, reading her mind. "Get some sleep so you don't look so exhausted, then come back and let Dad see you smile. You have to seem strong even if you're not. That's what we all need from you right now."

Once, years ago, when she was in despair over her marriage and could barely
move through the days, her mother had
come to her. She'd given a command—
go out and get your hair done and put
on a pretty dress. "You must learn to
act," Anna had said. "Put a smile on
your face. Put one on if you have to
paste it on." Iris had been furious, but
she had done what Anna said, and she
and Theo had patched up the marriage
that was so worth saving. Laura was
looking at her exactly the way Anna had
on that day.

Iris drew in a deep breath. "Jimmy . . .
and Theo's cardiologist . . . they want to
tell your father that his heart . . . that it's
been . . ." She stumbled over the words.

"That his heart is damaged."

"I don't want them to say that to him."

"Do you think he doesn't suspect it?
He's a doctor."

"But it doesn't have to be said. Not
yet."

"Maybe for you it wouldn't. But for
him . . . have you ever known him to
keep the truth from a patient? He always
tells them the worst right away. He says

they deserve that respect. That's what he wants for himself now. And you know it."

Laura's young face looked so much like that other one, the one Iris had resented and loved so very much. She was saying exactly what Anna would have said. And Anna had been right—almost all of the time.

"All right. Yes. I know that is what he would want."

It didn't matter how you felt; her mother had said that too. You put on a show for the people you loved. Iris had never been much good at that. But now it was time to start.

"I'll go home and change," Iris said. "But I won't have time to lie down. Tell Jimmy to wait until I get back and then they can give Theo the news. I want to be with him when he hears it. But I need to change my dress and fix my hair first. And I'll put on some rouge so I'm not so pale."

"Good. Dad always likes to see you at your best." But suddenly there was a quiver in Laura's stern voice. Her eyes were filling up and she turned away quickly to hide it. She was as scared as her mother. She needed Iris to pretend to be brave too.

"Laura," Iris heard herself say, "I will never fall apart again. No matter what happens. I promise."

Laura nodded.

"Now, can someone drive me home?"

"Yes. I've already asked her."

—

"I can't believe you told Christina to drive your mother back to the house!" Janet exclaimed later. "Of all people!"

"They seem to be getting along, don't they?" Laura said. Iris had gone home as promised, and returned to the hospital wearing Theo's favorite dress. Now she and Christina were sitting together in the waiting room talking quietly.

"But Mom doesn't even like her," Jimmy said.

"Mom and Christina are the same kind of woman."

"You can't be serious," Janet protested.

"I am, and they are. In the way that counts."

"You're a magician," Jimmy said.

"No," Phil said. "She's just smarter than the rest of us."

———

Iris kept her word that day. She stood by calmly while the cardiologist told Theo how much and what kind of damage there had been to his heart muscle. She listened as the man outlined the kind of care her husband would need when he came home. She never flinched or cried. She remained serene. She knew her daughter was proud of her; she thought her mother would have been too.

———

Theo sat up in his hospital bed, and listened to the cardiologist give him the news he'd already known—that he was a very sick man. The specialist was using technical terms—the words "myocardial infarction" were thrown around a few times—but what it all boiled down to was Dr. Theo Stern was sick. And he wasn't going to be getting better. Not really. Oh, he'd live a while longer if he

took all the precautions his distin-
guished colleague from the cardiology
department was now laying out so carefully, but he wouldn't be the man he had
been. Never again. Theo shifted in the
bed—he'd made the nurses crank it up
as high as it would go, because there
was no way he was going to take this
news lying down—and watched Iris.
She was sitting upright too, her spine
was as straight as a board. Her hands
were clasped lightly in her lap. She was
nodding and she looked perfectly calm.
Inside, he knew she wanted to scream.
Or maybe she wanted to curl up in her
bed like a child and close out the world;
he'd seen her react both ways in a
crisis. But someone had told her she
must be strong—probably it had been
Laura—so she was wearing a pretty
dress and lipstick that matched it, and
she was sitting upright and listening to
the cardiologist.

She was trying to behave as her
mother would have, Theo knew. Anna
would have been the rock everyone else
could lean on today, and now Iris was
trying to be that. Iris would always try to

live up to her mother's standards and she would always feel that she had failed. Theo knew that too. He looked again at his wife.

Ah Iris, he thought. *I wonder what you would do if you were to learn that your mother was a far more complicated woman than you ever dreamed. Because your mother had a secret, my darling. The perfect wife and mother, Anna Friedman, had a dark secret that I happen to know. And I will always wonder what it would do to you if you knew . . .* Theo shook his head impatiently. What on earth had made him start thinking about all of that at this moment? He must be losing his mind! Iris saw the movement and thinking that he was upset about what the cardiologist was saying, reached over to stroke his hand comfortingly. Oh yes, Iris was determined to be strong for all of them today. She was going to be Anna all over again.

———

The doctors said that it would be at least three weeks before Theo would be ready to leave the hospital. And as word of what had happened to Dr. Stern spread to his friends and colleagues, there was a stream of guests to his room, all making the same suggestion to Theo and Iris about the wisdom of moving to a . . . facility. Not a nursing home, everyone hastened to reassure, but some lovely retirement community where they could still have their own apartment. There would be a kitchen that would cook their meals in accordance with Theo's new restricted diet. And, above all, although no one mentioned this, there would be a staff trained to handle heart attacks if Theo should have another one.

"It would be the smartest thing they could do," Janet said. "If they'd agree."

Iris might have, but the Stern children knew their father never would. So their parents' home had to be adapted to the needs of a man who was now ill. Actually, the house was ideal for the purpose. During the years when Theo was retraining himself and the family hadn't had much money, he and Iris had sold their big beautiful home, and purchased this one, which was small and laid out for practical use rather than for show. When Theo was launched again, they'd thought about moving to a more luxurious place, but they'd come to love their neighbors, so they never did. And thank heaven for that, Laura thought. Because if they had, they'd be downsizing again. Instead, with a few modifications, their compact little house could be set up to accommodate Theo's needs and they could continue to live independently. Laura couldn't imagine her proud father existing any other way.

They'd been told by the cardiologist that Theo shouldn't climb stairs—at least not for the foreseeable future—so he and Iris would need a bedroom on the first floor. Laura suggested using the sun porch on the side of the house, which had been closed in and insulated years earlier.

"If you have any ideas about putting it together, please tell me," said her mother.

Of course Laura had ideas; after all, she'd been fixing up her own home for years. She called Robby and asked him if he could manage on his own with Katie for a while longer. She'd be home in time for Christmas, she assured him. Robby said she should stay as long as she needed to. He and Katie would decorate the house and he would even finish up the Christmas shopping on Laura's list. When Laura looked back later, she thought his voice had sounded a little odd and overly cheerful when he said all of that. But she told herself that he was just trying to be positive because he knew she and her family were worried about Theo.

Christina stayed on in New York too, and for the next two weeks she helped Laura paint walls, stencil woodwork, and sand floors. Even Iris got into the act, and while Laura knew her mother would never actually enjoy tufting a headboard, they did laugh a lot. And at night when they were finished working, Laura would whip up a meal for them.

"How do you do this?" Christina demanded one night as they sat down to dinner. "You just started cooking half an hour ago. You should write a book."

"Yes," Phil said. He'd been coming out to the house almost every night while Laura was there. Once he had brought a couple of friends and asked her to make her famous chestnut torte.

"He went to a gourmet cookware shop in the city and bought me a spring-form pan," Laura told Robby on the phone.

"It's sounds like you're having a good time."

She was, she realized guiltily. Now that her father was on the mend, she loved being near her family and back in the part of the country where she'd grown up. And of course she loved being so close to Manhattan. Sometimes when she was visiting Theo in the hospital, she'd take a break and walk around the streets, hoping to catch a snippet of a conversation in a language she didn't know, or to smell the aromas of a cuisine she'd never sampled as it wafted from the open doorway of a restaurant. At those moments, she would realize how badly she wished she could share such experiences with her daughter.

"I miss you and Katie," she said now to Robby. "I wish you were here."

I wish I could take Katie to see Swan Lake *at the ballet, the way my grandmother took me. We could go to Serendipity afterward for Frrrozen Hot Chocolate—that was always a favorite of mine. And I want Katie to see snow. That's what I want most of all, for her to see the way that soft white blanket transforms everything so you don't even recognize your own front yard. And to hear that eerie silence when the world is cold and still . . .*

"Well, stay as long as you like," Robby's voice broke into her thoughts. "There's no hurry about getting home, Katie and I have the holiday under control." This was the second time he'd told her to stay in New York in that same odd, overly cheerful tone of voice, and this time she didn't ignore it.

"Are you sure everything's okay? You don't need me?" she asked.

"Laura, for God's sake, I have an excellent command of the English language. If I said everything's fine, it is!"

Given that overreaction—and Robby's

strained cheeriness—she should have known something was up. But at that moment she was enjoying herself so much that she didn't want to think about what might be happening on the West Coast. So she pushed the phone call to the back of her mind, and for a few more days she let herself bask in everyone's compliments on her cooking and her decorating skills. She walked down Fifth Avenue and looked at the windows at Saks, which had been decorated for Christmas, and daydreamed about taking Katie to see them. She imagined watching her daughter learn to ice-skate. And she tried not to think about going back to California.

Chapter Ten

Sometimes, in a close family, it can seem as if your siblings know what you're thinking before you do. And they have a spooky way of sensing that you're about to make a change when you still think you're going to stay with the status quo. At least, that was how it felt to Laura when she looked back on the chilly night in late December when she found herself sitting in her parents' kitchen in Westchester with her three brothers. The work on the downstairs bedroom was finished, Theo would be coming home from the hospital the next day, and Laura was scheduled to leave for California the day after that. So the family had gathered for a good-bye dinner for Laura. And then somehow Iris, Christina, and Janet weren't around and Laura was sitting at the table drinking coffee with Steve, Phil, and Jimmy. It was Phil who asked the question.

"Laura, how long has Robby been working on his dissertation?"

It took her totally by surprise. "Excuse me?"

"It's been seven years, right?" Phil went on.

"You don't understand what's involved. Writing a dissertation takes time. He can't rush it . . ."

"You call seven years rushing it?" Her younger brother was going to be relentless. He could do that sometimes. "How close is Robby to finishing?"

"I don't see where that's any of your business," she started to say, but Jimmy leaned in.

"Not everyone is meant to be an academic," he said.

"Getting his doctorate is Robby's dream."

"We all have dreams, but sometimes

we can't make them into reality. There's no disgrace in that, as long as we accept it and move on," said Phil, who had done just that. His was the voice of experience.

"But wallowing in your failure and making your loved ones share it is just selfish," said Steve, her brother who had turned his own life around. His was another voice of experience.

"Is Robby going to be finished this year?" Jimmy asked. "Or next? Or the year after?"

It was a question she'd been asking herself—and refusing to admit she was asking it—for months. "He'll be finished when he's finished," she said. "Now, let's change the subject. Anyone want more coffee?"

But her brothers were the Stern boys—they didn't quit just because someone told them to. Especially not if that someone was their sister. "Maybe a fresh start would be good for both of you," Jimmy said.

"It might even be better for Robby than it would be for you, Laura," Steve put in gently. That made her eyes start to sting. Gentleness didn't come easily to Steve. "How much longer is he going to go on doing the dirty work for Professor Hawkins, and watching his contemporaries pass him by?"

"And how much longer can he stand knowing that he's the failure of his department?" Phil demanded. "You know that's what the rest of them are saying, Laura. Universities are nasty little hotbeds of gossip."

She did know it. The tears were now threatening to fill her eyes.

"I think what we're all saying is, maybe it's gone on long enough," Jimmy said.

"It *has* gone on long enough," Phil put in. "If Robby doesn't know it, then you should tell him."

Laura blinked the tears back. "I'd never do that! And we are going to change the damn subject right now!"

They saw how upset she was and they finally backed off. The subject was changed. But after they had all gone home for the night, Laura made herself be honest about the real reason why she'd reacted so strongly to their suggestions. She'd been having her own doubts about Robby's future and she'd been giving in to daydreams about moving back East. That was not only disloyal to her husband, practically speaking, it was impossible. Robby was thirty-three, which certainly wasn't old, but it wasn't twenty-three either, and he had a wife and child to support. He couldn't just start over in a new career. More important, he'd never wanted to be anything but an archaeologist and it would crush him to admit that he was failing at his dream. No, Laura's role was clear. She must keep on believing in him—and help him to believe in himself. Women had been doing that for generations, and she could do it too. Armed with that new resolve, she began packing for the trip back to California. But on the night before she was scheduled to leave, she got a phone call from Robby.

"It was a party, Laura, just a party." Robby's voice on the phone was belligerent. It got that way when he was scared. "It was just some kids getting together in someone's apartment to celebrate before they went home for the holiday break. They invited me to come over for a while, which was a compliment as far as I was concerned, so I lined up a sitter for Katie and I went. To a party in a private home. I didn't break any of Hawkins's damn rules about going to a bar with my students."

"He wasn't talking about going to a bar, Robby. He felt you'd used bad judgment."

"Well, I didn't. And I'm tired of being punished because some jerk on the alumni committee—who has more money than is good for him—didn't want to face that his daughter is a sick girl! That's what all of this was really about—"

"Robby!" she broke in. "What happened?"

"Nothing! Certainly not anything that should shock someone who works with today's kids. I mean, if Hawkins doesn't know by now that most of his students have experimented with pot—"

"Oh God. There were drugs at the party?"

"Pot, Laura. Don't say 'drugs' in that

melodramatic way. It was just a little marijuana."

"Which is illegal. Don't tell me you—"

"Of course I didn't do pot with my students! I'm not an idiot. And besides, I've tried the stuff, and I don't like it."

That was what he'd tell the students when he refused to smoke it. He'd say it in a way that would let them know that he wasn't disapproving of them. No indeed. Oh-so-cool-and-hip Mr. McAllister had already tried "the stuff" and he just didn't happen to like it. And of course he wouldn't mention the law the kids were breaking, or the rules of the university they were violating. Above all, he wouldn't say that he was going to leave the party if the drug use continued because he was bound by his job to report it. He'd stay, and he'd smile in that charming way of his, and he'd say, "Please don't call me Mr. McAllister tonight. That's my father. I'm Robby." That was his idea of setting boundaries, as he'd been told to do. Fear grabbed at Laura deep in her stomach and twisted it. She was sure she knew how the evening had ended.

"What happened next?"

"The party got noisy. Really noisy." There was a pause. When he spoke again the belligerent tone was gone. Now he was starting to feel sorry for himself. "That was my one big mistake, Laura. I should have made the kids keep the noise down. But to tell you the truth I was having fun—more than I've had in a while. So I didn't say anything. And of course one of the neighbors called the cops."

She could picture it. "I see."

"The locals called the campus police—town and gown courtesy, I think. So it wasn't as bad as it could have been."

"How bad was it?"

"They saw the pot. And they reported it. But only to the university. And the university didn't want anyone going to jail." He drew in a deep breath. His voice was getting wobbly. Now his eyes would be filling with tears. "The upshot is, three kids have been suspended, the boy who threw the party was expelled, and . . . and next year your husband will no longer be a teaching adjunct at Custis

University. Hawkins, the damn hypo-
crite, has informed me that he will be
canning me."

There it was. The knot in her stomach
let go. The worst had happened.

"He said he was going to keep me on
until the end of the school year so no
one would say he was firing me because
of the party," Robby went on. "He
seemed to think I should be grateful to
him, but I knew he was really covering
his own behind. He's afraid the whole
mess will reflect badly on him so he's
just going to bury it. He doesn't even
want to try to stand up for me."

"I guess that was to be expected,"
she finally managed to say.

"It didn't have to be, damn it! I'm a
good teacher, Laura. One of the best.
Everyone says so. He doesn't have to
do this!"

"What about your thesis?"

"Oh, I'm free to pursue that anywhere
I want to—just not with him as my advisor."

So Robby had finally done it. He'd
lost his slender foothold at the university. And since there was no way he'd

find a place in another doctoral program at another university without Hawkins putting in a good word, his dream was gone too. The dream that Laura had made her own for seven years.

"Laura, are you there? Look, if it does any good, I know I screwed up. I'm not saying Hawkins hasn't been gunning for me because he has. But I knew that and I should have been more careful. So I know you've got to be angry . . ."

She heard the hurt in his voice, but she didn't care. She didn't want to comfort him or try to find a way to make him feel better. The phone was in her mother's kitchen; she looked at the cabinets above the sink. They were badly scuffed; she wished she'd had time to paint them before going back to California. Back to . . . what?

"Robby, what about our house?"

"It's faculty housing. We'll lose it as soon as the school year ends."

And his salary would stop. It had never seemed like enough, but now that she knew it would be gone, it felt like a fortune. And it would be gone in . . . how many months? Four and a half? Then all they'd have would be her small savings account, and they'd need that for the move . . . *Where will we go? With a little girl and a huge dog and no job, how will we live?*

"Do you think you could talk to Hawkins, and explain?"

"Are you out of your mind? You want me to crawl to him? I won't do it. And there's no way I'm going back to Blair's Falls either."

That, at least, was a tiny bit of good news. Laura had finally seen his little hometown and she had not been impressed. Plus, her in-laws were about as fond of her as she was of them.

"My father would love to see me come home with my tail between my legs! The son of a bitch has been waiting for me to fail all of my life. And it would break my mother's heart. I can't do that to her . . . I can't . . ." Robby was sobbing. And she finally felt sorry for him.

"It's okay, Robby. It's okay," she soothed. Her initial panic was subsiding and now she could think again.

"It's not okay. I wouldn't blame you if

you were furious at me . . . I wouldn't blame you if you left me."

"I would never do that." *If I walked out on my marriage, that would break my mother's heart. I want to keep as much of this from my parents as I can.*

But there were other members of her family. Members who would be glad to hear that Robby had given up on his dream of a PhD . . . And they would want to do whatever they could . . .

On the other end of the phone, Robby had pulled himself together. "I'm sorry," he said, "I shouldn't have let myself . . . I shouldn't have done that. It was just . . . thinking about going back there . . . to Blair's Falls . . . I worked so hard to get out of that dump . . . and I swore I'd never go back . . ."

"We're not going there, I promise." Laura's mind was racing now. Steve had political connections all over the eastern seaboard because of the pro bono work he did, and Phil knew everyone in the financial community on Wall Street. Jimmy and Janet had a wide circle of influential friends. Surely one of her brothers could help Robby get another teaching job. A job here. Somewhere in the New York City area.

"Robby, I have to go now, I have to make a few phone calls. But don't worry, because we're going to be okay."

By the time she boarded the plane for California the next day, all three of the Stern brothers were already putting out the word that their sister wanted to move back home and their brother-in-law was looking for a job on the East Coast.

Next year I'll show Katie the snow, Laura thought as the plane lifted up into the sky.

Chapter Eleven

It was Steve who came up with a job for Robby. "Not teaching," he said to Laura when he called her with the news. "If Robby wants to do that again, he's going to have to ask Professor Hawkins for a recommendation and it doesn't sound as if the man would give him one." Laura hadn't told any of her brothers the extent of the disaster her husband had created in California, but they did know that Robby and his mentor had had a falling out. "Besides," Steve went on, "I think it might be better for Robby to be out of an academic environment for a while." He was being diplomatic.

Clearly, Laura's brothers had decided to handle her carefully. "There's a little museum in the Hudson River Valley, about an hour's drive north of Manhattan. It's called the Barker Museum and it's dedicated to the culture of the Native American tribes that lived in the area before the Europeans came—the Mohawks, the Mahopacs and the Mohegans, mostly. A couple of years ago I did some work for the place, and the guy who owns it liked me. His name is Leland Barker; he's extremely wealthy, his hobby is archaeology, and he's managed to put together a nice collection of artifacts. Leland built the museum, he's the chief source of funds and for years he's acted as curator—it's really a one-man show, but he's in his eighties now and he realizes he needs someone to take over."

"And you suggested Robby."

There was a pause on the other end of the line. She pictured Steve searching for the right words. "I'm going to be honest with you," he finally said. "Robby is overqualified for this job. But he's got an opportunity to build something there. Leland is well connected, he's got money and influential friends he's willing to call on. And he feels that this museum is his legacy. If Robby can find ways to expand it, and establish it as a more serious institution, Leland will back him all the way. Robby can make this job whatever he wants it to be."

If it were one of her brothers facing that challenge, the sky would be the limit. But Robby wasn't one of Theo Stern's sons. Still, it was a job. And it was in the Northeast.

"Steve, I don't know what to say except thank you."

"You may not thank me so much when you hear what kind of money your husband will be making. The Barker Museum operates on a shoestring . . ."

But Laura had already decided that this time Robby wouldn't be supporting the family all by himself. It was much too risky. She had another plan in mind.

"I just want Robby to be doing work he likes."

She repeated that to Robby when they sat at the kitchen table that evening, and she told him about the position.

"I don't give a damn what kind of work it is," he said. "I just want to get as far away from this town and Custis University as we can."

So Laura called Steve and told him Robby wanted the job. Then she emptied her rainy day fund, and with that as a down payment—she was going to buy this time, not rent—she flew east to find a home for her family. She wanted to stay in Westchester, within commuting distance from the city. "How about a co-op or a condominium?" the real estate agent suggested. "That would be within your price range."

But what she needed for her plan was a house. And it only took her a couple of weeks to find what she wanted. She and Iris were driving into Manhattan—Laura was staying with her parents—when they'd stopped for gas and she'd spotted the perfect place.

"Actually, you can still get some bargains in that area," the real estate agent said when she told him about it later. "There were many lovely old homes there that were turned into multiple dwellings during the fifties and the sixties. People are just starting to buy them and restore them." Then he'd checked the information on the house Laura had mentioned. "That property is a real fixer-upper. To be honest with you, it's been on the market for over a year because no one wants to take it on. Are you sure you wouldn't like to see something that won't require as much work?"

Laura was sure.

———

Up close, the house was even more perfect than she'd thought it would be when she'd seen it from the road. It sat on the top of a hill, at the end of a long, badly maintained gravel driveway. On either side of the driveway the branches of ancient trees bent to touch one another; in the summer they would form a green leafy canopy overhead. Behind the trees were shrubs in need of pruning, and formal flower beds, which were overgrown—she would have to wait until spring to see just how bad the damage was. Phlox would grow beautifully in these gardens. So would peonies, roses, lilies and fresh herbs. Laura was going to need fresh herbs.

Inside, there was more good news; although the house had been badly neglected the bones of it were fine. The plumbing and the wiring had been kept up to code, according to the real estate agent, and the roof was relatively new. Most of the problems were cosmetic: stained and peeling wallpaper, woodwork that would have to be stripped and parquet floors that were badly in need of refinishing. But the crown moldings and the wainscoting were original and magnificent, and even though someone had replaced the old chandeliers and sconces with ugly modern fixtures, the originals had been packed up and stored in what had been the old ballroom.

"What a fabulous room!" Laura said as she walked through it. "And it opens out onto that terrace and the back lawn. Perfect for a summer party."

But it was the kitchen that was her main concern. She held her breath as the real estate agent opened the big wooden door with the glass transom in the top. Then she breathed a sigh of relief. "Look at all the counter space!" she cried. "And that huge old sink! Of course, I'll have to get new appliances and the cabinets will have to be refinished, but that old tile floor is gorgeous, and it would be easy to clean. And there's plenty of room for a big worktable in the center." She turned to the real estate agent. "It's exactly what I need," she said.

Now it was time to put her plan into action.

———

She went to the library in her parents' neighborhood—what would she do without libraries?—and read up on small businesses. She worked out the cost of the repairs and restoration she'd need to do. Based on the work she'd done on the house in California, she was sure her figures were accurate. Then she asked the real estate agent for the keys to the old house because she wanted to show it to someone, and she spent the next two days shopping for food and cooking. When she was finished, she called her brother Phil and the next evening they drove to her dream house.

"I'm so glad you could come with me, Phil," she said as they finally stopped jolting their way up the driveway.

Her brother was staring up at her treasure. "When you said you wanted to treat me to a picnic at sunset, I didn't know you were planning to take me to the House of Usher."

"It's not that bad."

"Really?"

"What you're seeing are surface problems; underneath, this place is a real prize."

"If you say so."

"I just want you to promise to keep an open mind."

They unloaded the hamper of food she'd prepared and she led the way inside the house. She'd chosen to have her picnic in the old ballroom, where the last rays of sunshine were streaming through the long windows, so she spread a checkered table-cloth on the floor in there and set out cutlery and china.

"You've been so mysterious about all of this," Phil said. "I assume we're not trespassing . . ."

"No. The person who gave me the key to this place knows we're here." She opened a thermos and poured steaming soup into bright red mugs. It was a concoction of her own—rich, chockfull of mushrooms, and it filled the air with the scents of the red wine and rosemary she'd used. She sliced a loaf of crusty bread she'd baked that morning and arranged slices of an onion tart—also her own recipe—on a platter.

"Are you going to explain what's going on?" Phil demanded.

"Just try my soup, then I'll tell you." He took a spoonful. "Is it good?"

"Of course. It's delicious. Now, will you please—"

"I'm glad you like it. Because I think it's going to be one of the signature dishes for my new catering business."

"Are you serious?"

"I have this idea." Actually, she'd had it for quite a while, but she'd believed it was impossible. Now that she was finally talking about it, she found herself tripping over her own words in her excitement. "Most people hire a caterer for big formal events, that's the way it was out in California. But I think the women in this community might want something more casual. They're working at jobs outside the home now, many of them are commuting into the city. They don't have time to throw together a little dinner party for friends or pack up a picnic basket when the family goes to the beach. Stay-at-home wives used to do that kind of thing all the time; modern women are too busy.

"But people still want to entertain, and be social. They want life to be graceful and warm, it's just that no one is around to do the work. So I'll be there. If you want to have a romantic dinner for two for you and your husband, I'll deliver it on your doorstep, complete with wine and flowers from my garden. If you want to have a simple at-home wedding, I can provide the meal, and even make the table linens so they'll be color-coordinated with your bridesmaids' dresses. Your wedding cake will be unique because it'll be homemade." Excited now, she stood up and turned around, gesturing to the four walls of the ballroom. "And someday, after I've fixed it up, I'll be able to offer you this room with the beautiful nineteenth-century crown moldings if you need to accommodate two hundred guests." She turned to her brother and asked breathlessly, "What do you think?"

"It's obvious that you've been thinking about this for a while."

"Ever since I first started working for the caterer in California."

"How can I help?"

"I want to buy this house, and set up my catering business here. Robby and Katie and I will live here too. I have some money I've put aside from my baking, and it's enough for a down payment. But I'm going to need capital to get this place in shape, and to start the catering company. I have a business plan, Phil." She pulled it out of the picnic hamper and handed it to him. "If you look it over, you'll see that I'm projecting a profit after six months. I can do that because my overhead will be so small. I know you work with venture capitalists, and . . ." she drew in a sharp breath ". . . and I'm going to need investors, so if there's anyone you could talk to . . ."

"You have your investor."

"I don't understand."

"Me. I'm going to be your investor."

"I didn't mean . . . I wasn't asking you . . ."

"My money's on you, Laura. I figure I'll make a fortune off you. Because if you want this, I know you'll make it . . . What are you doing . . . Laura, you don't cry at a business meeting! Come on . . . you're getting my shirtfront wet!"

Later that night, as she lay in bed, too excited to sleep, she thought, *This is a real new beginning for Robby and me. This time it will be different. He'll be happy working at the museum—it's a perfect job for him with his charm and love of people—and he won't even remember California and Hawkins.*

And I'll have my business. Phil thinks I can make a go of it. And so do I. It'll be fun. Yes, this is a new beginning. My family believes in them. That's the spirit that brought them to this country. It got them through wars and tragedies. I come from tough stock.

The thought was incredibly comforting.

JOURNEY

Begin doing what you want to do now.
We are not living in eternity.
We have only this moment, sparkling
like a star in our hand and
melting like a snowflake.

MARIE BEYON RAY

Chapter Twelve

"Mom, you're not listening!" Katie stopped in the middle of the sidewalk, forcing Laura to stop too. "I was talking to you," Katie scolded. "And you ignored me. That's rude!" At the age of twelve Katie had strong beliefs about what was and was not acceptable behavior, and rudeness topped her list of the unacceptable. It was a code she had picked up from her grandmother. Iris would have cut off an arm before she ignored something that was said to her, and Katie adored Iris.

It had been that way from the beginning. When Katie, Robby and Laura had moved east three years ago, Laura had hoped her daughter would grow close to both Theo and Iris, and Katie did love them very much. But there was something special between Katie and Iris. Robby and Theo had both seen it when Katie was still a baby in her crib, and now most of Katie's conversations were peppered with the phrase, "Grandma says."

Laura looked at the small figure standing in front of her. *I'm a throwback to my grandmother and Katie is a throwback to hers. But Katie is stronger than Mom, I see that already. And it's as it should be. The new generation stands on the shoulders of the old—that's how it is in families.*

But now her daughter was standing in the middle of the sidewalk on Madison Avenue and frowning at her.

"I'm sorry. You're quite right," Laura said. "I was thinking about something else, and I was rude to you. Forgive me?"

Katie considered it carefully. "Yes, I will," she said finally. Harmony restored, she and Laura began to walk together again. "Grandma Iris says you're always rushing," she told Laura. "I think she's afraid that Daddy doesn't like it when you're not home for dinner and things . . . well, he doesn't . . . but I explained to Grandma that Daddy doesn't like to work and you do."

"Katie, that's not fair. Your dad goes to his job every day."

"But he doesn't like doing it. And he doesn't understand why you like yours so much."

She was so smart. "What did Grandma Iris say when you told her all of this?"

"Just that I must always respect my father. And I do, Mom."

"Of course you do. And you know, maybe I do rush around a little too much."

"Maybe. But you won't stop."

My child knows me.

The truth was, Laura loved being busy because after three short years her catering company was booming, and she still couldn't get over it. It had taken months to do the necessary renovations on the house, so she'd stayed in New

York to work on it, while Katie and Robby finished out the school year in California. By the time they'd come east with Molly, Laura had been halfway through the project. She'd fixed and decorated Katie's room first, before anything else. Then she'd concentrated on the areas she would need for her business. For six weeks she and a couple of workmen had worked on the kitchen and fitted it out with the professional equipment the law required her to have if she was going to prepare and sell food to the public. She'd planted her gardens full of the herbs she would need in her cooking and the flowers she would use to make the bouquets that would accompany the freshly prepared family dinners and food baskets she'd be delivering to clients. She'd painted the kitchen, the pantry, the laundry room and the back entrance where she kept her gardening tools, a cheery yellow, and she'd run up blue and white curtains for the windows. The hideous wallpaper in the dining room and the living room was stripped off, and the walls were painted a warm and inviting taupe.

The old chandeliers and sconces were back where they belonged and the bay windows were swagged with creamy draperies made from a bolt of silk she'd purchased at a discount on the Lower East Side in the city. She'd set up a corner of the living room as her office, where she could man her phones and take orders. Then she'd opened her doors for business and the rest of the renovations had been on hold. The ballroom remained unfinished, as did all the bedrooms except Katie's. Robby complained regularly about the peeling paint and crumbling plaster in theirs, but somehow Laura never seemed to get around to fixing it up. Later, she would realize that it was significant that the room that was the heart of a good marriage had not been a priority for her, and she would want to weep for Robby and herself. But at the time she just told herself she'd get around to it when she didn't have something more important to do.

Her company, which was simply named Laura's Catering, had been a success almost from the beginning. As she'd predicted, she'd started turning a small profit in the first six months, and by the time she'd been open for two-and-a-half years, she was doing well enough to pay her brother back and next year she'd be giving him a return on his investment. (Phil said he was going to set up a college fund for Katie with the money.) It seemed that in addition to Laura's domestic skills, she had a head for business.

Of course, she had made mistakes. In the beginning, she'd been thinking as if she were still in California and she hadn't grasped the full difference between a busy suburb on the outskirts of the world's biggest city and a sleepy little college town. She'd tried giving out free samples of her wares in the local mall, and it had taken her several weekends to realize that this was not the way to break into a market that moved at lightning speed and was crowded with products and services vying for the consumer's attention. On Phil's advice she had gritted her teeth and spent some of her precious capital to hire an advertising agency. But once they managed to get the word out, Laura's Catering had taken off. She'd been right about the busy workingwomen who needed a wife.

—

"Mom, did you see that?" Katie had stopped again. She pointed to a store window they had just passed. The words "Hospital Services Thrift Shop" were painted across the window in big black letters, and in slightly smaller print was the information that all items in the store were donated and the proceeds of sales would benefit two hospitals that were located in the area.

"What is it?"

"There's a picture in that window. It's really weird." Katie grabbed her hand, and pulled her toward the shop. "Come on."

They didn't have time to look at weird pictures, if they were going to catch the train back to Westchester. Laura and Katie had come into the city so Katie could attend her cousin Rebecca Ruth's birthday—the two little girls really didn't like each other much, but family was family—and Laura still had work to do when she got home. But she had already been reprimanded once by her daughter today.

"Okay, show me your weird picture," she said.

———

It was an oil painting with an ornate gilt frame, and it had been placed in the center of the somewhat jumbled window display so that it dominated the space. It was a portrait of a woman. She was dressed in the style of the early part of the century in a cream-colored gown with ruffled lace trim, and a long string of pearls falling over the lace. But it was the woman's face that made Laura gasp out loud. She would have known those huge dark eyes, that high narrow nose, that mouth and that hairline anywhere.

"See Mom?" Katie demanded. "Why do they have a picture of Grandma Iris in this window?"

Chapter Thirteen

The woman in the portrait couldn't be Iris. Obviously not. And yet . . . those distinctive dark eyes . . . and that mouth . . . and that nose . . .

"It has to be Grandma," Katie said at Laura's side. "She's not one of those people who look like lots of other people. She's special. So it has to be her."

"It certainly does look like her . . . very much . . . but it can't be, Katie . . ."

"Let's go inside and ask about it."

Laura glanced at her watch. Tomorrow morning she had to deliver seven breakfast baskets to a new inn that had just started using her services. If she missed the train she would have to work late that night to make up the time. But the portrait did look so much like Iris . . . She took Katie's hand.

"Come on," she said, and they went inside the shop.

—

"Yes, isn't that picture fabulous?" said the gray-haired woman who was tending the shop. She was wearing a name tag that said VOLUNTEER in red letters. "I'm afraid I don't know much about it. The man who manages this store knows the history of all of our donations, but you just missed him."

She lifted the portrait out of the window and propped it on a table so Laura and Katie could see it better. Iris's face—well, not Iris's face but the face of someone close enough to be her double—stared out at the dusty shop with a remote, haughty expression.

That isn't like Mom, at least. Mom never looked haughty a day in her life.

Still, the resemblance was eerie. Laura was starting to wish they hadn't come into the store—the picture was making her uncomfortable.

"I don't think the artist was anyone famous," the woman went on. "I'm sure he wasn't, because we would have saved this for our fine arts auction at the end of the year if he was. But I can tell you who donated it."

"That's okay," Laura started to say, but the woman was already bustling around the counter.

She pulled out a large black notebook. "All right, here we are," she said after a couple of seconds. "Oh, this is interesting. The donor was a woman named Leah Sherman; she used to own a boutique right here on Madison Avenue. It was a very elegant place. She sold real European couture, the kind of thing you don't see anymore." The woman smiled at Laura. "I remember it because my mother bought my first grown-up gown there. The store was called Lea, or something . . ."

"Chez Lea," Laura said, and now the uncomfortable feeling turned into a shiver. "My mother used to shop there. And so did my grandmother."

"What a coincidence. Although, perhaps it isn't. Most fashionable women
who lived around New York did shop at
Chez Lea back in the day."

"I guess," Laura said, only half listening. She was staring at the portrait
again; now she didn't seem to be able to
take her eyes off it.

"Mom, could we buy it?" Katie broke
into her thoughts. "It's for sale, isn't it?"
she asked the saleswoman.

"Yes, I can look up the price for you."

"We could give it to Grandma," Katie
said. "I bet she'd like to see it."

A shadowy memory came back to
Laura: she was in her teens and she and
her mother were spending a Saturday
together, when out of the blue, Iris had
said, "When I was a child I always felt
like an outsider."

At the time, Laura hadn't really
thought about it. Her shy mother had always been resentful of her own beautiful and charming mother, and this had
seemed like one more complaint about
her childhood. But now, as Laura looked
at the portrait in front of her and remembered her mother's words, she decided

for reasons she couldn't begin to articulate that her mother wouldn't want to see this painting of the woman whose dark eyes looked so much like her own. And furthermore, Laura didn't want to show it to her.

"We can't carry that thing around the city, Katie," she said. "The frame is so old, I'm sure it would chip." She turned to the saleswoman. "I'm sorry," she said.

"Well, perhaps I could interest you in something else. We have a couple of lovely watercolor sketches . . ."

"Not today, I'm afraid."

"Would you like to sign our guest book? We can put you on our mailing list."

It was the last thing Laura wanted to do, but the woman was clearly disappointed at not having made a sale. Laura signed the book.

"Now, are you absolutely sure—" the woman began, but Laura cut her off.

"I'm afraid we have to run," she said. She opened the shop door quickly, and ushered Katie through it. "Good luck selling that painting," she said over her shoulder to the saleswoman.

—

Theo hadn't gone to Rebecca Ruth's birthday party in Manhattan. He'd been planning to, but at the last moment, he'd felt a little tired so Iris had gone without him. Now he was sitting on the front porch—something he had never done before he got sick, certainly not in the middle of the day—watching three little girls play hopscotch on the sidewalk in front of him, and letting his thoughts wander where they would. As they did so often these days, they went to his late mother-in-law, Anna. And Anna's secret that she had carried to her grave—the secret that Theo would now carry to his. He had sworn he would never reveal it, and he wasn't a man to break his word. But he was finding that knowing it was a bigger burden than he'd thought it would be. He hadn't felt that way when he'd first learned about it, but perhaps your perspective on such things changed when you'd had a close brush with your own mortality.

He wasn't angry or resentful about knowing what he knew, he wasn't one to waste his time with that kind of mental whining. But he did wish he was still like the rest of Anna's family and was blissfully in the dark about one of the most important facts of her life. As he sat in the sunshine listening to the laughter of the three little girls playing the old-fashioned game, and waited for his wife to return home, he found himself wishing for ignorance.

———

Laura and Katie had missed the train from the city so Laura had gotten behind on her work, as she'd predicted. That was why it was one o'clock in the morning when Robby woke up, realized that she had not yet come to bed and finally found her in the ballroom.

"What are you doing?" he asked as he rubbed the sleep out of his eyes.

"The sweet rolls for tomorrow's breakfasts are baking, so I thought I'd come in here and get started on sanding this woodwork."

"My wife, the superwoman."

Robby was looking better than he had when they were in California. The puffiness around his jawline had vanished, and his slim waist was back. But Katie had said he didn't like working at the museum . . .

Are you happy, Robby? Is our fresh start working out for you? she wanted to ask. But she wouldn't because she was too afraid. Because if he wasn't happy, she didn't know what to do about it. And she didn't want to feel guilty about him. She knew that was selfish, but she couldn't help it. Everything was going so well for her; she loved her house and she was excited about her business, and she didn't care if it was one o'clock in the morning and she was still baking rolls and sanding woodwork. *I'm too happy to be tired, Robby. And I hope you're happy too.*

"I'd offer to help you," Robby interrupted her thoughts. "But we both know what happened the last time I tried to strip the wallpaper."

"That steamer is tricky," she said lightly.

"And I'm not handy."

"Not everyone can be a good janitor. You're the brains of this outfit."

I hate it when I do that—when I put myself down in that way. But I'm trying to make you feel strong by making myself less than you. And then it bothers me when you smile, like you are right now.

"Would you like me to make you some tea or a cup of hot chocolate?" she asked.

"No, thank you. You may be able to stay up all night, but I'm a mere mortal. I'm going back to bed." He headed for the door, then suddenly he turned back. "Laura?" he said. "Don't ever think that I don't know how remarkable you are."

She felt like she'd been found out in a lie. "I'm not—"

"Don't, all right? Give me credit for knowing what's in front of me."

"Well then . . . thank you."

The trouble was, she didn't know if he liked it that she was remarkable. He was getting harder and harder to read.

"Everything you do, you make it look so easy," he went on.

"Well, most things I do are easy. Making a slipcover or baking a cake isn't exactly brain surgery."

"The great Laura McAllister can-do spirit." He laughed. But he wasn't looking at her so she couldn't see if the laughter had spread to his eyes. "Someone should write a story about you. Maybe you should write it. Call the newspaper here. They have a woman's page."

"I couldn't call the newspaper and brag about myself. Besides, no one would be interested in me."

"With that can-do spirit? You're the damn American Dream, Laura. You're the Girl Scout who grew up to rule the world and the Little Train That Could all rolled into one!" He laughed again, and again she couldn't see his eyes. "Don't sell yourself short. Get the publicity. You'll sell hundreds of breakfast baskets."

"I don't know."

"The interest will be there. Because you're one of those people who never fails. Everyone likes to read about a winner." He yawned. "And now, I'm going to bed."

After he left, she still felt she didn't know how he felt about anything—not the house or his job, or their life. Or her.

If I had a perfect marriage I wouldn't have to wonder what he's feeling. I'd know because we'd talk to each other. But I'm not sure I know what a perfect marriage is anymore. And sometimes I think the less you say, the better.

She went back to sanding the woodwork. After a few minutes, Molly wandered in to join her. She settled the dog, whose joints were starting to get arthritic, on a pile of old sheets. "It's just you and me, girl," she said, and went back to work.

Chapter Fourteen

The suggestion Robby had made stuck with her. A story in the local newspaper would be a boost for her business. And, even though it embarrassed her to admit it, she thought it would be fun to see her name in print. Nana's granddaughter had an ego, it seemed. And what would Nana have said about that? She had always been so careful to keep herself in the background and let her husband shine.

I tried that and it didn't work, Nana.

Still, Laura tried to find ways to make it up to Robby. She made special dinners, with candlelight and wine. But by the time she'd put Katie to bed and walked Molly, it was usually too late for them to enjoy sitting down and eating a leisurely meal. Besides, Robby said sometimes her gourmet food was a little too rich for him.

So she told him she agreed with him that something must finally be done about their disgraceful bedroom. Robby swore that he would paint, hammer, and saw, if they could just please get rid of the ghastly wallpaper, and they both laughed. But it didn't take long for Robby to get bored.

"God, we've been sanding this floor for weeks," he said.

"Only a couple of days."

"Well, it feels like it's been longer. Can't we hire someone to finish it?"

"Finishing it ourselves is supposed to be what makes it so satisfying."

"For you, maybe. But I have better things to do."

Unfortunately, whatever those better things were, they didn't include his work at the museum.

"I'll tell you the truth, Laura," Steve said during a visit to New York, "Leland is disappointed in Robby. He was expecting him to be much more aggressive about getting attention for the museum."

So Katie had been right, Robby didn't like working at the museum. And being Robby, he wasn't putting any effort into the job. The job that had been handed to him on a silver platter, after he'd ruined his career by being stubborn and immature. But a loving wife didn't let anyone—not even her older brother—know that she thought her husband was being stubborn and immature. A loving wife defended her husband no matter what.

"I'm sure Robby is doing everything he can to build the museum's reputation. These things take time . . ."

"He's been there for three years, and he hasn't held one major exhibit. There was an offer of an exchange with a museum in Massachusetts that he never bothered to answer."

"The job he has is so loosely structured. Maybe he doesn't know what's expected of him."

"Well, that won't be a problem anymore. Since he doesn't seem to be able to take initiative on his own, Leland's appointing a board of directors that will be doing regular oversight. They'll keep it low key for now, no one wants to insult him because he's my brother-in-law, but he's going to have goals he has to reach."

Laura braced herself for the explosion when Robby heard the news. But he never mentioned it—and neither did she. By that time she was busier than she'd been before, because one of the inns that had been buying her breakfast baskets had called to ask if she could cater an event for them—a cocktail party that would benefit an arts program for low-income kids.

"And of course you said yes," Robby said when she told him about it.

"Look at it this way: now I won't have time to finish sanding the bedroom floor, so you can hire someone after all."

"Ah, the perks that come from having a successful wife."

——

Overnight, Laura was plunged into a whole new world. She had to hold a tasting for the charity's planning committee so they could decide on the appetizers. She had to hire waiters and bartenders, and she had to rent tables and chairs and a tent. She had to buy tablecloths and napkins, and baskets for her signature homegrown flower centerpieces. She had to figure out the cost per head for the guests.

"Are you sure you want to take on something as elaborate as this?" her mother asked. It was Sunday afternoon, and Katie and Laura had had lunch with Iris and Theo. This was a weekly ritual Laura had begun after Katie arrived in New York. She wanted her child to have as much time with her parents as possible. Especially Theo—for reasons she didn't want to admit, even to herself. While his recovery after the heart attack had been satisfactory—that was what the doctors said—he certainly wasn't a healthy man. In addition to the medicine he carried at all times, there was now an oxygen tank discreetly tucked away in the new first-floor bedroom. He hated using it and tried not to when his children and grandchildren were around, but the fact that he needed it was a new development. Iris avoided talking about it, probably in deference to his wishes, but Laura had noticed that whenever Theo had a setback with his health, her mother seemed to become more worried about the health of Laura's marriage. Now she repeated, "Are you sure about this job?"

"I have to try it. It's only cocktails and hors d'oeuvres, not a full meal. It's a bigger job than I've ever done before, but as parties go, it's relatively simple, so it's a good way to start expanding my business."

Iris picked up a plate and began rinsing it carefully. "Don't you and Robby make a good enough living now? Why do you have to expand?"

"I guess . . . because I enjoy the challenge. I want to see how far I can go . . . the way you did, when you went back to school and got your doctorate."

Iris put down the plate and looked at her. "I waited until my husband was ready for me to do that."

I knew it, Laura thought. *What she's really worried about is Robby's reaction.*

"Are you saying Robby isn't ready? Has he told you that?"

"No. He wouldn't."

Not in so many words. But he could let her mother know—very subtly, of course—how overworked Laura was. And how little time they had together. "This is nineteen eighty-two, Mom. Women don't feel they have to put their lives on hold until it's convenient for everyone else."

"I know that. And I know what I'm going to say will seem old-fashioned, but . . . you have a good man, Laura. He's a good father . . . and he's a good husband . . ."

Is he? How do you know that?

"He's never even looked at another woman."

And there was the answer—her mother's criteria for a good husband. Perhaps it was her pain about Theo's cheating, even after all these years, or maybe it was just that an insecure woman like Iris would always prize fidelity above all else.

"I still think, in the end," Iris went on, "that a marriage is a seventy–thirty percent proposition. At best. And the woman is the one who must give the seventy percent. I don't care how much the times have changed."

Out of nowhere, stupid tears stung Laura's eyes. Her mother had never criticized her before—not like this, not over something so serious. It shouldn't matter so much, but it did.

"I give one hundred percent," she flung at her mother. "All the time. And Robby knows it. He and I are just fine."

"Good," said her mother. "That's all I wanted to hear." She reached over to kiss Laura on the cheek. "Marriage isn't easy, but when it's good, it's one of the greatest joys I know."

———

Later that night Laura lay in bed next to Robby. He was already asleep but she was having trouble drifting off. She closed her eyes, but the talk with Iris kept coming back to her. Her mother was modern in many ways, but when it came to men and women, Iris was not really a part of her own generation. Her standards came from the last century; she felt a woman who had never been married had not had a full life, and it was a woman's responsibility to make a marriage work. And while it was painful when a man cheated on his wife, she had an obligation to try to forgive him because men would be men. Laura was sure her mother would not have felt the same way about a cheating wife.

Laura was getting drowsy at last. Her mind began to wander as minds do, on the edge of sleep. An image of Iris's face floated through her consciousness—but in the image, her mother's dark eyes were tragic. Whenever someone or something had disappointed Iris, that was the way her eyes would look, as if she'd just suffered a horrible loss. Laura could remember the expression from her earliest days. And she could remember promising herself that she would never do anything to cause it. Yet, now as she drifted into sleep, she felt responsible for the tragic look, and she wanted to protest that she hadn't done anything. But then, as happens in dreams and nightmares, her mother's eyes became the eyes in the portrait she and Katie had seen in the thrift shop. Once again, Laura felt the same unease she'd felt in the store. But then the painting faded away and she was asleep.

—

Theo was breathing easily but deeply. Iris relaxed in the bed next to him because this was her cue that he was asleep. But she didn't close her own eyes; she was too troubled. *Why was I so hard on Laura earlier?* she thought as she stared into the darkness. *I'm not a fusty old-timer who thinks a woman shouldn't have any life but her husband's. I wanted my own career and my own fulfillment and I got them . . . But not at my husband's expense, that's the difference.*

Robby seems lost these days; he doesn't talk about his work at the museum at all. I remember when he was a student, how excited he was about his future and what he wanted to do. He had so many dreams. Now it's Laura who has the dreams. She's happy, but he isn't, I can tell. And that's not healthy for a couple.

I want Laura's marriage to be a good one. Mine wasn't always. Theo and I always had love but we hurt each other. That's not what I grew up with—my parents did everything they could not to hurt each other. They were good to each other—and they were good for each other. That's what I want for Laura and Robby, I want them to be like my mother and my father, not like Theo and me.

And yet, even as she thought that, distant memories of quarrels between Anna and Joseph crowded into her mind. There hadn't been many, but the few had been bitter and extraordinarily painful. And it was always her father who had started them—out of jealousy. There had been a couple of times when he'd come close to accusing Anna of being in love with another man. It had been unfair of him and terribly wrong. Still, there had been that way Mama had of seeming to hold back . . . But no, the truth was, her father, who had been the strong rock of Iris's life, had always been insecure about his wife. And insecurity could play with anyone's mind.

But I don't want to think about that now. I don't want to remember the times when he suspected her of the thing he never could have forgiven. She was innocent and in the end he knew it and they were happy. As I want my daughter to be. My daughter who is so like my mother.

At her side, Theo was still breathing peacefully. She listened to him for a moment. These days she waited until she was sure he was all right before she allowed herself to slip off to sleep. Her husband was doing as well as could be expected given the severity of his heart attack, but there had been two minor scares recently—one of them in the middle of the night. That was the reason for the oxygen tank standing in one corner of the bedroom. Iris tried to feel comforted by the fact that it was there, but the truth was, it frightened her. The only thing that really reassured her was the sound of Theo's breath going in and out in a steady rhythm as he slept. So she lay next to him and listened. It was a useless little exercise, but she seemed to need to do it.

———

Theo waited until he was sure Iris had gone to sleep before he opened his eyes. She didn't know he knew she monitored his breathing now, wanting to be reassured that he was safe before she'd let herself sleep. Once that kind of hovering would have annoyed him, but now he found it touching to be so well loved—particularly after all they'd been through together. He turned his head—very slightly, so he wouldn't wake her—to look at her face as it rested on the pillow next to his. Iris. Wife. Beloved.

We've had such a journey together, my darling. I wish I could find a way to thank you for taking it with me. But I know that anything I say like that will only frighten you. At least, it will right now. Maybe later, when I'm closer to . . . well, maybe I'll find the right time later on.

Chapter Fifteen

"Just checking on my investment," Phil said on the phone. It was three days before the cocktail party Laura was catering for the arts foundation and he had called her to find out how she was doing.

"There's a big difference between putting together a few breakfast baskets and making cheese puffs for three hundred people. And it has to be cheese not crab, because crab is too expensive. The foundation wants to make as much money as it can."

"You'll do it."

"I finally managed to convince the

president of the board of trustees that sangria will be a better choice than the punch her mother always served her garden club. The waiters can walk around with pitchers so we don't have to rent a punch bowl."

"That's my girl."

"I also had napkin rings made out of dried flowers—the guests can take them home as souvenirs—and the students in the arts program designed the name tags."

"Whoa! Is all of that the job of the caterer?"

"No. But no one else is thinking about those little details and they make all the difference."

There was a pause on the other end of the phone. "You really like this, don't you?" said Phil.

"Why wouldn't I? I get to decorate and cook and shop . . . all the things I love to do . . . and when it's time to clean up, which isn't all that much fun, I pay this nice kid who's earning money for college to come in and help me. It doesn't get much better than that."

"I envy you."

"You want to make napkin rings and cheese puffs?"

"No. But I guess . . ."

"What?"

"I'd just like to do something I'm passionate about."

"Oh." She'd known for a while that he was unhappy with his work, but when he let it slip like that, she didn't know what to say to him. "Phil . . . I . . ."

"Sorry, I shouldn't whine. I'm good at what I do and I make a lot of money."

But in our family we don't work just for the money. We want to earn a living, but we want our work to be our passion too. But she couldn't say that, because Phil had walked away from his passion.

"Knock 'em dead at the fund-raiser, Laura."

"Will do."

———

The party was a success. Everyone agreed that the napkin rings had been a great touch and no one actually believed the president of the board when she claimed that the sangria had been her idea. A week after the foundation sent Laura her check, an art gallery on the Hudson River contacted her about catering the opening of a new exhibit. And following Robby's suggestion, she'd contacted the local newspaper, which not only did an article about her, they invited her to write for them. "It's going to be an advice column for the woman's page," she told Robby. "Readers will write in with questions on cooking or refinishing cabinet doors, and I'll tell them how I'd do it."

"So now you're a writer." There was a funny edge in his voice.

"It was your idea, Robby," she said quickly. "I never would have thought of it without you."

See, Mom? I'm trying to please him and give him all the credit. I'm still Nana's granddaughter.

But he didn't even bother to smile.

—

"Let's get out of here," Robby said. "We need a vacation."

"It's a bad time for me. I've got the column to write, and I've been offered my first wedding. I'll be doing it all—the food, the flowers, the decor and the music."

"Turn it down."

"I can't. I've already accepted it."

"Tell them you're too busy. Tell them to go to hell, I don't care. Anyway, you are too busy. We don't have any time together."

But that wasn't the real reason he wanted to go away. *He wants to distract me,* she thought. And it was something new. *My business is getting too big for him now, and he's trying to slow me down.*

"Come on," he said. "Let somebody else plan the reception for some spoiled rich girl's wedding. Lord knows there will always be another one getting married."

"Breaking into the wedding market is the next big step for me—for any catering business. And this is my first opportunity."

"Well, I'm taking time off. I haven't been back to Ohio in six months, and it's been longer than that for you."

"I know that."

"My mother is all alone. She doesn't have anyone."

"Yes, Robby, I know."

In one of life's ironic strokes, Robby's father had died a few months after they moved to New York. And almost overnight, it seemed to Laura, Robby had changed his mind about his hometown. Now he loved to go back to Blair's Falls for visits, and he seemed to have totally forgotten that he'd once called the place "that dump."

"I see your parents all the time," he said angrily.

"Yes, and I'm very grateful to you . . ."

"Well, I think my mother deserves some attention too."

"If it were any other time . . . Robby, I've worked so hard, I need to make the most of what I've gained."

But he didn't want her to do that. That was the whole point.

"Why don't you go without me?" she said a little desperately. "Give your mother my love and tell her we'll all come out to Ohio during the summer. That's a slower season for me."

"I want to take Katie with me. Her

spring break at school is coming up and Mother's been asking to see her."

"That's fine."

———

But as it turned out, it hadn't been fine for Robby to leave. Not as far as his employer was concerned.

"Robby took off for two weeks," Steve fumed to Laura over the phone. "Right at the time when all the kids are out of school and parents are looking for things to keep them occupied—like a trip to their local museum."

"It was the only time Katie was free to visit his mother." A good wife defends her husband. No matter what.

"Robby didn't ask for the time off. He just announced that he was going and he went. That kind of thing doesn't sit well with a board of trustees—or with a man like Leland, who is already wondering why he's paying Robby. You better tell him to get his act together. There's only so many more times I can save his job for him."

But when she tried to talk to Robby about it, all he would say was, "The trip was worth it, Laura. When I saw the look on my mother's face . . . she was so happy to see Katie. It did her a world of good."

That wasn't quite the way Katie told the story. "Grandmother Mac—and I really hate that name, Mom . . ."

"But that's what she asked you to call her. What about her?"

"She just cried and cried when Daddy and I left. She said she misses Daddy so badly it's like having her right arm cut off."

"That must have been very hard for Daddy."

"It was, I could tell. He loves her a lot. But Mom . . ." Katie trailed off.

"What is it?"

"I have to tell you something kind of bad . . . about me . . ."

"If it's about you, it can't really be bad."

"Yes, it can. Sometimes . . . I don't like Grandmother Mac. I mean, I know you're supposed to love your elders, and I try . . . but she's always crying around Daddy and making him feel bad about something . . . And she says you're selfish."

"Selfish?" Laura was too surprised to be angry. "Why?"

"Because you wanted to move back to New York so you could be near your family and she never gets to see Daddy and me."

"Your father wanted to come here! He couldn't wait!" The surprise had worn off and the anger came.

"But Grandmother Mac says . . ."

"I don't want to hear any more of what Grandmother Mac says!"

"You don't like her either, do you?"

Laura drew in a deep breath; her outburst had been wrong—although it had felt good. Now she didn't want to make it worse. "Your Grandmother McAllister and I are very different kinds of women. It isn't easy for us to like each other but we have to try. And most of the time we don't do too badly."

"But you don't like her," Katie said. It was clear that as far as she was concerned that was the final word on the subject. Laura decided to let it go. But that night when Laura was tucking Katie into bed, it seemed that the trip to Ohio was still on her daughter's mind.

"I do like Daddy's Uncle Donald though," she said as Laura pulled up the bedcovers.

"He's very nice."

"He worries a lot because there won't be anyone to take over his department store when he's gone."

"When did he tell you that?"

"He said it to Daddy, and I heard them talking. They didn't know I was listening." Katie yawned. "I'm just glad we don't live in Blair's Falls. I like it here."

"Me too."

"And if Daddy gets lonely sometimes because he's here with your family instead of being with his own, like Grandmother Mac says he does, we'll take care of him, won't we, Mom?"

"That's my job," Laura said, and she tried to smile.

———

"How could you let your mother say things like that about me?" Laura demanded when she and Robby were alone.

"Laura, give her a break, she's not as young as she used to be and she wants to know her granddaughter better."

"And saying rotten things about me is the way to do that?"

"She's lonely—that's all. She wishes I'd come back home, and bring my family with me."

"You never wanted to live in that town. You couldn't wait to get out."

"I know. But I can't say that to her, can I?"

"She told my child I'm selfish."

"She's jealous. She just wants Katie to know about my side."

"When did you and I start having sides?"

"You know what I mean. Katie is a lot closer to your family than she is to mine and my mother resents it. I know it's not your fault and I don't blame you for it. Don't you blame me for the things my mother says. Now, let's drop this."

She had a choice; she could do what he said and drop it, or she could let him know how angry she was. She could scream and they could have a fight. In the movies and in novels when a couple had a big blowup, it cleared the air and they felt closer afterward. And of course her parents had fought. But her parents had had passion, so perhaps in some deep way they'd felt they could risk having battles. She and Robby had to have peace because they couldn't take the chance.

She dropped it, and got into bed.

Chapter Sixteen

"I'm having lunch in the city today. With a writer—the one who wrote the article about me for that magazine, *Woman's Life*," Laura said. When the story had appeared a month earlier, somehow Robby had forgotten to read it. "She says she has a project she wants to discuss with me."

"What kind of project?" Robby asked.

"I don't know. Lillian—that's her name, Lillian Anderson—was very mysterious. We'll be having a late lunch, so I probably won't get home before six. I'm leaving a roasted chicken in the oven for you and Katie for dinner tonight."

—

"I want to write a series of Laura McAllister books," Lillian announced through a stream of cigarette smoke. She used a black cigarette holder, the frames of her outsized eyeglasses were black and so was the headband that held back her blond bob. She was very dramatic when she spoke. "I am going to make us both a fortune, and you'll be a household name!"

"You want to write a book about me?"

"I want to write one *with* you—and it'll be more than one book. Essentially they'll be an extension of your how-to column, but for an upscale reader. The books will be hardcover with all the bells and whistles, including tons of gorgeous photography featuring you demonstrating how to make finger sandwiches, or regrout a bathroom, or whatever. I'll collaborate with you on the text."

"But I'm not an expert on doing those things. I write my columns for a few hundred readers who know I don't have any training. I just suggest what works for me."

"That's the point, dear! You're Every-woman. You've never been to a culinary institute but you can cater a wedding—and bake and decorate the wedding cake. You're not a professional gardener, or a professional decorator, but you do all of that as well. And you are able to explain it simply, so other women can do it too." Lillian stubbed out her cigarette. "The way I see it, these books will really be about a lifestyle, Laura. A gracious one that is slipping away. If people want it today they have to pay a professional to do it for them, and most folks can't afford that. But you're offering them a way to create some of it for themselves."

Laura's mind flashed back to her grandmother's house. "It was so generous," she said softly. "That's what we all remember. There was so much generosity and care."

"In those old-fashioned homes our mothers ran? Is that what you mean?"

"And our grandmothers. That was how they said they loved us, with the meals they cooked, and rooms they decorated, and gardens they planted."

"Gardening and generosity—I never thought of it like that."

"Neither did I before this minute."

"So, I'm getting the feeling that you'd like to work with me on this?"

"Yes. I want to."

"Thank God! Because I've already sold the idea to Crescent Publishing."

"Crescent Publishing? They published a book by my husband's college professor."

"Yes, they're a classy outfit. And now they're trying to break into the more popular market. They're very excited about you."

—

"My first book will be titled *Laura's Weddings*," Laura told Phil. "I'll teach my reader—doesn't that sound grand? 'My reader.'"

"Very grand. Go on."

"I'll teach her everything she needs to know to put together an at-home wedding. I'll show her how to make her own invitations and arrange her flowers, and there will be several chapters on picking a menu and recipes. I've even got a pattern for a little pouch to hold the bird-seed the guests will throw at the bride and groom."

"Why are you starting with a book about weddings?"

"Because I'm going to be doing Steve and Christina's." Steve had finally asked the ever-so-patient Christina to be his wife. "They're getting married the second week in June so the timing for the book couldn't be better, and all the photography for the illustrations can be done in my house because the wedding will be in my ballroom, and I've built a brand-new kitchen for the catering portion of the business in the basement, so—"

"Hold on. You're telling me you managed to convince Steve to let you put his wedding in your book?"

"It'll really be about me and what I do."

"But still, this is Steve we're talking about. It took him forever to ask Christina to marry him because he hates fuss."

"Yes, but I promised him that all the publicity would mention that he works for a not-for-profit organization that can always use donations, and he didn't mind so much."

"You are a manipulative woman."

"I prefer the word persuasive."

"You bribed him."

"I had to." Laura laughed. "I wanted him to agree. Lillian says the book will be much more personal and appealing if the wedding I'm planning is a family affair."

"Oh, I understand that—but you're still manipulative."

——

Laura hadn't realized how much preparation went into the publishing of a book; it seemed to her as if Lillian was sending her daily notes about chapter headings and the correct way to spell "genoise." But the real work on the project, as everyone liked to call it, couldn't begin until a photographer was chosen.

"I know just the man," Lillian said. "He's amazing. You'll adore him and he'll make you and the wedding look like a million bucks. I'll set up lunch for us."

"I'll be waiting to hear from you," Laura said.

She waited for two weeks without hearing a word.

"Maybe this whole book was just a figment of my imagination," she joked to Robby.

"That would make me feel a lot better about Crescent Publishing" he said. And he wasn't joking.

"Really? It would?" She tried to keep the edge out of her voice.

"Come on, Laura. They publish serious educational textbooks. Not tips for the happy homemaker. But I guess even a publishing house like Crescent will do anything to make a dollar."

"I'm sure you didn't mean that the way it sounded."

He had the grace to be ashamed. "I'm sorry. I just can't help remembering when I was the one who was going to write books. Important ones about civilization and the history of mankind, fool that I was."

"There's still time . . ."

"For what? I've been away from my

real work for so long I don't even remember who I was."

"You could go back to school ...
maybe now it would be easier because
there's less pressure. I can support us."

*Why do I keep trying? Because I feel
so sorry for him. And I'm tired of feeling
sorry for the man in my life.*

"Oh yes. That would be the final hu-
miliation, wouldn't it? You already support us, my darling. I couldn't have
afforded that fancy new car you
bought—"

"I needed it for the business ... when
I drive to appointments with clients—"

"That's not the point," he said as if he
were talking to a child who wasn't very
smart. "On the miserable salary I
make—and don't think I ever forget for
one minute that I owe my job to your
brother's charity—I could never compete with you."

"Robby, we're a couple. There's no
competition between us." But that was
a lie, and they both knew it.

Robby turned away. "I'm just saying,
don't be surprised if wiser heads have
prevailed over at Crescent Publishing,

and that's why you haven't heard from this hack writer they've assigned to you or the photographer you've never met. They could have decided the book isn't up to their standards and they're not going through with it."

Even though Laura knew he'd just said it to be unkind, it rattled her. She tried calling Lillian Anderson, but the woman's answering service said she wasn't available. She started to call her editor at Crescent Publishing, but then she decided that would seem like she was worried about the project—which she was by then, but there was no need to let anyone know that. And then she had something more important than her book to worry about.

—

"What are you talking about, Robby?" she demanded. It was a couple of days after their conversation about Crescent Publishing, and Robby had come home from work even though it was the middle of the morning. "What do you mean, you quit your job at the museum?"

"I couldn't do it anymore—okay? I

couldn't keep on taking orders from Leland Barker's crew of rich, smug bastards."

"So you just walked out?"

"They think because they've managed to make a lot of money it means that they are qualified to tell me what to do. Well, they're not. I'm the archaeologist, Laura. I'm the professional!" He was shouting, defending himself, but his voice was close to cracking. In spite of all his anger, he was scared. And his pride had been hurt.

I'm so tired of feeling sorry for him.

But she couldn't seem to help it. "What are you going to do now?" she asked more gently.

Instantly, his eyes lit up. "I have an idea. You were the one who suggested it, really."

"I did?"

"You said you'd support us if I wanted to go back to school. Well, I'm not going to do that, I'm finished with university life, it's too political, and too cutthroat. But I know I could write that book I always dreamed of."

"You want to write a book?"

"I know I haven't always followed through when I said I was going to do something. And maybe I didn't try as hard as I could have to please Leland Barker. I never wanted to work at the museum, that was your brother's idea— and yours. But this is different, Laura. This is something I really want to do. Just give me six months, and if I don't have half a manuscript in shape to show to a publisher, I promise you I'll take any job you want me to."

If she didn't say yes, he was going to be miserable. And he was going to make her life miserable. He'd hang around the house all day long while she tried to run her business and plan Steve and Christina's wedding and work with Lillian. If Lillian ever bothered to return her calls.

"Don't give yourself a deadline, Robby. Take as long as you need."

—

Robby rented a small office for himself in town. He said he couldn't write at home, because Laura's catering business caused too much confusion and noise. He was up and gone every morning by eight. When he'd worked at the museum he had waited around so he could drive Katie to school, but that was now Laura's job.

One morning, she awakened a half hour late. She grabbed an old corduroy skirt and a faded sweater, pulled them on and, not bothering to put on hose, jammed her feet into a pair of shabby loafers before running downstairs to make Katie's breakfast and take her to school. When she returned, she headed for the kitchen. Normally when she was cooking or doing anything around the house, she wore a coverall. She had several of them, which she'd designed and sewn herself, all in bright colors and cut to flatter a figure like hers with her long slender legs and small waist. Laura liked to look pretty when she was working.

This morning, having gotten a late start, she didn't bother to change her clothes but went straight to work rolling out the pâté brisee for the mushroom tarts she'd be serving at a cocktail party later in the week. But just as she was getting started, Molly scratched at her knee, asking to go outside. The dog was old now and didn't see well, so she often got lost, and preferred to have a human companion when she ventured out of the house.

"All right, all right," Laura said. She popped the dough into the refrigerator. "I'll come with you."

It was one of those early days in spring that can break the heart. The sky was turquoise blue, deep, yet clear enough to see through, with little puffs of white cloud scattered over it. The sun had warmed the ground, and green shoots were starting to poke up from under the mat of dried brown lawn left by winter. Underneath the old oaks that lined the driveway leading up to the house, the violets and lilies of the valley were preparing to flower, and in Laura's gardens a few early crocuses and daffodils were sending out tentative blooms.

Laura led Molly down the steps of the wraparound porch and onto the grass. The old dog sniffed the air with a grunt of approval, and suddenly, without warning, began to run. The house was far back from the road and Molly would tire long before she reached it, but Laura kicked off her shoes and chased after her anyway. The brittle grass pricked her bare feet, her hair was flying and so was her skirt, and for a moment she was sixteen again and the only care she had in the world was deciding which of three smitten young men she'd choose to escort her to the spring dance.

"Molly, you demon, enough!" she called out, laughing. The dog stopped her mad dash, and laid down, panting happily, as Laura ran up and sat down on the grass beside her. Molly began rolling around on the warm earth in ecstasy.

"Oh, that must feel good," Laura said. "If I could, I'd join you."

"Me too," said a masculine voice behind her. She whirled around to see a man standing in the sunshine.

"Hello," he said. "I'm Nicolas Sargent. I'm the guy who's going to be taking your picture."

Chapter Seventeen

His hair was black and it was curly; stray tendrils of it fell onto his face. That was the first thing Laura noticed about him. That, and his eyes, which were not brown, as she would have expected in a man with such dark hair, but a light color, somewhere between green and blue. They were fringed with lashes that were almost too long for a man. He wasn't handsome in a conventional sense—his features were too craggy for that, and his mouth was too wide. But there was such intelligence in those green-blue eyes. He was dressed like a teenager, in blue jeans, a T-shirt and work boots, with a leather jacket slung over his shoulder.

He was shading his eyes from the sunlight. And he was staring at her. She wondered how long he'd been doing that. Without thinking, she pulled her skirt down to cover as much of her bare legs and feet as she could. He shook his head slightly as if to clear it. "Lil didn't tell you I was coming this morning?" he asked. His voice was deep, with a slight huskiness to it.

"No."

"I should have known! She's been rewriting an article she did, and when she's working like that she shuts out everything else. I bet you couldn't get her on the phone either."

"No."

"Lil's talented, but she can be flaky."

"I see."

I'm a grown woman with a child and a husband and a business. It's absurd for me to be tongue-tied.

"I wish I had known you were coming," she said, and looked down at herself. "I'm not exactly dressed . . . this isn't the way I dress for a business meeting . . . when I'm meeting someone for the purposes of business."

Idiot!

"Yes, I was hoping for the coverall," he said. "The one Lil says you wear when you refinish the floors while baking bread and—I think she said you also parted the sea at one point?"

"No, no, I just walked on it."

And now she was flirting with him like a schoolgirl. As if she weren't pathetic enough sitting in the dirt in her old clothes with her windblown hair and her bare feet. But he was smiling, and his green-blue eyes were sparkling. He was enjoying this. Enjoying her. It had been such a long time since a man had . . . "Lil makes way too much of what I do," she said.

He stopped smiling. "I think I'll judge that for myself," he said seriously. And when he was serious, those green-blue eyes could send a shock wave through to the inside of your bones.

She stood up. "I need to bring Molly inside," she said. She grabbed the dog's collar, and she and Nick walked back up the hill, stopping briefly so she could retrieve her shabby shoes. When they reached the house, he opened the kitchen door for her, and she went in with Molly in tow, being careful not to let herself accidentally touch him. Which was ridiculous.

She served him tea, the quintessential old lady's drink, as benign and boring as the color beige, and brought him into her office in the living room to drink it. The kitchen would have been too informal.

"How long will we be working together?" she asked, all business.

"That depends on you. According to Lil I'm to document every phase of your work on the wedding from beginning to end."

"There's always some last-minute job to do right up until the day of the wedding."

"Then I'll be in your life for the next three months."

Three months. He'd be coming to her home, and he'd be "in her life," as he'd put it, for the next three months.

Laura didn't see Nick for several days after that initial meeting. He had other assignments he was finishing, and she had other jobs she was working on, in addition to Steve and Christina's wedding. When he finally came back, he was scheduled to shoot pictures of her empty ballroom and terrace. Since the wedding dinner would take place in the ballroom and the cocktails would be served on the terrace, he'd get shots later of Laura decorating these areas and setting up the chairs, tables, buffets and wet bars that would be needed. Lil, who had reemerged from her seclusion and was now working with Laura again, had explained all of this.

Even though she wouldn't be in any of the pictures Nick was taking on the first day, Laura had pulled her hair up high on her head, so it fell into a shiny mane down her back, and she'd worn her prettiest coverall in her favorite shade of pink.

Nick arrived in his car, and behind him two assistants—a boy and a girl—drove a van that was loaded with equipment. It hadn't occurred to Laura that he probably wouldn't come alone. She told herself that she should have known.

Nick and his helpers began unloading big boxes made of wood and metal from the back of the van. Inside the boxes were cameras, lights, cables, toolboxes, gels, light filters and a whole array of gauzy white screens and umbrellas that, Nick told her, were used for shadowing and depth. This somewhat cryptic statement was the only thing he said to her all morning; he went straight to work and soon he was totally absorbed in what he was doing.

He was all over the ballroom: climbing ladders, hanging lights, setting up his shots, working for some specific vision that he alone could see. His assistants—they had finally introduced themselves as Diana and Jeff—bantered with him as they followed his orders skillfully and quickly. Often they seemed to know what he was going to want of them before he asked for it. Diana particularly seemed to be able to read Nick's mind. Laura watched her and wondered if she was more than an assistant to him. She wasn't a pretty girl, exactly. But she had a quick smile that was delightful, and it was clear Nick relied on her more than Jeff. Telling herself that was none of her business, Laura left the ballroom and went to her desk. She had her own work to do.

Lil had asked her to describe how she was going to decorate the ballroom, so she did some preliminary sketches of the flower baskets she planned to hang around the room. As far as Laura was concerned, flowers were the jumping-off point for any wedding. Once you knew what the bride's favorites were, it was easy to choose a color scheme, music and even the food. Christina loved daisies, and this had suggested hanging baskets with big yellow organdy bows, and a fresh, springtime menu.

Laura started sketching, but it was hard to concentrate with all the laughter coming from the ballroom. The morning passed and she hadn't gotten more than a couple of ideas down on paper. A shadow fell over her desk. "Have lunch with me," said a voice she realized she would have recognized anywhere. "And by the way, the coverall lives up to its reputation." The admiration was soft in his green-blue eyes. Then he added briskly, "It'll photograph beautifully when we take shots of you."

———

She suggested that instead of going out for lunch, she could make sandwiches for herself and Nick, and he said yes. Jeff and Diana had already driven off to eat at some chain restaurant, so they were alone in the house. She thought for a moment that maybe she shouldn't have made the offer, but it was too late. Besides, there was nothing wrong with offering a man a grilled ham and cheese sandwich. And there was nothing significant about the fact that she was using her most expensive Gruyère cheese and Black Forest ham. And anyway, Diana and Jeff would be back in less than an hour. So there was no reason for her hands to be shaking as she slid the sandwich into the buttered pan. But they were. She hoped he hadn't seen it.

"Diana and Jeff seem very competent," she said. "Have they worked with you long?"

"Jeff is an intern, straight out of photography school, and he'll be around for another six months. Nice kid, but I'm not sure how good his eye is. Diana's been with me for ten years. I don't know what I'd do without her."

She didn't want to know more ... shouldn't need to know more. But she couldn't seem to stop herself. "Ten years! My, that's a long time!" she heard herself say in a horrid, perky voice.

"Yes. It'll be rough for me when she goes."

"Will that be happening any time soon?"

I'm just making polite conversation. Casual, polite conversation.

"Probably when I finish the shoot for this book. She and her girlfriend want to move to San Francisco."

"Oh." Diana had a girlfriend. It was not what Laura had expected to hear and it surprised her. Suddenly she felt frumpy and old-fashioned. He lived in a young, sophisticated world where people were not surprised when girls had girlfriends. She wasn't prejudiced about such things but they did surprise her. The people he knew would be up on all the current fads. The women would wear chic hairstyles and the latest fashions and they would go to trendy bars and restaurants. She wore pink coveralls and spent her days making yellow organdy bows for hanging baskets of daisies. She was hopeless. And yet, Diana was not his girlfriend. She told herself there was no reason for her little sigh of relief.

A smell filled the air. "Oh no!" she wailed as she looked down at the frying pan. Scorched cheese, bread and ham were sticking to the bottom. "I can't believe I did this. Any idiot can make a grilled cheese sandwich!" She dumped the pan in the sink and opened her freezer full of party food.

"What are you doing?" Nick asked.

"Finding something to defrost and cook. I don't have any more Gruyère, so I can't make sandwiches unless you'd like peanut butter and jelly."

"Are we talking about some kind of

exotic version of peanut butter you've ground yourself and a homemade jam?"

"No. Commercial peanut butter and plain old grape jelly in a jar. My daughter brings her friends home sometimes and they don't like my fancy cooking."

"Oh, I want a peanut butter and jelly sandwich." He laughed. "I bet I'm the only person you've ever made one for."

She laughed too. "The only person over the age of twelve."

The sandwiches tasted surprisingly good. They washed them down with milk and for dessert they had some brownies with raspberry icing that she had left over from a baby shower she'd catered.

After he'd finished his brownie, Nick leaned back in his chair. "This whole thing . . . writing this book with Lil . . . getting all this attention . . . it's unsettling for you, isn't it? I mean, you like it, but you don't know quite how to handle it."

"I . . . Does it show that much?"

He shook his head. "You're very good at hiding it. I happen to be a very astute fellow."

"It's just that I've never really had a great talent for anything. I'm not musical, or artistic. I'm not even that smart—certainly I'm not as smart as my brothers and my parents."

Or my husband, she could have said. But she found she didn't want to mention Robby.

"My mother has her doctorate, and my father is a brilliant physician. My brother Steve—he's the one who's getting married—is a lawyer who goes around the country saving people. There's Jimmy, who's a doctor, and Phil, who's a very successful financier. And then there's me. I'm the . . ." She trailed off, not wanting to finish.

"The pretty one?"

"The happy one. That's my job. To be happy. No matter what."

What was she doing? It would sound like she was whining, and he wouldn't understand.

But he did. "That's a hard job."

"It can be." She never opened up like this. And it wasn't because she felt relaxed being alone with him here in her kitchen. She wasn't relaxed at all, her pulse would be racing if she were to check it. It was that she wanted—no, she *needed* him to know her. And it had to happen now. Because in less than twenty minutes his assistants would be back from lunch. And in three months he would be gone from her life for good.

"It's because I'm like my grand-mother," she said. And she told him about being a throwback to Nana, who had made such a beautiful life for her husband and her children. While she talked, she went to the sink to clean the scorched pan, and without interrupting her, he took it from her to dry. They were both careful—at least she was, and she thought he was too—not to let their hands touch.

"And here I am, doing the same kinds of things Nana did . . . only she did it all for the family and I do it for my busi-ness," she finished up her story.

"A very successful business," he said, and once again, there was no mistak-ing the admiration in his eyes. It was so . . . exhilarating. Suddenly she was ashamed of herself. What was she do-ing, getting carried away because a total stranger was impressed with her? What was it that Robby had said? That she catered parties for rich, spoiled people. "I'm not exactly coming up with a solution for world peace . . ."

"How trivial of you," Nick said.

"That's me, the flighty type."

They both laughed at that. But then his face got serious. "In my family I'm the trivial one." He was looking off into space, and she knew that now he was going to tell her about himself, and he was doing it because he needed her to know him as much as she'd needed him to know her. "My father is dead now, but when he was alive he was a professor of English literature. He taught at Harvard, among other places. My mother was an opera singer with a promising career before she married and had me and my younger brother, Sam. Sammy, by the way, does something esoteric with mathematics that I will never begin to understand. He has also taught at Harvard."

We're two of a kind, she thought. *That's what he wants me to know. In spite of the bright shining world he lives in, we're two of a kind.*

"As I'm sure you can imagine, my parents weren't very happy when their elder boy—the one who was named after his father—quit school to spend his time interning with commercial photographers. The important word in that sentence was 'commercial.' As far as my folks were concerned, it would have been all right if I'd gone the artistic route, running around the country taking gritty pictures that would never sell, and having little shows in small galleries that no one has ever heard of. Starving in a garret would have been noble. But when I finally got my first job, it was at an ad agency. I took pictures of coffee and canned soup." He smiled a little sadly. "I always wanted to make money, you see. And I did. Because I really enjoyed getting lighting right, so that a cup of coffee looked like it was steaming in the print ad. I love what I do."

I know. I watched you today. I saw you working harder than either Jeff or Diana, and I knew you did it because you love what you do. I know that about you.

"And now people like Lil ask for me to work with them." He looked a little embarrassed and his face got red. "In fact, they compete to get me. I'm in demand. And I love that too." He folded the dish towel he'd been using. "My father would say I'm wasting my time."

She forgot her earlier restraint and reached out to touch his hand. "No, you're not." His hand was warm, and his fingers were long and strong. She pulled her hand back. His green-blue eyes blinked. "I love what I do too," she said.

"I know that."

He was staring at her and she was staring at him, and the silence in the kitchen was roaring around them. He was from a scarily sophisticated world she didn't know. And she was married.

"I should get back to work. My daughter will be home in a couple of hours," she said.

Saying that Katie would be coming home broke whatever spell had been going on. As she had meant it to. But she'd wished it hadn't.

"And I need to finish setting up the lights," he said. He left the kitchen.

The next time he came to the house, he didn't have lunch with her. After that one time, he went out to eat with Jeff and Diana.

———

But something had happened to Laura during the brief moment they'd shared in her kitchen. After that day, she found it harder and harder to keep from criticizing Robby. It seemed to her that he complained all the time about everything. Sometimes when she was listening to him, an image of Nick, laughing at something she'd said, would flash through her mind. She would banish the thought fast. She could not, would not, compare the two men. It wasn't Robby's fault that she'd had peanut butter sandwiches with a man who smiled at her and laughed at her jokes. She was the one who had changed, not him. So when she went to sleep at night she was not going to let herself think of green-blue eyes.

Instead, she dreamed of her mother's

huge, disapproving, dark ones. And then the eyes in her mother's face became the eyes in the portrait she and Katie had seen in the shop on Madison Avenue.

Chapter Eighteen

Katie was going to be a junior brides-maid in Steven's wedding, so Iris and Theo had driven out to Laura's house to see the child model her gown. They were in the kitchen, eating the salad Laura had prepared for lunch and chatting while they waited for Katie to emerge from her bedroom.

"How does Robby feel about having all those people in his house, photographing everything?" Iris asked. "It seems like they've been here forever."

Laura looked at her mother taking a forkful of avocado and had to block an image of herself sitting at this same table with Nick. "It's only been three months," she said. "And the photographer has finished for the moment. He won't be back again until the day of the wedding, to take the final shots for the book. Then that will be the end of it."

And I won't see Nick again.

"I have to say, I'm glad. It must be hard to have your privacy invaded. Maybe you should think again about hiring out your home for parties—"

"Wasn't that the reason why Laura and Robby bought this house?" Theo broke in. "I thought it was understood that Laura would use it for her business."

"We always planned to live over the shop, Mom."

Iris looked through the kitchen door to the ornate dining room beyond it. It would never have been her taste, Laura knew. Her mother liked things sleek and modern. It was Anna who'd had a beautiful old Victorian house. "You may have planned that, but people are allowed to change their minds," Iris said. "Maybe living over the shop isn't as easy for Robby as he thought it would be."

"I'm sure if Robby feels that way, he'll tell Laura about it. A man doesn't need his mother-in-law to fight his battles for him," Theo said. And from the distaste in his voice Laura was sure he'd over-heard Robby complaining to Iris.

Why not? Laura thought wearily. *Robby complains to his own mother every night on the phone.*

"Well, here I am," a little voice behind them said. Katie walked into the room.

—

Theo watched his granddaughter make her way toward them. She was walking a little self-consciously, a little girl on the verge of becoming a young lady, wearing her very first party dress. There was a picture of Iris at her age and as everyone always said, Katie looked just like her. But, oh, what a difference there was between them! Iris had been afraid even at that young age that she wasn't pretty. It was clear that Katie wasn't troubled by such thoughts. Her head was high as she walked toward them, and her eyes were shining.

"Katie, you're as pretty as a picture," Iris said.

And she did look like a picture; a slightly quaint and sweet illustration from a child's fairy tale. There were no ruffles on the dress, no lace or bows to overwhelm Katie's small frame. Two fabrics had been used, one was silky, and over it, the second was light as gossamer. The long skirt floated down to Katie's feet, adding to her fairy-tale appearance. And although the dress was yellow and Theo would have thought that would not be a good color for a little girl whose complexion tended to be sallow, this was such a light creamy shade that it was flattering. More important, somehow the charming little dress captured everything that was unique and special about Katie. Clever Laura, for of course it was she who had chosen the pattern and had it made for her daughter. She'd done well. But then, Laura always did do well.

He looked at her now, and he frowned slightly. She wasn't happy these days.

She pretended to be her usual cheerful self, but he could tell. And he was certain he knew why. Something had changed inside her, and she had realized that she was no longer in love with her husband. Now she was trapped because she was a good woman and she would not walk away. He'd known many such women over the years—he had comforted a few in ways that a married man should not have, if truth be told—and he'd always thought it was a small tragedy. Particularly if the husband was the kind of self-serving, self-pitying man his son-in-law had become.

Theo turned to look at his wife, who was praising Katie in her party dress. Iris still thought of Robby McAllister as the bright young man who had had so much promise when he married Laura. Well, not everyone fulfilled their promise, that was just a sad fact of life. And sometimes a person like Laura exceeded all expectations—that was a fact of life too. But Robby was jealous of her because of it. And Theo had seen her try to make him feel better by playing down her own accomplishments. Should she have to do that to save her husband's fragile ego? Shouldn't she be proud of herself and say so?

But what about the marriage, he could hear Iris cry. What will happen to it if Laura continues to be more successful than Robby is? And it was true that when Theo was Robby's age he couldn't have stood that. But that was another time. And damn it, this was his daughter!

His tricky heart fluttered unpleasantly in his chest, reminding him that he wasn't supposed to get agitated. Well, he couldn't help that any more than he could help eating the occasional forbidden piece of pastry or sneaking a bit of salt onto his food. A man had to have his pleasures, no matter how much his loved ones tried to protect him from them.

But now he was exhausted. That had been happening more often lately. The truth was, he probably didn't have a lot of time left. He still couldn't talk to Iris about it; she was determined to keep him alive forever. But the doctor in him knew it to be a fact. Since his heart attack, he'd had two minor incidents, and then a few weeks ago, there had been a more serious one. He and Iris had agreed not to tell the children about that one because there was no point in scaring everyone at such a happy time, but when a day like today could tire him so badly, it was not a good sign.

He wasn't sure how he felt about that; obviously he didn't want to die, no one did. But he had already cheated death twice: once when he'd had his heart attack, and another time, so much earlier, when he alone of his entire family had survived the slaughterhouse that was Europe during the thirties and forties.

He had had the chance to establish a second family. A beautiful strong family of Americans who had a birthright to be as happy as it was in their nature to be. All of them, it seemed, except his Laura. Anna always said she was the one in his family that no one would ever have to worry about, but Anna had been wrong. The boys would take care of themselves. With the typical male instinct for self-preservation, they would see to it that they had what they needed. But Laura, his lovely smiling girl, would break her heart trying to please everyone else. And that was wrong. Someday he would have to tell her that. Someday soon. Before it was too late. The fluttering in his chest had turned into tightness. He took a pill out of his coat pocket. Instantly Iris saw it.

"Theo? Are you all right?" she demanded as she leapt to her feet to get him a glass of water. "It's all my fault, I shouldn't have let you stay out so long."

"I'm a grown man," he protested. But he took the glass of water, and allowed himself to be clucked over. His wife ended the visit and he was grateful for it. As he walked with Laura—slowly, and carefully—out to the car, which Iris would drive home, he said, "Your mother and I are proud of you." It was the best he could do.

———

After her parents had driven off Laura walked back to the house slowly. As she'd told her mother, Nick's part of their project was all but done. He had photographed the preparations as they went forward, step-by-step; now all he had to do was come back on the wedding day to finish up his shoot. One day. Twelve hours.

It wasn't as if they'd been able to spend that much time together. They hadn't talked seriously again—not after that one lunch. But they didn't seem to need to do that; it was as if a connection had been established between them and all they had to do was be in the same room to feel it. Laura couldn't explain it, she didn't even want to try, she just knew that the feeling had gotten to be as necessary to her as eating or drinking. She found herself looking forward to the little moments during the day when he would take a break in his work and so would she. They'd have a glass of water or iced tea and they'd chat about everyday things. Things that would be much more important later when she looked back and remembered who had said what—or when she replayed in her imagination the way Nick had brushed the hair out of his eyes. Or the way his fingers had curled around his glass. She and Nick laughed a lot during those short breaks; she would remember that too— although she couldn't always remember what they had laughed about. Maybe it was just that the world seemed like a happier place when they were standing side by side, drinking iced tea. The strange part was, she never doubted that he was feeling everything she was feeling.

She liked to watch him work. He'd set up a shot patiently and meticulously, and then he'd beam with pleasure when he'd gotten exactly the effect he wanted. She enjoyed the way he made her feel when he was taking pictures of her, the care he took with angles and lighting as if she were some rare and beautiful creature. Once, when Diana and Jeff were off in another part of the house, he made her sit at her kitchen table and talk about her childhood. She chattered on about her family, and Nana's house, and pets cherished and long gone, while he took shot after shot of her with his handheld camera.

"Those pictures will be terrible," she told him when he finally said they were finished. "I didn't even put on fresh lipstick."

"They're what I wanted. They're pictures of you talking about things you've loved."

The way he said it stirred something inside her that was frightening. "How will you use them in the book?" she whispered.

"They're not for the book, they're for me."

After that, there were times when she'd look up from whatever she was doing, to catch Nick staring at her. The air between them would crackle with tension, and she would want to run. But then Nick would crack a joke and she would laugh and the tension would melt away. Until the next time.

So three months had flown by without Laura noticing it. And then one afternoon—was it only a few weeks ago? because it seemed so much longer—as he was standing in her doorway, ready to leave, Nick had said, "Tomorrow I'll be done, Laura. Except for the shots on the wedding day." And his voice, which was always so alive, was flat.

For a moment she hadn't understood him, it was like he was speaking a foreign language. "What do you mean?"

"I've finished my work. After tomorrow, I won't be coming back anymore. Until the wedding. For one day." They had stared at each other then, and she had felt like something inside her was ripping apart. But before she could say anything he had turned and walked out the door.

The next day he'd worked quickly and quietly—they both had. There had been no iced tea, no joking, no little moments of chat. He'd taken his final shots, then he'd told Diana and Jeff to pack up the gear and meet him back at the studio. He'd barely said good-bye to Laura, and he'd driven away without a backward glance.

Now Laura looked around her. The sun was shining; people had been saying what a lovely summer it was. She knew in her mind that it was, but she couldn't make herself see it. Ever since the taillights of Nick's car had disappeared at the end of her driveway it was as if a gray fog had descended around her, blocking out everything else.

Chapter Nineteen

No matter how down she felt, Laura had
a wedding to put on. There was a cake
to be covered in buttercream daisies
and roses, there were tables to be set
up in the ballroom and the flower baskets to be hung around it—those pretty
baskets that she'd designed to suggest
springtime and romance—and there
were more flower garlands to be draped
over the balustrades of the terrace
where the newly married couple would
circulate as the cocktails were served.
And if it felt like a cruel joke that she was
creating a party to celebrate love and
joy when her own days were so gray,

she told herself to get over it. At some point this obsession—or whatever it was—with Nick would go away. His absence would starve it to death. Or, at the very least, she would grow accustomed to the aching she felt inside. She would have to.

So three days before the wedding, after Katie and Robby had gone off to school and work respectively, Laura had jammed on her old straw hat to protect herself from the sun, picked up her checklist and started for the backyard. She always hired a crew of part-time workers for the final push before a big event, and she wanted to write down everything that needed to be done so that they wouldn't waste valuable time.

First, she was going to check the gazebo; she'd had it painted earlier in the spring, but since this was where the ceremony would be held, she had to make sure the work had been done properly and no touch-ups were needed before the folding chairs were set up.

It was not yet nine o'clock but it was

already warm outside. The rose gardens that surrounded her back lawn were in full bloom. Laura's bleak mood lightened as she climbed the steps to the gazebo. She closed her eyes and breathed in the flower-scented air. What did the smell of roses remind her of? Some spice, but she couldn't place it. She'd have to ask Nick. She opened her eyes. She was going to have to stop thinking like that. Nick was gone—he would be, after one more day—and she was going to have to accept it.

But she wasn't going to have to accept it just yet. Because Nick was standing in front of her.

Laura whipped off the ugly old hat. "I didn't . . . I thought . . ." she stammered. "I thought you weren't coming back until the wedding."

"I wasn't supposed to." He climbed the three steps up to the platform of the gazebo. He was standing close to her now. Somehow it felt like that first morning, when he'd found her playing on the lawn with Molly. It had been warm then too. Was it a million years ago? The sweet, heavy air was all around her, making her dizzy. *I've been so unhappy,* she wanted to say to him. *I've missed you every day.* But the air and the heat and dizziness were making it impossible for her to speak.

He seemed to be having trouble too. "Laura," he finally managed to get out, "I came because I..." He stopped. "Because I wanted..."

And then her back was against the post of the gazebo and his mouth was on hers. And it was soft and firm all at once. There was a sigh from one of them, or maybe it was both of them, she wasn't sure, and then his mouth—his firm, soft mouth—wandered over her face and neck and she was clinging to him to keep from sliding down to the floor of the gazebo, because all the strength had left her legs. His body against hers was warm and strong and his green-blue eyes were shining, and when he finally pulled away from her, they both were breathing hard, as if they'd just run for miles.

"I had to come here," he said.

There were things she should say now. Responsible, mature things. Even with the warm, flower-scented air swirling around her, and with the feel of his mouth and hands still on her, she knew this. But he reached out to stroke her hair, and she let her head tilt to one side so she could feel his fingers. And she couldn't think of one responsible thing to say.

"I've lost my hat," she said instead.

"And a thing of beauty it was too."

That was when they both started to laugh. They laughed because they didn't know what else to do. They laughed because they were both the kind of people who loved to laugh. For a few moments the silent air rang with the sound. Nick drew her to him again. "No more hiding now," he whispered. "It's out in the open now."

The words brought her to her senses—a little, at least. "Nick, I don't even know you . . ."

"Yes you do. But what specifically did you have in mind? Favorite books? I read junky detective novels, biographies, and when I'm being grand, I'll dip into a little Shakespeare. Music? I listen to opera because my mother sang it, but basically I like anything with a beat. Food? Whatever you cook."

"That wasn't what I meant."

"You can learn the rest. We have time."

"No we don't. We can't . . ."

He wouldn't let her finish. "This is right. Laura. We didn't ask for it or plan it. But it's right. And you know it, darling."

She did know it. And when he put his arms around her it all seemed so easy. But of course it wasn't. Or was it?

There was a sound coming from the front of the house, she and Nick turned to see a car coming up the driveway. It was followed by a second. The first driver beeped the horn in greeting, and two of Laura's crew, Angie and Marina, emerged from their vehicles and began chattering loudly as they made their way to the kitchen door. The workday had begun.

"Talk about bad timing!" Nick said.

"Or was it? Should I be glad we've been interrupted?"

"I don't know."

He nodded. "I should go."

"Yes."

He started for the driveway, then turned back. "I've been lonely without you."

"I know."

"I'll see you at the wedding."

"Yes, at the wedding."

"Just remember that I . . . Oh God, I love you, Laura. I didn't want to, but I do."

"Thanks for the compliment." She tried to make a joke because otherwise she was going to start crying and the crew mustn't see her tears.

But this time he didn't laugh. "You know what I mean."

"Yes," she told him. "I do."

He turned to go. But then he turned back. "I love you, and we can work this out," he said, then he left her standing in the sunshine.

Maybe somehow they could.

She started back to the house. The grayness was gone now. All around her were colors that were almost too bright. *He loves me. Nick loves me!*

But then pain, hard and deep, sliced, and she stopped moving. *I have a little girl. I'm a married woman. I have a family I can't disappoint . . . I have a mother I can't disappoint . . .* She started walking again. *No, damn it, that's ridiculous. I'm an adult. A woman my age should not be worried about what her mother thinks. It's absurd.*

She almost managed to convince herself of that, and for the rest of the morning she felt freer than she had in years. Then the mail came. Mixed in with the pile of bills and advertisements was a postcard. It was from the thrift shop on Madison Avenue—the one where she and Katie had seen the portrait with the big dark eyes. Iris's eyes.

Laura threw the postcard in the trash. *I'm not superstitious,* she told herself. *I don't believe in signs and omens. The store is having a sale and they contacted me—that's all.* But the damage had been done. She remembered the portrait. And the portrait reminded her of Iris.

I love you, Nick had said.

I love you, please don't disappoint me, her mother had said all of her life.

We can work this out, Nick had said.

Be my golden girl, her mother had begged silently with her big tragic eyes.

Chapter Twenty

There had never been a more perfect day for a wedding, everyone agreed. Laura had been up early, unable to sleep. She'd checked the tables in the ballroom and the rows of sparkling champagne glasses sitting on the bar, ready to be filled. She'd opened the refrigerator to see the neat trays full of hors d'oeuvres waiting to be removed and baked. She'd done all this, but of course this last-minute review was not the reason she'd been awake before dawn.

Nick was coming. She would see him again. It made her heart sing like it belonged to a teenager. Although she couldn't remember ever feeling this sharp-edged joy when she was young. No, this emotion was reserved for adults who had learned the hard way how incredibly rare and precious it was. And yet . . .

There are people I can't disappoint.

And yet . . .

My heart is pounding just at the thought of seeing him again.

———

When he walked in the front door, he was wearing a suit.

"It's the first time I've seen you dressed up," she said.

"Same here," he said. She wasn't a member of the wedding party—she had to work, overseeing everything—but she had dressed for the day, and her lace tea gown was the same soft yellow as the dresses the bridesmaids were wearing. It was a very flattering shade for a redhead.

She and Nick smiled at each other awkwardly, like two kids about to go to their first dance.

"The last time I felt like this, I had a corsage in my hand," he murmured.

"And I was wearing one."

Behind him, Diana and Jeff were coming through the door with his equipment. Behind her, the waiters and waitresses were assembling for their last-minute instructions. The wedding was due to begin in twenty minutes.

"I'll start setting up for shots of the ballroom while it's still empty," he said.

"And you should probably get a picture of us putting the top on the cake," she said.

But neither of them moved. "We'll talk later," he said finally.

"Yes, later."

—

The ceremony was conducted by a justice of the peace since neither the bride nor the groom was religious. When the man began speaking Laura looked over at Robby, who was sitting with her family. She watched him lean in and whisper something in Iris's ear, and she watched her mother smile back at him. This moment wasn't easy for Iris, Laura knew.

Iris was glad that Steve was getting married and happy about the wife he'd chosen. But it was hard for the daughter of Joseph Friedman to watch another of her children marry without the old rituals or a rabbi. Laura had been the first in the Stern family to have such a wedding and Iris had mourned for the entire day. Now, as she smiled at Robby, she just looked wistful. We do get used to things, Laura thought. A little, at least.

But the promises the couple *were* making were the same as those made in a traditional wedding. *Everyone who gets married makes them, with or without mentioning God,* Laura thought as she watched her brother and Christina. *We say to each other, I'll stick it out with you, no matter what. I'll be the one person who loves you, no matter what. You can trust me, no matter what. Those are the promises we make . . . I made those promises once.*

The ceremony was over. Across from her, Nick was taking pictures of Steve kissing Christina as if there were no one else in the world. In the seats, Robby reached over and squeezed Iris's hand as everyone clapped for the bride and groom. Next they would all go to the terrace. Everything was moving along beautifully. Laura looked at Steve and Christina smiling at each other. *I made those promises once.*

The band on the terrace was playing, and people chattered over it as the cocktails were served.

Lovely, lovely day.

This terrace is divine.

What a beautiful place to hold a wedding.

Did you ever think anyone would get Steve Stern down the aisle?

Waiters carried platters of hors d'oeurvres: crisp little bites of buttery pastry and savory fillings. On one side of the terrace, Laura saw Robby fill a plate for Katie. On the other side, Nick was taking pictures of the flower garlands. Laura's head began to ache. From the moment Nick had said the words "I love you," her world had had a brightly colored glow. But now it was starting to fade. She began shepherding the crowd into the ballroom for dinner.

———

Everyone was seated at the tables. Salads followed the appetizers, the service smooth as a well-oiled machine. Dinner music played under the clatter of silverware and china and the roar of one hundred and fifty people talking. Jimmy, who was the best man, made a toast and there was laughter. Phil said a few words and there was more laughter. Theo stood up to speak and there wasn't a dry eye in the room. The food kept coming in a steady stream: asparagus in a lemon vinaigrette; rice with mushrooms; tournedos of beef, chicken marsala or salmon poached in wine, take your pick.

The bride danced with the groom. She danced with Phil, who had walked her down the aisle—her father had died when she was a child. She danced with Jimmy. Nick was everywhere taking pictures of the dancers, making sure he was getting the right shot. Robby was beside Laura and he wanted to dance.

She let him lead her out to the floor. Nick stopped taking pictures.

Iris wanted a family portrait and so all the Sterns lined up. Laura stood between Iris and Robby. Katie was in front of her. Nick told them all to smile. She watched him take her picture as she was surrounded by her husband, her daughter and her mother. And she watched him see what she'd known since the ceremony. She had made promises. She was the kind of person who kept the promises she'd made.

The wedding went on. The cake was cut. There was more dancing, there were more good wishes for health and happiness. Finally the bride disappeared, and reappeared dressed for travel. The bouquet was thrown and caught amid squeals of laughter. The couple ran to the groom's car as the birdseed Laura had provided was tossed. And they were gone. All the months of planning, all the weeks of hard work, had culminated in this day, and it was over. The guests began leaving.

It was such a beautiful party, Iris.

Theo, you must be so proud.

Good job, Laura. I've never been to a better wedding.

And then finally it was quiet.

In the living room, Laura's family rested on chairs and sofas, shoes kicked off, holding the obligatory post-mortem. In the ballroom, Nick was packing up his cameras. Diana and Jeff were outside loading up the van. Laura went to the ballroom.

His back was to her, but he must have felt her coming because he straightened and turned. She walked to him, and he took her hands. His were cold—icy cold—she thought perhaps hers were too.

"I can't," she said.

"I know."

—

She walked with him to the back door, where his van was waiting for him in the driveway. They passed the living room, where her brothers, her niece, her sister-in-law, her daughter, her father, her mother and her husband were all sitting. The back door wasn't visible from the living room but you could hear the voices. And presumably they could hear hers.

She and Nick stood facing each other. She wasn't going to cry.

"It's okay," he said softly.

"Speak for yourself," she tried to joke, and they both managed to smile, which was the best good-bye they could have. The only one. Nick left and she turned back to the family that was waiting for her. And the promises she'd made.

———

"It was so nice to see Robby and Laura dancing together. They're such an attractive couple, don't you think, Theo?" Iris asked, as she pulled down the covers on her side of the bed. The long wedding day was over, and she and Theo were home and getting ready to go to sleep. "Don't you think, Theo?" Iris repeated. He knew she wanted him to agree with her; she was all but demanding it. At his side of the bed, Theo sighed quietly.

Iris wanted him to say that he thought Laura and Robby were still a good couple. He didn't, not anymore. There was a certain something you felt when a man and a woman were right for each other. It was in the air when they were together. It was like . . . what was it the young people said? It was like the vibrations . . . the vibes . . . they sent out. Theo climbed into bed and leaned back against the pillows. He closed his eyes. There was no mystery about that "something"; it was the man-woman thing, and old as the hills. It was the attraction that no one could explain, but it had been entrapping the human race since the beginning of the written word, if not before. Sex was at the root of it, but it was usually more than that. Sometimes it inspired the very best of human art and thought, the tales of Tristan and Isolde, or Romeo and Juliet, had been reconfigured over and over in poetry, music, theater and dance. Sometimes that same sexual attraction could turn dark and ugly, bringing on degradation and despair. Poets wrote about that too. But it was one of the most powerful forces mankind knew, maybe the *most* powerful one. And like the fire it was often compared to, once it had started to burn it was almost impossible to stop. And once it had died it was almost impossible to rekindle.

At his side Iris was still waiting for him to answer her. Theo opened his eyes. "What did you think of that young man?" he asked. "The one who was taking the pictures."

"I really didn't notice him that much." But she had, Theo was almost positive about it. Iris was too smart about people and too instinctive not to have sensed the man-woman pull he had sensed between their daughter and the photographer. Iris wouldn't admit this, certainly not out loud, but his wife was no fool.

"I thought that man, whatever his name is, was kind of silly, if you want to know the truth," she said after a second. "Taking pictures as if it was the most important thing on earth." Oh yes, she had noticed the photographer.

"Well, Steve and Christina will probably think it was pretty important when they're looking at their wedding album,"

Theo said. "And those pictures will be used for Laura's book."

"That darned thing! I know it's a big honor for Laura and I am proud of her, but the sooner she's done with it, the better. It's been too much of a drain on her time, and Robby isn't happy about it."

"I wish Robby had better things to do with his time than go tattling to you."

"You don't understand. Robby needs support. It hasn't been easy for him . . . he had so many pressures and expectations . . . and I hate to speak badly of someone who's died, but that father of his . . . well, you met the man . . . you know the kind of damage a parent like that can do to a boy . . ."

It was the same kind of psychobabble she'd used to excuse Steve when he was giving them so much trouble. "I'd hardly call a man who is in his thirties a boy, Iris."

There was silence. Then she said in an anxious voice, "He'll find his way. It's just taking him a longer time than most. Laura has to be patient. She has to be there for him."

Be there for him. That was another of the psychobabble phrases Theo detested. And what if his daughter got tired of being patient and *being there*? What if she wanted to experience joy again? What if she decided she wanted a man who was her equal, not an overgrown schoolboy still nursing the wounds of his failure?

A thought occurred to Theo. How would he feel about a divorce in his family? As far as he knew there had never been one. There had been plenty of infidelities, particularly back in the old country—that was, after all, the European way. And in families of a certain class especially, it was almost always the men who indulged, which was also European—and very old-fashioned.

But this was not Europe and it was not the old days. American women considered themselves as free as any man to find love and sexual satisfaction where it pleased them.

So how would you feel, Theo, if Laura had an affair? Lord knows you've had them. Steven and Jimmy were not virgins when they were married and neither is Phil as a single man. And to be fair, you wouldn't want them to be. But Laura, your beautiful Laura?

Theo closed his eyes again. The weariness that was now his nemesis was threatening to take over his body. But his mind went on.

Iris wants Laura to be a saint, the way she imagines her own mother, Anna, was. But I know differently about Anna. So how would I feel if Laura is more of a throwback to her grandmother than anyone knows?

Theo opened his eyes. *I don't have an opinion,* he realized. *It's a new time, one I don't understand. A new generation is making the rules and the decisions, and unlike Iris with Laura, I don't want to control what happens.*

———

Why do I feel so alone? Iris wondered as she turned out the light on her nightstand. *Most people would say it's natural because my son got married today and I've lost him. But I haven't. If anything, now that Christina is my daughter-*

in-law, he'll be in my life more than he ever was. I love that girl.

So this isn't about Steven, its about Laura. But I already knew that. Today, when I watched her, it was as if I was a child again, watching my mother. I remembered all those old feelings— that Mama was hiding something, that she was holding something back. I've never felt that before with Laura. We've always been so close, so open with each other; I've been proud of that. But it hasn't been like that for a while now. I don't know if I could stand it, if she and I became like my mother and me.

Robby had better start paying more attention to his marriage. I defend him to everyone because I remember the shining boy he was, and I know he's still a good person. And he's my daughter's husband and the father of my granddaughter. But something is going on with Laura and he's not seeing it.

"That photographer should do something about his hair," she said, and her voice was angry in the darkness. "It hangs in his face like he's a stupid schoolboy."

But Theo had fallen asleep.

Robby was downstairs, and Katie was asleep in her room, after having hung her creamy yellow party dress on her closet door so she could see it when she dozed off. Laura's tea gown was hanging on the front of her closet door too, but she couldn't bear to look at it. She never would be able to again. It was the gown she'd worn when she'd said good-bye to Nick. The pain was just starting to sink in. Throughout the day she'd been so busy covering her emotions that she hadn't had time to feel them. But now her family had gone to their various homes, her cleanup crew had done the heavy work and would be back in the morning to do the rest, and she was sitting in front of her vanity. And the pain had begun to throb. She wanted to sit quietly, and try to absorb it, and to mourn. But Robby had come into the room and he was talking to her.

"I just got off the phone with Mother,"

he was saying. "I've decided to go see her. She hasn't been feeling too well, and to be honest with you I need a break. I know you haven't noticed it, but I've been having a rough time. Your brothers seem to think I shouldn't have quit my job. I've gotten a lecture from every one of them, and—"

His voice finally got through the mist of sorrow and loss. "I'm sorry," she broke in. "What did you say?"

"I don't know how I could make it much clearer. Don't tell me a member of the brilliant Stern family doesn't understand English."

"Robby, please."

"I'm going home for a visit. I want to see my mother and I need to clear my head."

She forced herself to focus on him. To put her pain aside. "What about your writing?"

"I knew you were going to bring that up. You're just like your brothers. You think I should be working nonstop because I quit that job Steve arranged for me as a consolation prize for moving here . . ."

"That's not what I was saying and it wasn't what Steve did it for."

"All right then, it was charity. A gift he cooked up to keep the little man busy while his sister became a household name. I suppose I'm lucky you're still using 'McAllister,' by the way. Thank you, dear, for putting me on the map."

"That is unfair in so many ways I don't know where to start. Steve didn't—"

"Your brother has nothing but contempt for me! Your whole damn family does! And why shouldn't they? I let them treat me like a weakling."

"My brothers don't feel that way. Nor do my parents."

"Don't try that with me, Laura!" He was shouting. Just like his father used to.

Nick, I gave you up for this!

"I let you walk all over me!" Robby ranted on. "I never should have let you push me into moving here."

"I didn't push you. You wanted to come."

"Don't tell me what I wanted. Don't put words in my mouth. I came here and I took your brother's lousy job for your sake. I let you wear the pants in our family and I became a nothing."

She was so sick of trying to be good. Sick of trying to be good to him. "And what the hell did you do, Robby?" she burst out. "You got fired from one job because you wouldn't do as you were told, and you quit a second one because you're the great Robby McAllister and the work was beneath you. How is any of that my fault?"

He was startled. He'd never seen her like this before. "You work all the time. Your business is more important than I am, how do you think that makes me feel?"

"I don't care! I don't give a damn about your precious feelings!"

In the silence that followed, her words seemed to echo throughout the room. It wasn't completely true, but it was more honest than she'd ever been with him. And the trouble with that kind of honesty was, there was no way to take it back. But she tried. "I didn't mean it that way, Robby," she said.

But suddenly he was not fighting anymore. "Yes, you did," he said quietly.

"You meant it exactly the way you said it."

"I was angry . . ."

"No. This is about a lot more than anger, don't you see? You've lost all respect for me. That's what I've been trying to tell you."

I have, but not for the reasons you think.

But she wasn't going to say that, wasn't going to risk honesty again.

"I need to get your respect back, Laura. I need to get my self-respect back." He was eager now, and there was a trace of the old sweetness too. She remembered their college days when he'd find a poem by Emily Dickinson that he knew would delight her, or when he'd hear a new song he wanted her to hear, and he'd race across campus to share it with her. She remembered the way he had looked at her when he'd put Molly in the back of the car because he knew she loved the dog and couldn't bear to leave her out in the desert. He had wanted to make her happy then, and in his own way, he was still trying to do that now. She wanted to cry.

"Let me get out of here for a while, I'm starting to hate this town," Robby said. "I'll get my head together and come back and we'll make a fresh start."

Suddenly she didn't want to cry anymore, she was just tired. Too tired to try to point out how many fresh starts they'd already made, or how many times he'd tried to get his head together. Maybe he was right and it would do him good to get away. Maybe a miracle would happen. And if it didn't, at least if he was in Ohio she could finish the work on her book without him wanting her to stop what she was doing to make dinner or to take time out to go someplace, and then sulking when she said she couldn't.

"When do you think you'll go?" she asked.

—

Robby left the next week. He kissed her before he walked out to his car—he was driving to Ohio—and she stood in the doorway and waved good-bye. Then

she closed the door and went back inside and made herself a cup of coffee,
and listened to the whir of her refrigerator in her silent kitchen. She and Robby
had been separated before, of course.
But this time . . . she wondered if she'd
miss him.

Chapter Twenty-one

"Robby's gone to Blair's Falls, and Laura says she's not sure when he's coming back. Something's wrong," Iris said. The worry lines were creasing her forehead, and she was biting her lip.

"It's not a separation," Theo soothed. "He went to visit his mother."

The worry lines relaxed a little. "I wish Laura could have gone with him."

"She had to work. There's the reception she's catering for that pianist." The reception was to be held in Manhattan, and the pianist in question was a young girl who was the big new name in the classical music world. The job was very glamorous and a big coup for Laura. "It's the first time she's done a party in the city. This is important to her."

"So is her marriage."

And they were back to Iris's concern . . . no, it was a fixation . . . with Laura's marriage. Unfortunately, her motives weren't as pure as she liked to think. It was true that Iris genuinely believed in marriage and she couldn't imagine a full, joyful life for any woman without it. But it was also true that she didn't want her daughter to fail at the thing at which her mother had been so brilliant. Theo shook his head. Mothers and daughters, he would never understand that relationship. They loved each other so much, certainly Iris and Anna had, but Iris had always been in competition with Anna—not that she'd ever admit it. Laura had been Iris's secret weapon in that competition. It was as if Laura could vindicate her mother in her struggle with her mother. Theo shook his head again. It was all so very feminine . . . and so very convoluted.

He should probably try to say something that would put his wife's mind at ease . . . But no, he wasn't going to have to. Because Iris was looking at her watch, which meant that her agile mind had just switched to an even greater concern than Laura's marital status. Him. Sure enough, she came bustling to his side. "Good gracious, Theo," she said. "I've been going on and on, and it's time for you to take your nap."

There had been a time when he would have argued that naps were for children and he would have given her a hard time. But these days he was always grateful for a rest. Not a good sign, but to be expected. That was what he had to remember. It was to be expected. He allowed his wife to lead him into the bedroom and soon he was lying in bed with the lights turned off, supposedly trying to sleep. But his mind returned again to the never-ending puzzle of Iris, Anna and Laura. And Anna's secret. Which was at the heart of the puzzle. He could still remember the fateful afternoon when he'd learned the secret. The man who had told him the story was named Paul Werner. Before that day, Theo had only known him as an old friend of Anna's. Theo closed his eyes and in his mind he was transported back to the late sixties, when his life was in shambles.

The immediate cause of his misery had been a terrible accident. It had occurred during a furious quarrel with Iris, when she'd closed a car door on his hand. She hadn't meant to do it, hadn't seen his hand, but his fingers had been severed and in a few seconds his career as a plastic surgeon had ended. That was all it had taken; some words spoken in rage, a car door slammed shut and a hand that was in the way. And his life as he had known it was over. He couldn't earn a living, and since he had always lived beyond his means, he hadn't had a penny of savings. He was soon drowning in debt, and Iris was drowning in guilt. She couldn't be in the same house with him, and he had been living in his office.

Theo had pulled down the blinds and was playing Verdi's *Requiem* on the stereo when Paul Werner had knocked on his door. He'd let Paul in—he'd never been sure why, since he barely knew the man—and after a bit of prodding Theo had spilled all the details of his desperate situation. To his amazement Paul had offered to support him and his family while he trained himself in a new branch of medicine. Paul had claimed he was making this outrageously generous offer because of his old friendship with Anna, but Theo had dismissed that lie and demanded the truth. Then it had been Paul's turn to tell his story—the one he'd been carrying inside him for almost forty years.

When she first came to America from Poland, Anna had worked as a maid in the home of Paul's parents, Florence and Walter Werner. The Werners were an old and respected New York family with deep roots in the German Jewish community of the city. All of this Theo had known. But he hadn't known that while Anna was working for the Werners, she and Paul had fallen in love—helplessly and, as it turned out, hopelessly, because Paul was already engaged. His fiancée was a girl of his own class and his family had been hoping for years for the match. Unable to disappoint them, Paul had married his fiancée, knowing that Anna was the only woman for him. A heartbroken Anna had married Joseph Friedman, knowing that Paul was the love of her life.

Joseph had prospered and become a wealthy and influential real estate developer. Paul had taken over his family's bank and prospered too. Both marriages seemed sound. But the love between Paul and Anna had not died or dimmed, and when fate threw them together several years later, they had finally consummated the passion that had started when she was a servant in his family's house. Out of that act of love, Iris had been born.

This was Anna's secret. She had tried to keep it from Paul, but he had discovered the truth. He had wanted desperately to have some kind of connection with his child, but Anna had been terrified. Still, he had managed to engineer the occasional meeting with the two of them. For reasons she had never been able to articulate, Iris had not liked those encounters and she had disliked Paul Werner.

Now, Theo opened his eyes and stared up at the ceiling. The bedroom was cool and so silent he could hear the bedside clock ticking. Wherever she was in the house Iris was moving quietly so he could sleep. But his mind was too full.

"Iris is my daughter," Paul had said when he finished his tale. "Now you know what's hidden." And then he had threatened Theo. "And if you ever re-peat this, I'll kill you and then I'll kill my-self."

Theo had sworn that he would never tell anyone—not because of the threat, but because he agreed with Paul that Iris must never, ever know the circum-stances of her birth. However, it was be-cause she was Paul's daughter that Theo had been able to justify borrowing the money—he couldn't have taken it as a gift—that had rescued him and his family.

It had taken Theo years to repay Paul, and during that time Paul had only asked for one thing. "Stay in touch and tell me how Iris is doing—how you all are doing. Your children too." Theo's

children, who were Paul's grandchildren. The only grandchildren he had
since he and his wife were childless.
"Do you want to know how I've kept
track of my daughter all these years?"
Paul had demanded once. The pain in
his eyes had been almost too much to
bear. "There's a shop on Madison Avenue where Iris and Anna buy their
clothes. It's called Chez Lea." It was one
of the most expensive stores in Manhattan, and back in the days when Theo
was throwing his money around, he had
encouraged Iris to patronize the place.
He nodded.

"The owner of that store is a woman
called Leah Sherman. She knows about
Iris . . ."

Theo couldn't stop an involuntary
intake of breath. "Why take the
chance—?" he began to say, but Paul
cut him off.

"I've known Leah since she was a
child, and I would trust her with my life.
For all these years she has given me
what no one else could." He paused.
"Iris is the only child I have. I've kept
away from her because Anna said it was

too dangerous. I can count on the fingers of one hand the number of times I've seen Iris face-to-face, or managed to say a few words to her. I've forced Anna to let me meet her . . . but it's been so little . . . so little." There was a pleading note in his cultured voice now. "A man wants to know his child. And the only way I could get any information about Iris was through Leah. Whenever Anna or Iris came into her shop, Leah could be my eyes and ears. It wasn't enough, but it was the best I could get and I'm not ashamed to say that I let her spy on them for me. I've been that desperate."

Paul Werner was a proud and private man, and Theo thought it must be costing him greatly to make himself this vulnerable. But Paul had let the floodgates open after years of silence and now it seemed that he needed to talk. "I don't even have a picture of Iris. Do you know what I do when I want to see her face? I have an oil painting of my late mother. Iris is the exact image of her, so I look at that portrait and tell myself it's of both of them. I suppose that sounds crazy or foolish to you."

No, Theo had wanted to say, *it's just so very sad.*

He and Paul had talked one last time about all of these things on the day when Theo had handed Paul the final check of repayment for his loan. Theo had tried to express his gratitude again, but Paul had waved him off. He had looked down at the check in his hands and he'd said softly, "These years since we started our arrangement have been the best I've known. For the first time, I've felt I was a part of Iris's life." There were tears streaming down his face, and he didn't try to wipe them away. "I could never give her a doll for her birthday. I never knew what her favorite color was, or her favorite subject in school. When you married her, your wedding was in all the newspapers because Joseph Friedman was an influential man. Not because of me—because of Joseph. I stood in the crowd outside the temple and tried to catch a glimpse of my child as she ran to the limousine. That was all

I could do. But now, I'm a part of her life."

"I'm glad you feel that way," was all Theo could think to say.

"Whatever I've given you—and I'm not minimizing it, I know what that money has meant to you, but it can't compare with what you've done for me. Just know that."

Theo had known it. And even though he never could—or would—have revealed any of this history to Iris, in time he'd been able to convince her to change her mind about her mother's old friend. She had come to care about Paul, and that had given Theo great satisfaction. Paul had died several years ago, and Theo had been grateful that Iris had made peace with her father, even if she hadn't been aware of it.

—

In the bedroom, Theo sat up. He wasn't tired anymore. It was as if remembering the past—even those days that had been so charged with emotion—had refreshed him. He found that happened sometimes these days. He walked out of the bedroom and found Iris sitting with a book in her lap. But she was not reading it; it was clear her thoughts were far away. When she heard his footsteps behind her, she jumped to her feet, ready to do whatever he needed. She was like that now, always on the alert in case he was in trouble.

"Are you all right? Did you sleep?" she asked. He heard the anxiety in her voice even though she was trying to cover it.

What will she do when I am gone? May the God she believes in, that I do not, help her.

"Yes, yes. I had a nice rest." He made his way to his chair and sat. She sat opposite him. "You looked so pensive when I came in," he said. "Tell me what you were thinking."

She laughed a little. "Oh, just that it's interesting the way our minds work. I've been so worried about Laura and Robby . . . well, you know that. And to be honest with you, I was sitting here thinking about that photographer. Then for some reason I started thinking about Paul Werner. I was just wondering to myself why I made the leap in my mind from that arty-looking photographer with his awful hair to Paul Werner, who was such an elegant man."

Ah, my Iris, you do know why. When you were a child you sensed what was between Paul and your mother. Now you know in your heart that the same thing is there between our daughter and that young man. But you can't admit it, and you're afraid.

But he wasn't going to say it, because she was sitting up very straight like a good little girl hoping to hear that the things that frightened her were all in her imagination. And it was his job to protect her from the things that frightened her, at least for a while longer. While he was still here.

"Are you asking me to explain the way your mind works?" he asked with a grin. "After all these years you are still a mystery to me, my darling. And I hope that never changes."

And after he had kissed her, and she had kissed him back, he asked her what they were having for supper, and she said soup. She went into the kitchen to heat it up for him, and as they ate it together at their kitchen table, he thought how simple life really was. You could solve so many of your problems with a grin and a kiss and a bit of soup. And he wished, oh so much, that he had known that years earlier.

Chapter Twenty-two

It was summertime. Robby hadn't come back from Blair's Falls yet—he'd been away for almost two months—and Katie had gone to a sleepaway camp, and wouldn't be home until the end of August. Laura still didn't know when Robby was returning; he never mentioned it when they spoke on the phone. However, he seemed cheerful and busy—doing what, she wasn't sure. So for the first time in years, Laura had no one to feed but Molly, and the only voice in the house was her own. But that wasn't why the gray fog had descended on her once again. She missed Nick. It was that simple. Sometimes the missing took the form of a dull ache that stayed with her throughout the day, sometimes it was a sharp, fast pain that hit her without warning. Either way, it hurt. And there was no way to stop it.

The only thing that had helped was work and she had thanked God that for a while she was very busy. She and Lillian had finished writing the book and were editing the final draft. The reception for Mai Ling, the concert pianist, had been a success, and several Manhattan organizations had expressed interest in hiring Laura's catering company in the future. (To Iris's delight, Phil had gone to the reception, where Laura had introduced him to Ms. Ling and they seemed to like each other.)

But then—and it was as if it happened overnight—the book was finished and had been sent off to the publisher, and there were no new catering jobs until the fall. This was nothing new, summer was always Laura's slow season, and normally she used the time to work with her gardeners; she now had two of them tending the fresh vegetables and flowers that were her trademark as a caterer. This was also the time of year when she spent hours with her accountant doing the paperwork that had piled up during the year. But now, when she was in the midst of her gray fog, she knew she'd go out of her mind if she had to spread mulch in the glaring sunshine, or sit inside adding up columns of figures.

She thought about going north to see Katie, but the proprietor of the camp frowned on parents visiting until the kids had had a chance to settle in. And besides, Laura didn't want to go anywhere until the fog had lifted. It would have to eventually, she told herself; in spite of what all those Victorian novels said, no one actually died of a broken heart.

But the fog didn't lift.

———

"I'm not happy with some of the pictures that were selected for the book." Lillian's voice on the phone sounded exasperated. "Everything Nick shot is beautiful, of course, but from a storytelling perspective I think we have some better choices. I told him you and I would come to his studio one day next week to take another look at his proof sheets."

I'm going to Nick's studio. I'll see him again! Laura's heart began to pound. But then she came to her senses.

"Lillian . . . I'm afraid I can't get away."

"All week long? You must have one day free. This is important."

Lillian was right. The pictures were as important to the book as the text she and Laura had slaved over.

But dear God, how am I going to do it? How am I going to see him again and then walk away?

"Laura, are you still there?"

"How about next Wednesday?" she said with a gasp. And hoped Lillian hadn't heard it.

"Be at Nick's studio at noon."

Today was Thursday. There were six days to wait.

———

She didn't seem to need to eat very much, and she wasn't sleeping more than a few hours a night. Yet she was never tired. She worked longer and harder than any of her crew in the gardens and still had energy left over. Sometimes she found herself shivering, she didn't know whether it was from excitement or fear or a combination of both. And it didn't matter. She had only six days to wait. Then there were four days. Then there were two. Then it was Tuesday night.

She washed her hair, and brushed it dry so that it gleamed. She pulled clothes out of her closet until almost everything she owned was spread on her bed. Finally she selected a pink wraparound dress—she liked the way it accentuated her slender waist—a little orange jacket to go over it, high-heeled sandals that made her feel like a model on a runway when she walked in them, and her favorite coral earrings. She laid it all out on her chaise, then she climbed into bed and waited for the morning.

Wednesday morning was bright and sunny. But Laura might as well have been in Alaska in the dead of winter. She piled her gleaming hair on top of her head with hands that shook. They shook when she put on her lipstick and

pulled on the pink dress, which suddenly seemed too revealing and showy.
She thought about changing into something else, but she didn't have time. If
she missed the train into the city, she
would be late.

Besides, she told herself, *you're being
absurd. It's been weeks since you've
seen him. And you told him it was over.
New York is full of girls who are younger
and prettier than you are. He's probably
moved on to someone else already.*

But he hadn't. She would have known
if he had, because they had that connection that had started on the first day
she met him.

*Even if he hasn't found someone new,
that doesn't change anything. You're still
married. You're still a grown-up.*

But she felt like a girl—a scarily reck-
less girl.

*This is a business meeting. Lillian will
be there. What can possibly happen
while she's there?*

And in the end, that was the only re-
assurance she could give herself; nothing would happen because Lillian would
be there.

Thank God for Lillian. It became like a mantra for her as she drove to the railroad station and stood on the platform waiting for the train, and when she sat in her seat on the trip into the city. *Thank God for Lillian,* she repeated over and over in her mind. *Nothing will happen because Lillian will be there.*

———

Nick opened the door to his loft. He didn't say a word, he just stared at her with those beautiful, beautiful green-blue eyes. If she hadn't known it before, she knew now that there hadn't been a new woman in his life.

"Hi," he said after a long wait. She thought about running.

"May I come in?" she asked. He stepped aside so she could enter, then closed the door behind her. "Would you like something to drink?" he asked. He needed to do something because he was nervous. She knew this because she was so nervous herself.

"I . . . Some water?" she managed to say.

Along one wall of the loft there was

what looked like a galley kitchen with a sink. As he hurried over to it, she began walking around, studying everything intently—anything to keep from looking at him.

She hadn't known what a photographer's loft would be like—she had imagined a glamorous place with chrome and leather chairs and huge avant-garde photos on the walls. Nick's loft looked more like an old-fashioned workshop. There was a big worktable in the middle of the room, and a forest of standing lights, as well as cameras and other equipment, were stored neatly in a corner. The ceiling was high, and it was encrusted with intricate crown moldings. There were frosted Palladian windows that were covered by long shades, and the hardwood floor beneath Laura's feet had been scuffed from long use before it had been restored. In one corner of the space there was a conversation pit consisting of a deep sofa, three comfortable-looking chairs, an oak coffee table and a thick Oriental rug.

Nick brought her the glass of water. She took it and thanked him and then they were staring wordlessly at each other again. "So this is where you work," she finally said, to break the silence.

"Yes. I live here too. Behind that door over there, I have a living room and a full kitchen and my . . . and my bedroom," he stumbled. The word with all it's suggestions floated in the air. The water in the glass Laura was holding, splashed. Nick took it from her.

"Your hands are shaking," he said. She'd forgotten how tender that husky voice could be. But she couldn't let herself think about things like tenderness.

"Take a look at yours," she said. He smiled and she could feel herself smile back and that was even more dangerous than the tenderness.

"Where's Lillian?" she asked quickly. The tendrils of hair were falling in his face the way they always did. He was wearing his standard outfit, the blue jeans that looked so well on a man with a narrow waist and long legs, and the T-shirt that outlined the contours of his chest. "Is Lillian here yet?" she asked again.

"She's not coming."

Oh God.

"She called to say she's got a nasty summer flu. She said she tried to phone you to let you know, but there was no answer at your house."

"I'd probably left for the train station already."

"That's what she thought."

She should get out of there. She should say she'd come back later when Lillian was there. But she couldn't make herself form the words.

"Laura . . ." he said softly.

I should get out of here.

"If you only knew how many times I imagined you being here like this."

I should get out of here right now.

"I thought I'd give you champagne and fill the place with roses . . . make it as beautiful as you are."

But God help me, I don't want to go.

"I don't need champagne and roses, Nick," she said, and her voice was as soft as his.

Somewhere in the hallway outside his loft, a door slammed shut. Someone called out something, but the words were too muffled for her to understand. She waited for Nick to move to her. As he had to now. Because there was no turning back. When he was standing in front of her, she watched him look down at the wraparound dress that empha- sized her narrow waist and her breasts. And then she took off the jaunty little or- ange jacket.

Her dress was made of a silky jersey, and only the tie at the waist kept it to- gether. His fingers were sure as he un- did it, remarkably so considering that they were still shaking. The silky jersey slid to the floor, and her pretty sandals were off—she never quite knew how. He carried her to the sofa and knelt beside her. His mouth was all over her, her neck, her throat, her lips. He was kissing her, and his hands were caressing her while she was pushing away fabric and undoing buttons and buckles. And then he was over her . . . and smiling down at her . . . and she could hear his breath, and his heart beating . . . or maybe it was hers . . . and when at last he cried out, she followed him with a cry of her own.

So it had happened. All the denying and struggling had come to an end. Nick was lying beside her, peace in his eyes, his fingers tangled in her hair, which had come out of the pins she'd used to pile it up. And she knew she should be feeling guilty, but she couldn't. Not then. It would come later, of course; it had to. But at that moment all she could feel was joy.

There was an afghan on the sofa. Nick pulled it up over them, so they were in a cocoon. He drew her closer to him, and her head found a place on his shoulder where it fit perfectly. Outside the loft, below on the street, the traffic of the city was blaring, she could hear it dimly through the closed windows. People were rushing around doing all the things responsible New Yorkers must do on a beautiful Wednesday afternoon in July. But she was inside her cocoon with Nick. And now she could sleep.

———

When she awakened, at first she didn't know where she was. An ornate ceiling she didn't recognize soared above her head, and there was an afghan wrapped around her that she knew she didn't own. Then she remembered. She turned so she could see Nick lying on the sofa next to her. But he wasn't there. Scared, she lifted her head.

"Hi." Nick was sitting in the chair on the other side of the sofa. He was dressed and he'd turned on a lamp.

"You're there . . . for a moment I thought . . ."

"I'm right here." He came across the room, knelt at the side of the sofa and kissed her. It was a different kind of kiss now, it was gentle because there was no more urgency. But maybe there was something a little sad about it too?

"What time is it?" she asked.

"Ten after four, I was about to wake you."

"Why didn't you?"

"I like watching you sleep." He stroked her cheek. "Your clothes are there." He pointed to a neat pile. "Would you like some coffee before you go?"

And now she understood the sadness. "I don't want to leave you," she said.

He hesitated for a moment, then he took a deep breath. "I don't want you to. But I think we'd better start getting used to it . . . don't you?"

She looked in his eyes and saw what he'd been realizing while she slept; that saying good-bye to each other was a part of their life now. They would say good-bye instead of sleeping side by side and waking up in each other's arms. They would never have the luxury of wasting their time together, because the word "good-bye" would always be hanging over them.

"This is so unfair to you," she said. Her heart would break if he agreed with her.

He kissed her again. "I'm a big boy, Laura." He stood up. "Let me make you that coffee. There's a train you can take at six. I checked."

"I'd stay if it weren't for poor Molly. I didn't leave any food for her and . . ." She had to stop because—stupidly and ridiculously—she was starting to cry.

"Don't, darling!" He knelt down again. "No tears. That's not what we're about.

All right?" She wiped away the tears and nodded.

She dressed while Nick busied himself in the kitchen. Then he handed her a steaming cup and sat in his chair again. After a moment, he said, "I know I can't have . . . everything I want. You're married. You have responsibilities. But this is so right. Because it's good . . . you know it is . . . and there's no way something this good can be wrong . . ."

"I'm afraid it can."

"No. As long as we don't hurt anyone, it won't be."

"But someone always does get hurt."

"Because people get careless. We won't do that. We'll make sure no one ever finds out."

"But what about us? What about you and me?"

He turned away then. "I'll take whatever I can get for as long as I can have it. And no matter what happens it will be worth it to me." He turned back to her, and he tried to make his voice light, but the green-blue eyes were pleading. "Your turn."

He'd said she had responsibilities—

and she did. She was a person who made her promises and she kept them. But he'd also said this was right and good. That was the truth too, undeniable, unbelievable and unarguable.

"I'll take whatever I can get for as long as I can have it," she said.

———

The next weeks seemed to whirl by. She worked, of course, when had she not worked? Her gardens had to be tended, and requests for parties and events to be planned for the fall started to come in. But it was Nick and being with him that dominated every thought. They met in his loft—she was familiar with every inch of his private living quarters by now—as often as they could. She became adept at subterfuge . . . and lying. Whenever she ran into the city for a few hours of stolen happiness she claimed to be doing research for a new book. She told this lie to her workers, her parents, her brothers and sometimes even her editor—everyone but Katie. Katie called on Tuesday and Thursday evenings because that was when the campers were allowed to use the phone. Laura saw to it that she was always home before dark on these nights, so when her daughter called there was no need to explain—or to lie about—anything.

Robby called regularly too, and she was stunned at how easily she was able talk to him. Although talking with Robby these days meant listening to him. He seemed to have fallen in love with the town he had once fought so hard to get out of. Now he referred to it as "the real America," and he spent a lot of time telling Laura how friendly everyone in Blair's Falls was.

"You'll find them a little conservative politically," he said with a laugh. "You may have to pull back a bit on some of your opinions when you come out here to visit."

It was the first she'd heard that she would be going out to Ohio. Or that she would be trying to impress the people in Blair's Falls.

"And it might be best to keep mum about your brother Steve dodging the draft during Vietnam," Robby went on.

"And all that do-gooder work he does now."

She thought about reminding Robby that he hadn't exactly lined up for military duty himself. She also thought about asking him when he was coming home. But she didn't want to know.

—

As the days turned into weeks with no mention of his return, her husband urged her again and again to come out to "the real America." She got more and more adept at putting him off. Most of the time she had good reason. Her book had been printed, and advance copies of it were being passed around to critics. The response had been resoundingly favorable, and the publicist who had been assigned to her by her publisher had begun setting up press interviews for her—which were based in New York, not Ohio. The biggest feather in her cap—her publicist's words, not hers—had been an interview, which had already aired, on the country's highest-rated morning talk show. In addition to promoting the book, Laura had told funny stories about salvaging kitchen disasters, and her adventures with her pressure cooker, which she admitted scared her half to death. Everyone loved it, and they loved her. The show's producer had called to ask how she'd feel about doing a five-minute segment for them twice a week. Laura had acquired an agent to handle the negotiations.

Everyone was happy for her. "This will make you a household name, book sales will go through the roof," her publicist crowed. Nick made a videotape of what he called her star turn, and they watched it together on his television while they ate the Frrrozen Hot Chocolate he'd ordered from Serendipity because he knew she loved it. Her family and friends kept her phone ringing with congratulations and Katie said over the phone that her mom had been really cool. Only Robby was not enthusiastic.

"It seemed a little self-serving," he said. "Did you have to brag about that book so much?"

"The idea was to promote it."

"Well, when you come out here, you'll have to tone it down some. People in this neck of the woods don't like it when someone toots their own horn."

There had been a time when this would have made her angry and she would have had to swallow that anger to avoid an argument. Today she was too focused on her wristwatch. If she didn't get off the phone that minute she'd be late getting into the city to see Nick. "Robby, I have to run," she said.

Forty-five minutes later as the train whisked her into Manhattan she'd already pushed the phone call to the back of her mind. Robby was getting more and more entrenched in his hometown, that was obvious. She didn't want to think about what that might mean in the future. She was going to have to deal with her marriage and her husband sometime. But today the sun was shining, there was a light breeze in the air and Nick was waiting for her.

And so her days went—busy, golden days. She and Nick never talked about the future. What was there to say, after all? There were decisions ahead, painful, big decisions—so much for no one getting hurt—and she couldn't bear to think about them. So she lived for the present. She and Nick both did. But then, suddenly, the summer was almost over.

"Katie will be coming home next week," she told Nick. She didn't have to add that their carefree days had ended. They both knew she wouldn't be able to linger in the city until seven at night when Katie was back home. The future they had been avoiding for weeks was suddenly much closer.

"Let's go away for a long weekend," Nick said. "We could leave next Friday."

"But we've never gone anywhere together."

He gave Laura a twisted little smile. "That's my point."

So they began the bittersweet process of planning a discreet getaway. Bitter because without saying it, they both knew this marked the end of a halcyon time they would never have again. But the weekend itself would be sweet. They could lie in bed for as long as they liked. They could wake up in the morning together and have breakfast. Or take a walk and hold hands. Or go to the movies. She and Nick had never been to the movies together.

The question of where to go for their getaway proved to be more complicated than Laura had imagined. The problem was Nick. Because of the work he did in the arts, fashion and publishing, he was well known in the kind of circles where people "summered" in fashionable vacation areas along the East Coast. Places like the Hamptons, the Berkshires, or the shores of Connecticut and New Jersey were off-limits because he might meet someone he knew. But traveling too far away from the city wasn't a solution, because he and Laura didn't want to waste the precious time they had together in airports.

They finally settled on an old hotel in a sleepy area of the Catskills that had once been a thriving resort but was now struggling for survival. The customers who booked reservations at the Grande Inn were mostly families looking for a bargain rate on a room with sleeping cots for the kids. It was as far away from being a glamorous spot as anyone could imagine.

It was also terrible. The sheets were cheap and scratchy, there were no towels in the bathroom until Laura called the desk and begged for some, and there was a musty smell in the closet. In the dining room, there was only one well-meaning, but frazzled, young girl waiting on the tables. The food she served was not only badly prepared, but by the time it arrived, it was stone-cold. At their first breakfast, Nick had reason to be grateful for that fact, because the waitress spilled a cup of coffee on him. Then she burst into tears and raced into the kitchen, leaving Laura to mop him up.

"Let me help you, Ms. McAllister," said a middle-aged woman from the neighboring table. She bustled over and began dabbing at Nick's jacket with her napkin, while Laura had a moment of panic, wondering how she knew the woman. The mystery was cleared up after a second. "I recognized you from the TV, and I just wanted to say how much my daughter and I loved you on *Good Day USA,* Ms. McAllister. Debbie's sitting right over there ..." She waved in the direction of her table, where her husband and three children were getting ready to leave. The oldest, a skinny girl of about eighteen or nineteen, waved at Laura. "I know she'd love to have your autograph," the woman said.

Totally taken aback, Laura said, "My autograph?"

"It's not every day that we get to see a real live TV star in person. If you don't have any paper, I do." The woman reached into a pocket and whipped out a used envelope and a pen. She held them out to Laura. "Make it out to Debbie. I named my girl after Debbie Reynolds. I must have seen every movie she's ever made. I just love her—don't you?"

Laura had never been that impressed with Debbie Reynolds. "I ... well ..." she stammered.

"I know you're much too young to remember when Debbie was married to Eddie Fisher and that nasty Elizabeth Taylor stole him away, but I'm here to tell you, Debbie handled that with class and dignity. Eddie must have been out of his mind is all I can say. Although he certainly got a bit of his own back when Liz left him for Richard Burton. What goes around, comes around—don't you agree?"

Across the table Nick was barely managing to keep a straight face.

"I . . . guess . . . ," Laura said unsteadily. She grabbed the envelope, signed it and handed it back to the woman, who shook her hand with a crushing grip and finally, mercifully went back to her own table. A few seconds later she and her family waved good-bye to Laura and exited the dining room. Nick broke into whoops of laughter.

"Some help you were," she scolded him. "You almost made me start laughing at that poor woman."

"That 'poor woman' had you in her sights from the second you walked into the room," he said. "She was sitting over there just waiting to pounce. Besides, it was fun watching you handle your first fan."

"I never expected anything like that—a total stranger coming up to me and starting to talk. What if I was eating and I had something stuck between my teeth?"

"The price of fame, darling," he said as he wiped his streaming eyes. "The price of fame." Then he sobered up. "But I should have realized that people would recognize you from that TV interview. It was stupid of me not to think of that."

She hadn't thought of it before that second either. "Does this mean we have to go home?" It would be so unfair if they did. She and Nick were asking for so little, just one weekend in an awful old hotel in the middle of nowhere!

"We're okay. That was a fluke," Nick said. But to be on the safe side, maybe we should stop eating in the dining room here."

So after that, Nick bought their meals in a diner and they ate them in their room. But even so, the three days were heavenly and they passed way too quickly. It seemed to Laura that before she knew it, Nick was back in his loft and she was in her house missing him with an ache that was like a physical pain. Then Katie came home, and everything changed.

Chapter Twenty-three

Some of the changes were what Laura had expected: although she still went into the city to be with Nick—nothing could change that—their times together were much shorter. And there were fewer of them. But a bigger change was in Laura herself; now she had to face the fact that no matter how much she'd told herself that being with Nick was right, it wasn't something she wanted her daughter to know about. That had to mean that there was at least something wrong about it. Katie's return had brought with it a dose of reality.

And there was an even stronger dose to come.

"My Uncle Dan wants to turn the family store over to me," Robby said during their nightly phone call.

"What?"

"He told me last spring that he wanted to retire, and since he didn't have any children of his own, he wanted me to have the store, if I had an aptitude for running it. That's what I've been doing these last few months."

"You've been . . . working for your uncle?" Laura tried to grasp what he was saying. "In Blair's Falls?"

"I've been learning the ropes at the store, Laura, to see if I have a feeling for retail. And to find out if I like the work. Uncle Dan and I agreed that I needed to test myself."

"You and your Uncle Dan agreed that you were going to do this? Just like that? Without even asking me?"

"Yes. Because I knew this was the only way."

Because he knew she never would have gone along with it.

"I've made so many mistakes, Laura.

I've had so many failures. Before I told you about this I wanted to be sure. And now I am."

Oh dear God, why didn't I see this coming? I should have seen it. When he didn't come home, I should have known something was up . . . But I was glad he wasn't home.

"What about your writing?"

"In all those weeks that I went to that office, I didn't write one word; that's not the career for me. Look, I know this is coming out of the blue, but try to keep an open mind. I think you and I and Katie could be really happy here in Blair's Falls."

He thinks I'd be happy living in his hometown near his mother, who hates me? He thinks I'd want to leave my family and my business . . . and Nick. But I mustn't think about Nick. Not now.

"Robby, we can't just pick up and leave. We have a life here."

"You do. I have nothing. And that's not good for us. You need a husband you can be proud of. And I need to get my pride back."

"I know you've been depressed. And

things haven't gone well for you. But moving isn't going to solve that."

"It will. Because I'll be making money—you won't be paying all of the bills. And we'll be on my home ground."

"Your home ground? This isn't a game, where somebody wins and somebody loses."

She heard him draw in a breath. "Remember when we were in college and we were young and dumb and we thought we had all the answers? Back then, I never would have dreamed I'd hear myself saying this, but when it comes to men and women, I think some of the old-fashioned ways are best. I'm not saying women need to stay at home like my mother did, God forbid, but I think most men still want to be the head of the household." He chuckled ruefully. "Maybe it's that our egos aren't strong enough." Then he got serious again. "I just know I can't be the man who's introduced as your husband. And I see that coming, Laura. Your book will be published, and your business is growing. You're going to be even more successful than you are now. Where does that leave me?"

"You can be whatever you want to be. Do whatever you want to do. And I'll back you."

"I don't want you to back me. Not by supporting me financially, or giving me a pep talk as you're running out the door to your next business meeting. I want you at my side."

"I understand what you're saying . . . but to do this . . . ?"

"It's a fresh start for all of us, Laura. You think I want this just for me? I'm doing this for our marriage. And for Katie. She needs two parents who are happy."

And if it makes you happy to be in Ohio, then I'll be happy too. That is truly the way you feel.

"Robby, you can't just throw this at me."

"I know. You have to come out to Blair's Falls for a real visit—you've always just run in and out. And then we'll wait until after New Year's to move. I know it would be better for Katie if we could do it now so she could start the school year with her classmates, but it will take time to wind up everything in New York."

Laura hadn't agreed to move, she hadn't even agreed to go out to Ohio to visit, and he was talking about Katie's classmates and her new school as if it had all been decided.

"And this gives you plenty of time to help Katie adjust to the idea."

What about me? How am I supposed to adjust to it?

But arguing would be useless. Robby's mind was made up. Uncle Dan had already promoted him to the position of store manager, with a promise of a vice presidency to come. Now it was Landon's Department Store and Blair's Falls that would solve all of their problems.

———

In the weeks that followed, Robby sang the praises of Blair's Falls to Laura every night on the phone. He told her that during the summer he had already joined a couple of clubs in the town—he'd been that certain Laura would uproot her life for him. Membership in both organizations was limited to prominent men in the community, he told her proudly. It took everything she had not to say that he was so damn prominent because his uncle had handed him a business on a silver platter.

At the end of every phone call, Robby would urge her again to come out to Ohio for a real visit. And she would keep on finding excuses not to go. And the next day, she would run to Nick's loft where they would lock the door and for a few hours they would pretend that the world outside didn't exist.

"I don't know what I'd do without this place, and you," she said to him one afternoon as she was leaving to catch her train.

"You won't have to find out, I promise." He liked to make everything light when they were parting.

"I mean it. I've loved so many people, but you're . . . necessary. I need you. I don't think I've ever needed anyone except Katie."

"I need you too. Frightening, isn't it?"

"Frightening in a good way, or a bad way?"

"Now you're fishing." She reached up and kissed him. "In a good way," he whispered. "In the very best way."

———

As Laura rode home on the train the conversation came back to her. She needed Nick—in the same way Christina needed Steven. The same way her mother needed her father.

What do you know, Mom? All of my life I thought I was like Nana. She loved Grandpa, but I never thought she really needed him. Not like you need Dad. And now . . . I need Nick. We're two of a kind, after all, Mom.

But Laura needed the wrong man. That was what Iris would think.

Chapter Twenty-four

"Katie, there's an empty cab on the corner, hurry!" Mom began running up Madison Avenue, with her hand up in an attempt to hail the taxi. Katie, who had been dawdling behind her, now slowed down even more. "Katie, come on!" Her mother turned back to urge her, and in that instant a man with a briefcase stepped into the street and took the cab. "Damn it!" Mom swore, which was something she almost never did unless she was really upset.

Good, Katie thought with sour satisfaction.

"Honey, didn't you hear me tell you to

run? We could have gotten that one. Now we're going to be late." They were going to Uncle Jimmy's apartment for dinner.

"You always are," Katie muttered just loud enough for her mother to hear.

Mom looked hurt—and surprised. She didn't expect this kind of thing from Katie. Katie didn't expect it from herself. "I don't know what's gotten into you," Mom said. "Would you like to explain this attitude?"

Katie shrugged elaborately and began walking up Madison Avenue. After a second her mother followed.

Katie was scared, and feeling scared was making her angry. Not that she was going to tell her mother that. Their family was falling apart; it wasn't Mom's fault, Dad was actually causing it, but Mom was always the one who fixed things. Only now she wasn't. And while it wasn't fair for Katie take it out on Mom, she couldn't stop it. Even though she was actually on her mom's side.

The trouble was, you couldn't get mad at Dad, because it would be like getting mad at a puppy or a little baby.

Dad was always coming up with plans that were going to make them all so happy, but they never did. Now he'd come up with the worst plan yet. He wanted to move them to Ohio. Anyone who knew Mom would know she didn't want that. But instead of telling Dad she wouldn't go, she was acting like he'd never said anything. It was like she thought he'd drop it if she just didn't mention it. But once Dad had an idea in his head he never dropped it. Mom should know that.

Katie didn't want to go to Ohio any more than her mother did. She liked her school—except for arithmetic, but she was going to have to take that any-where—and she had friends here. There were only two of them; Katie wasn't the kind of person who said hi to dozens of people in the school halls every day, but those two friends were really great. She didn't want to lose them. And she didn't want to live far away from Grandpa Theo and Grandma Iris. Katie had come to love them both an awful lot. She didn't feel the same way about Grandmother Mac, who made you take your shoes off when you walked into the house, and when you were trying to tell her something you could see that she wasn't really listening because you were just a kid and she was the kind of adult who thought you wouldn't have anything worthwhile to say. No, there was no way Katie wanted to move anywhere and especially not to Ohio, and she wanted her mom to do something about it fast.

"We'll have to walk to Uncle Jimmy's apartment. We'll never get a cab in rush hour," Mom broke into Katie's thoughts. "I'm sorry, honey."

For a moment, Katie was sorry too. Mom tried so hard, and Katie shouldn't have made her lose the cab. But Katie wasn't about to say that.

Her mother sighed. "Still sulking, I see."

They walked up Madison Avenue in silence. Suddenly, Katie looked around. She didn't come into the city often with her mom and the streets tended to melt together, but this stretch of Madison Avenue was looking very familiar. Then she remembered. A year ago when she and

Mom were coming home from Rebecca Ruth's birthday party, somewhere around here they'd seen the weird picture that looked exactly like Grandma Iris in the thrift shop window. She started scanning the store windows. After a couple of seconds she saw what she was looking for on the other side of the street. She ran to the corner, caught the tail end of the "walk" light and dashed across Madison Avenue.

"Katie, what are you doing?" her mother cried out.

But Katie was safely on the other side. She heard her mother calling out again, but she raced to the shop and peered into the big window. The picture wasn't there.

After a minute or two, her mother ran up behind her. "You scared the life out of me," her mother panted. "What did you mean by running off like—" She stopped short and looked at the window. "This is that shop," she said.

"Yes. The one with the picture," Katie said. "But it's not in the window."

Her mother let out a breath. "Oh. Well, they've probably sold it."

But Katie didn't want to give up so easily. She turned back to the window, and by putting her eyes right up to the glass and squinting she could see all the way to the back of the shop.

"Katie, that picture is gone. Let's go."

But Mom was wrong. "It's still here! It's on the back wall, right over there. We can go inside and look at it again."

"No, we can't. There's no point in going in to look at the picture if we're not going to buy it. We'd just be wasting the saleswoman's time. And anyway, we're late," Mom said in a tone Katie had never heard from her before. Then she grabbed Katie's hand and almost dragged her away from the window.

"Why are you being so weird?" Katie demanded as they resumed their walk up Madison Avenue. "I hate it when you're like this."

—

Katie's words came back to haunt Laura later that evening, after they were home from the city and Katie was in bed. Laura settled into a chair in the living room. The truth was, she was feeling weird. And very, very guilty.

Robby is pressuring me every night to come west. Nick doesn't pressure me about anything, but he should. We're sneaking around now, that's what it feels like anyway, and it's humiliating and degrading. Nick deserves better. And Robby deserves more too.

This is unfair to everyone, and I should stop it. But I'm stuck. Me. The one who could always make up her mind in a flash. Sometimes I think I'll just tell Robby I'm not leaving New York. This is where I belong, and I've earned the right to be here. But for the first time in years I'm hearing hope in his voice. He's getting his confidence back, and he's working so hard. For us. For Katie and me. But I love Nick.

I know divorce doesn't have the stigma it once had, people end their marriages all the time. But I don't know how they do it. I have a daughter who loves her father. I stay awake nights worrying about what it would do to Katie if Robby and I split up.

And what about the rest of my family?

My brothers think they're so liberated, but I'm not sure how they'd react if they knew I've been having an affair. How would my father take it? He was no saint when he was younger, but he's an Old World man, and they have different standards for men and women. And of course I know how Mom would react. But I love Nick.

Laura went to bed. And the next morning, as she did almost every morning, she told herself that she was going to stop being a coward. She was going to make a decision and live with the results. But not today. She just couldn't do it today.

Chapter Twenty-five

Iris loved the first weeks of a new school year. She liked walking into a classroom and seeing the bright faces of the freshmen turned toward her, waiting to hear what she had to say. She knew some of these youngsters were sitting there because they had to fulfill an academic requirement, but there were always others who were genuinely excited about the subject—and hopefully they would be about their professor too. During the course of the semester she would discover who the eager ones were, and she would enjoy their energy and enthusiasm.

An even greater pleasure could be found in the familiar faces who returned for her advanced classes. These were the students who knew what she had to offer them and wanted more of it. Teaching them was a privilege that genuinely humbled her. So she was pleased when one of her favorites came up to her as she was entering the main building of the university on a crisp morning in October. The girl's name was Debbie.

"And you can't call me Deborah, even though that would be more dignified," Debbie had said during her first student meeting with Iris. Then she'd rolled her eyes. She wasn't a pretty girl, but Iris liked her sense of humor. "It's just plain Debbie, because, heaven help me, I was named after Debbie Reynolds."

Now Debbie joined Iris and they walked together down the hall toward Iris's classroom. They were chatting about the summer, when Debbie said, out of the blue, "By the way, that woman who writes about lifestyles—Laura Mc-Allister—she's your daughter, isn't she?"

"Yes."

"I met her this summer . . . well, I

guess it was more like I saw her. At first I couldn't believe it was her. I mean, we were in the dining room of this old horror of a hotel in the middle of nowhere. My family was there because my dad is really cheap, but I couldn't figure out what she'd be doing in a place like that. She'd just been on television talking about her book—the one that everyone is buying now. But when I saw her it wasn't out yet."

The book had been published a month ago. And Laura's interview with *Good Day USA* had been on the air about two weeks before that. Iris tried to think back to the end of the summer. She was positive Laura hadn't mentioned going anywhere. "Are you sure it was my daughter?" she asked.

"Oh yes, it was at breakfast, and Mom got her autograph for me on a napkin. I didn't put it together then that she was your daughter or I probably would have gone over and introduced myself."

Something cold and nasty stirred in the back of Iris's brain, but she pushed it a way. Debbie was wrong. She had to be . . .

"Although I might not have interrupted her," Debbie went on. "She and her husband were so happy just being alone with each other. You could tell it was like a second honeymoon or something."

Laura's husband? A second honeymoon? Robby had been in Ohio all summer long.

"Forgive me for saying so, Professor, but your son-in-law is yummy! He and your daughter make a beautiful couple, she's so pale and patrician-looking and he's a little bit wild, with all that curly black hair falling in his face."

Robby's hair was light brown, and cut short. The photographer . . . Nick . . . had had black hair. The cold nastiness filled Iris's brain again and she flashed back to Steven's wedding. She'd watched Laura say good-bye to Nick at the end of the day, and she'd had the feeling that there was something . . . But she hadn't wanted to believe it. But now . . .

She and her husband were so happy just being alone with each other . . . it was like a second honeymoon, that was what Debbie had just said. Only it hadn't been Laura's husband, and it wasn't a second honeymoon. Suddenly Iris felt dizzy.

"Professor Stern? Are you okay?" Debbie looked worried. "I'm sorry, if it was out of line for me to say that . . ."

I'm scaring the girl, Iris thought wildly. *I can't let her see how upset I am. I can't let anyone see. I never could hide my feelings. Why didn't I learn to do that?*

"I just meant . . . you could see how much in love they are. And they've been married for a long time too." Poor Debbie dug the hole deeper.

"Please excuse . . ." Iris managed to gasp. "Forgot something . . . my office." She ran down the hallway, leaving the bewildered Debbie looking after her.

Somehow Iris got through the rest of the day. She taught her classes, and she managed to make sense when colleagues and students talked to her. But all the time in the back of her mind were the words "you could see how much in love they are." And in her imagination she saw her daughter and the photographer standing in the doorway of Laura's house.

———

"You don't know she's having an affair, Iris," Theo said.

"Of course she is! She went away to have a horrid, ugly little . . . tryst. With that man, that *Nick*!" Iris spat the name out.

"You don't even know for certain that it was Laura your student saw at that hotel."

"Laura signed an autograph for her."

"Maybe Laura decided to get away for a weekend and she ran into—what is his name? Nick?—while she was there."

"The hotel was an old wreck, Theo! The kind of place where you go to hide, not for a relaxing vacation. What are the chances of the two of them just happening to decide to go to a place like that at the same time? And they were having breakfast together."

"Still, there could be an explanation."

"You know better than that." What she did not say was, *You, of all people, know.*

But he understood. "All right," he said. "Say she is having an affair . . . I can understand it, Iris, and you should too."

"She's married!"

"She was too young when she married Robby McAllister. I said so at the time."

"Robby was a fine young man . . . a remarkable young man, we both agreed on that."

"He *was.* Do you like the man Robby is today?"

That stopped her. But just for a moment. "You don't get married for better or for better, that isn't what the vow says."

"Oh Iris, my dear! You know very well that a vow is made in a vacuum. A life is lived every day, and sometimes the things we thought we could do, we can't."

She listened to him, and thought angrily, *This is how he excused his own infidelities over the years. This is the way all liars and cheaters do it.*

"So what should I have done during

our hard times, Theo? Should I have walked away? Had an affair?"

"Of course not."

I almost did once, although you never knew it, my dear husband. I didn't go through with it because I'm not like you. I didn't find excuses, although I had plenty. I didn't cheat because I have honor. And now, God help me, it looks as if my daughter, of whom I have always been so proud, takes after you. The bitter words came to her lips and tongue. Words she was surprised to find she still could have said after all the years. But she wouldn't say those words because she had learned the hard way how little good they did. And how much harm. And besides, Theo, who she loved in spite of everything, wasn't a well man, and she shouldn't argue with him like this.

"I had such a good example growing up," she said more calmly. "I saw how a couple could pull together. My mother stood by my father during the worst of times, when he lost everything, she never said one word of complaint. And even when the money was coming in again, Papa wasn't the easiest hus-band. But she brought out the best in him. She put up with his failings and she loved him devotedly."

There was a pause, Theo seemed lost in his own thoughts. Finally he said, "Your father was a mensch. He was worthy of her devotion."

But not necessarily her love, Theo added to himself. *He wasn't the right man for your beautiful, cultured mother. I think I always knew that, in the same way that I knew Paul Werner was the right man for her after he told me the truth.*

Life is messy, Iris, and humans cannot always live by the rules. You don't want to accept that, but I think you know it's true.

Iris's voice broke into Theo's thoughts. "I'm going to talk to Laura."

"No!"

"Of course I will. I'm her mother, I have to make her see that what she's doing is wrong."

"You think she doesn't know?"

Or maybe it isn't wrong. I'm glad Paul and Anna stole whatever few moments of joy they could get. I think it was a tragedy that they didn't have more.

"Leave it alone, Iris. I'm begging you."

"I don't want my daughter sneaking off to be with her lover!"

And I don't want her to wind up like her grandmother.

"She'll find her way, Iris. She's a good, honorable person and she'll do what's right if you leave her alone. You have to believe that." His heart was starting to pound now, he shouldn't have let himself get so excited.

Iris saw it. "Let me get your oxygen . . ."

But he waved that aside. "I'm saying this as much for your sake as for Laura's. Because someday the children will be all you have."

"I don't want to hear such talk."

"Then promise me you will not say one word of this to Laura."

"All right, I promise. Whatever you want."

———

Iris had given her word. And she would keep it. But in the days that followed whenever she talked to Laura on the phone she had to bite her tongue until she thought it would bleed. *How could you do this to me?* she wanted to scream. *Don't you know that cheating is the one thing I can't bear?*

A part of her brain knew that she was overreacting, but it didn't seem to matter. She tried to make sense of her feelings. In the evenings, after her day's work was done, she would run a hot bath and soak in it, hoping to soothe away her anger. But her longtime panacea didn't help. *Why?* she asked herself. *Why am I taking this so much to heart? Of course it is not something any mother wants to hear about her child, but I'm too upset.*

I'm worried about Katie, that's why I'm feeling this way. That child picks up on things. No matter how clever Laura is, no matter how much she thinks she is getting away with this, Katie will know something is wrong. A sensitive little girl will always know.

But even though the concern about Katie was real, Iris finally had to be honest with herself. She was furious because she felt betrayed by Laura. And so when Laura and Katie came for their usual Sunday night dinner, Iris wasn't sure how she was going to get through the meal.

———

Sunday dinner at Grandma Iris's house was usually one of Katie's favorite times. Her grandmother wasn't the kind of great cook that Mom was, but Katie liked the food she served. It was plain and easy to eat; dishes like meatloaf and baked potatoes. Most of all Katie liked the good feelings that were in the air when her mother and her grandparents were together. They really liked one another. At least, they used to. But tonight something was wrong with Grandma Iris. Katie frowned. It seemed something was wrong with someone all of the time lately. Right now, Grandma Iris was barely talking to Mom and when she did say something her voice was harsh. Grandpa Theo was watching Grandma like he was afraid she was going to explode or something, which wasn't good for him, because the doctors had said he shouldn't have a lot of stress after his heart attack.

Katie had had it. It seemed to her as if all the adults were sad and angry and there was nothing anyone could do for them. She tuned out the sound of their voices, and turned away from her grandmother's frowning face. Her eyes landed on a picture hanging in the place of honor on the wall behind the head of the dining room table. It was a portrait of her grandmother's mother—her name had been Anna Friedman—and it was one of Grandma Iris's most cherished possessions. It had been on the wall for as long as Katie could remember.

Great-grandmother Anna had died before Katie was born but there were a whole lot of stories about her in the family. Everyone said Mom was just like her. Mom certainly looked like her, Katie thought as she studied the portrait, and the gown Great-grandmother was wearing in the picture was something Mom would have chosen too. Mom liked full skirts that kind of swished around her legs when she walked and this gown's skirt looked like it would do that, plus it was pink, which was Mom's favorite color.

Her mother was sitting at the far end of the table, telling Grandpa Theo about the *Good Day USA* television show asking her to do a segment twice a week. Katie looked back and forth between her mom and the portrait on the wall. It was strange that a dead person could look so much like someone who was still alive, and you could see it in the painting. Then she remembered another painting that resembled someone she knew.

"Mom," she called out. "Did you ever tell Grandma Iris about that picture we saw in the thrift shop?"

"I don't think your grandmother would be interested in that," Mom said really fast, at the same time that Grandma Iris said, "What picture, Katie?"

"It's in that thrift shop on Madison Avenue—the one where they give all the money they make to the hospital where Grandpa Theo used to work. It's a painting of a woman and she looks just like you, Grandma."

"There's not that much of a resemblance," Mom said.

"Yes there is. You even said so yourself, Mom." She turned to her grandmother. "The woman in the picture is wearing old-fashioned clothes, and she's kind of stuck-up looking, which you aren't at all. But her face is like yours—her nose and her mouth, and especially her eyes. They're big and dark—"

"A lot of people have dark eyes," her mother broke in.

What was Mom doing? It was like she was saying Katie was a liar, when she was only reporting what they'd both seen. "But this woman's eyes were shaped like yours," Katie said to her grandmother, determined to make her point. "And you know yours aren't like everyone else's. You really should see it, Grandma."

"Don't be silly, Katie," Mom said. "She has much better things to do with her time."

But Grandma Iris said, "If Katie thinks it looks so much like me, maybe I'll make the time to see it. Where did you say the shop was?"

"It's on Madison Avenue, on the same cross street as the Metropolitan Museum. Oh, and that's another thing—when Mom and I asked the saleslady if she knew the name of the woman in the picture, she didn't. But the woman who donated it used to have a store right near where this thrift shop is now. And it was a place where you and your mother used to buy your clothes . . . it had a French name. Shay something."

"Chez Lea?"

"Yes, that's it."

"For heaven's sake," Grandma Iris said. "I haven't thought about that place in years. Yes, absolutely I will go to that thrift shop and have a look at your mystery painting, Katie. I have a dentist's appointment in the city a week from next Wednesday, and I'll do it then." She turned to Katie's mom. "It's on Madison Avenue, one block over from the museum—right, Laura?"

Mom nodded, but she looked really upset. What was wrong with her? And what was wrong with Grandpa Theo?

Suddenly, Katie realized he'd been quiet the whole time they'd been talking about the picture, and that was un-usual because he always had an opinion on everything. She turned to him. It seemed to her that his face was kind of white. And he was holding on to the side of the table.

"Grandpa, are you okay?" she asked.

He let go of the table and smiled at her. "I'm just fine, *Liebchen.*"

"You do look pale, Theo," Grandma Iris said. "Let me—"

"If you try to get that oxygen tank, I'll strangle you, Iris." He turned to Laura, "What I would like, my dear, is some brandy."

"Right away, Dad."

——

Thank God for brandy, Theo thought, as he swallowed the amber liquid Laura poured for him. It was a remedy as old as the hills—or, at least, as old as Theo's medical school days in Austria. It dilated the blood vessels and kept the blood pressure from shooting through the roof, and felt a hell of a lot better going down than holding a nitroglycerin tablet under the tongue. More important, it didn't stop a conversation the way the cursed oxygen tank did. Theo didn't want the conversation to stop. Nor did he want to draw the attention of his women to himself. He needed to think, and think fast. When Katie had started talking about an oil painting of a woman who looked like Iris he had felt like a character in a surreal play. Because if what Katie was saying was true, then in some cruel twist of fate, she and Laura had stumbled on what was probably the only evidence in existence of Paul and Anna's relationship.

It couldn't be, Theo argued to himself as he sat rooted to his chair in his own dining room, which had suddenly become as alien to him as the surface of the moon. It was just a coincidence; it had to be. The picture in that shop could not, must not, be the portrait of Paul Werner's mother. He smiled reassuringly at his womenfolk; meanwhile, in his mind he was comparing the story he had learned from Paul with Katie's stunning statement.

The woman in the picture is wearing old-fashioned clothes, and she's stuck-up looking, which you aren't at all, Katie had said to her grandmother. *But her face is like yours—her nose and her mouth, and especially her eyes. They're big and dark . . .*

I don't even have a picture of Iris, Paul had said on the fateful afternoon when he'd told Theo his story. *Do you know what I do when I want to see her face? I have an oil painting of my late mother. Iris is the exact image of her, so I look at that portrait and I tell myself it's both of them.*

And then there had been the final exchange between Katie and Iris: . . . *when Mom and I asked the saleslady if she knew the name of the woman in the picture, she didn't,* Katie had said. *But the woman who donated it used to have a store right near where this thrift shop is now. And it was a place where you and your mother used to buy your clothes . . . it had a French name. Shay something.*

Chez Lea? Iris had asked.

Yes, that's it.

That was the damning detail that Theo couldn't ignore. Because Paul had told him that the only other person in the world who knew his secret was a woman named Leah Sherman—who was the owner of the boutique called Chez Lea. Where Iris and her mother used to shop.

. . . the only way I could get any information about Iris was through Leah, Paul had said on that gray afternoon in Theo's office so long ago. *Whenever Anna or Iris came into her shop, Leah could be my eyes and ears. It wasn't enough, but it was the best I could get and I'm not ashamed to say that I let her spy on them for me.*

That was the confirmation, if Theo had actually needed it, that Katie was right about the woman in the portrait she had seen. The woman resembled Iris because she was Iris's paternal grandmother. The proof—incontrovertible and undeniable—of Anna's infidelity and Paul's paternity was sitting on a dusty shelf in a thrift shop in Manhattan. Those two had given up the possibility of years of love and joy to protect Iris, and now it seemed their sacrifice was for nothing. It would be washed away by this monstrous cosmic joke in the form of a forgotten old portrait.

Because Iris was determined to see it. Theo shook his head to clear away his ghosts and forced himself to listen to a discussion that was taking place between Laura and Iris. Iris was repeating that she was going to be in the city for her dentist's appointment and she intended to run over to the thrift shop and take a look at this strange portrait for herself. Laura was trying to convince her not to do it, but after a couple of seconds it was clear to Theo that Laura was going to lose the argument. In ten days, Iris would be staring at a portrait that would destroy all of her most fondly held beliefs—and illusions. She would be devastated. Unless Theo could find a way to stop it.

Chapter Twenty-six

Most people, Theo knew, would not have believed that he was a romantic man. A flirt, yes, and perhaps a ladies' man, although that was not a term he would have preferred. But he was sure Iris would have said that he was too practical a man of science to take on the role of Lancelot riding off on his white charger to protect his ladylove. And Iris, fragile as he knew her to be in some ways, was too practical a person to need that kind of grand gesture. Or so it had always been in the past. But now it seemed that in their old age they were to play the parts of damsel in distress and knight in shining armor after all. And if the knight did his job properly, the damsel would never know she had been saved from the dragon—or, in this case, an old painting. Because there was one fact Theo was certain about: his wife was not going to see the damn thing.

He had a brief hope that perhaps the fates might be with him, that the picture had been sold since Katie and Laura had last seen it in the shop. So on the morning after his granddaughter dropped her bombshell, he waited until Iris had left for the college, and he called the place.

"Oh yes, we still have that picture you described. It's a hard piece to sell," said the man who answered the phone. It was clear that he was more informed about the store's stock than the woman who had waited on Katie and Laura. "The artist was popular enough in his day, but that was at the turn of the century, and I'm afraid his work hasn't stood the test of time. As for the subject of the picture, she might have rated a few lines in the social columns back then, but she wasn't anyone memorable. *Sic transit gloria mundi* and all that."

"Do you happen to have the woman's name?" Theo asked.

"She was one Florence Werner."

"Thank you." But of course Theo had already known it.

"I could do some more research about the painting, and get back to you."

"That won't be necessary. But I would like to come to your store to see it. I'm in the city regularly," Theo lied. He had only gone into the city four times since his heart attack, and in each instance he'd been with Iris, who had done the driving. His family felt that he shouldn't undertake the trip often, and when he did he should not be unattended. He had agreed with them. Until now.

———

The best way to get himself into Manhattan, he decided, would be to go on the train. It would take longer than it would if he were in a car, but he wasn't up to driving. He didn't want to take any foolish risks. He would drive himself to the train station, he could handle that, then he'd let Metro-North get him into the city, where there would be taxis to carry him to the thrift shop and back to Grand Central Terminal. It would require more exertion than he was used to, but he would pace himself carefully. He had to admit that he was rather enjoying planning this outing without a babysitter. And so far it didn't seem to be doing him any harm. As he'd been making his plans, he'd waited to feel the skipped heartbeats, the pounding in the chest and the shortness of breath he'd come to know so well. There hadn't been so much as a flutter.

He set Friday as his date since Iris wasn't going into the city until the following Wednesday. She had a full schedule of classes on Fridays, so she would be out of the house by nine and would not be back until six. He'd have plenty of time to accomplish his mission.

———

"This is splendid," said the elderly man with the silk cravat who had identified himself as the manager of the thrift shop. "I'm so pleased that you've come in, Mr. . . ."

"Stern . . . off," Theo supplied. Before that moment, he hadn't thought about using an alias.

The man led him to the interior of the shop. The lighting was dim, but Theo could see that there was indeed a portrait propped up on a shelf. "Even though you told me not to, I did a little research for you. As I said, the lady in this picture was one Florence Werner, nee De Rivera. The Werners were one of the more prominent Jewish families in the city in the early part of the century." The man lifted the picture off the shelf and handed it to Theo. "There she is," he said.

And there she was indeed, with her slender neck and her narrow waist—and most of all, her face. There was no mistaking that face, with those big black eyes, that mouth, and that nose. They were the familiar, much-loved features of the woman Theo had been looking at for more than three decades.

Naturally, there were differences be-

tween Iris and her ancestress. As Katie
had said, Florence Werner did have a
grand attitude that Iris, bless her, would
never acquire. But no one who knew Iris
would ever doubt that in some way this
woman was related to her.

"How much?" Theo asked the man
wearing the silk cravat. "I want to take
this with me."

He paid the man, and asked him to
take the picture out of its heavy antique
frame—shocking the dapper manager,
who pointed out that it was probably
worth as much as the painting—but
Theo didn't want to try to lift it. The
painting itself was light and the manager
wrapped it and tied a string loop at the
top for a handle. Theo carried it out of
the store, and hailed a cab to take him
back to Grand Central Terminal.

It wasn't until he was stepping off the
train in Westchester that he felt the first
little twinge of protest from his heart. He
thought about sitting on one of the
benches on the train platform to rest,
but it was already after four and his plan
was to burn the picture in the backyard
before Iris came home. He put a nitro-

glycerin tablet under his tongue and waited until the twinge subsided. He told himself to walk slowly to his car.

The pain didn't come back until he had entered his house. It wasn't a bad pain, and once again, it vanished quickly with medication. All the same, he wished Iris were home. He thought about lying down on the couch in the living room and waiting for her. But then he remembered that he couldn't lie down yet. Because he was still holding the portrait. The portrait Iris must not see. He had planned to burn it, but now he thought he'd rather not make that kind of effort. Not at this moment. He went to the sideboard and poured himself a brandy, which made him feel better—but he still didn't want to push it.

So where to hide the portrait until he was feeling more himself? They didn't have many closets in the house, and the few they did have were small and full to the bursting point. It would be impossible to conceal a large painting in one of them. The same was true of all other potential storage places he could think of; everything was so full. He and Iris had accumulated so many things during all their years together . . . so many things . . . and so many years . . . He forced his mind to stop drifting.

The only place where the picture would be safe from Iris was the cellar. Going all the way down into it, and then climbing back up the stairs would not be a good idea for a man who had been experiencing chest pain—even though it was better since the brandy—but there was a ledge on the wall at the side of the staircase. He could walk down a couple of steps, put the painting on the ledge and come back up to wait for his wife. Two steps weren't going to hurt him, and the painting would be safely out of sight on the ledge.

The two steps didn't hurt him. But holding the painting up to put it on the ledge brought the pain back. Excruciating pain. Pain he knew from his last heart attack. His legs buckled with the force of it so that he had to drag himself back up the two steps, and he only managed to get halfway through the cellar doorway before he collapsed. But the portrait was hidden.

He came to slowly, fighting his way through mists. He was in a hospital room—intensive care. He wanted to ask what had happened but he didn't seem to be able to form words. Or maybe he was just too tired to try. Doctors and nurses came in and out of the room— speaking in soft, soothing voices. He wanted to tell them not to bother being so kind. *You don't have to be so careful with me,* he wanted to say. *I'm one of you, I've seen this happen before and I know what's going on.* He wanted to re-assure them that it was all right. *I wasn't sure it would be,* he would tell them. *Right up to the end I didn't know how I would feel about dying, but now I am dying and it's all right. I've been a lucky, lucky man, you see. How could a man who has been so lucky have any re-grets?* He would have said all of this if he could have formed the words. And then he would have told them all his wonderful, glorious joke. *I am here in this bed because I went on a lover's quest,* he would have said. *I am Tristan.*

I, the practical man of science, am Romeo. They probably wouldn't have understood, but Paul Werner would have. So would Anna.

———

Faces passed in front of him and he would have liked to have talked to them. To his sons, all three of them with desperate smiles, hoping he wouldn't see their red, wet eyes, he would have said, *Please, know what you have done for me. You healed my heart and made it whole. You gave me laughter and tears and a purpose. Because of you, my name will live on when so many others were lost. Please remember that, and don't be sad.* When Laura's bright face and dry eyes passed in front of him—no weeping for her, at least not where anyone would see it—he would have said, *Be happy, my little girl. You are good and beautiful and strong and do not be afraid of that. Be happy.*

Iris's face did not pass in front of him in the same way that others did. Hers was a constant he could see whenever he floated back to his hospital bed from the mists that were taking him away more and more. He didn't mind the mists, because in them time was fluid. Sometimes he was a boy playing outside the mountain lodge his family owned in the Arlberg, sometimes he was a young father at the beach watching Steve and Jimmy running at the edge of the ocean. In the mists he was strong again, able to run after his wayward boys, and able to tell his daughter how beautiful she was. When he came back from the mists, he was in his hospital bed, lying on his back, with machines hissing and beeping. And he was unable to say what was in his mind and heart.

He would have given in to the mists already, if it hadn't been for Iris. She sat upright next to his bed, holding her body together with her arms, with her love in her eyes. For her sake, he would have tried to stop the process that he as a doctor knew he'd already begun. *But I can't stop it, Iris. Not even for you. And the truth is, my darling, I don't want to. I'm so tired.*

But before he could float away there

was something he had to do. He had to find a way to say these words to Iris: *I told you something many years ago, while I was still so full of rage and pain. I said, "When I die, there will be no funeral for me. No rabbi who never knew me saying words that have no meaning for me, over my dead carcass." That is what I said to you, and I have never told you that I have changed my mind. I still don't believe in your religion, my Iris. But I know you will need it. So sit shiva for me, if that will help you. Say the Kaddish for me and give yourself whatever comfort you can. And then go on to smile and live. That is how you will honor me, Iris. That and remembering that I love you.* These were the words he had to say. He had to say them before he could go.

And so the next time the mists came for him, when he looked over to the place where Iris sat and saw her, he didn't let himself float away. With a huge effort of muscles and blood and nerve cells, he gathered up all his strength and he pushed the words he needed from his brain. The mists rushed at him, but he threw them back, and forced the words he needed to his lips. At his side came the sounds of machines, of the monitors attached to his body, whining out warnings. But he kept on pushing. People ran into the room, Iris's face was the color of his bedsheets, her eyes were huge and black with panic, and there was a roaring in his own ears that drowned out the monitors, but he had to keep on pushing. Had to keep on fighting. And then, finally, miraculously, a word came out of his mouth. It was only one word, not the speech he'd wanted to make. But it would have to do. Because that one word had taken all his strength. It was up to all of them now, Iris and his children, to do what they could. He was finished. The mists came back and now he let them overtake him.

—

"Oh my God," Iris cried. "What happened?"

"He said your name, Mom," Jimmy told her.

"Even though the doctors told you he'd never talk again," Steven said.

"That's how much he loved you," Phil said.

"Good-bye, Daddy," Laura whispered.

Chapter Twenty-seven

Iris wasn't going to cry. She had promised herself she wouldn't and she could keep that promise—as long as she didn't let herself think too much. That had always been her biggest failing: she thought too much. Mama used to say that, and Theo had said it more than once too. Not lately, but back in the days when they were young. The days that were gone forever. But she wasn't going to think about that. She wasn't going to think about what was gone.

It was afternoon, and her children were sitting around her in her living room, waiting for her to tell them what she wanted them to do; their father had died that morning. But she wasn't going to let herself think about that. If she did, there was a scream in her throat waiting to burst out. Her survival depended on focusing on what was in front of her. She studied her children's faces.

Steven, her brilliant oldest, was weeping silently, tears he couldn't stop pouring down. He would relive all the bad times he had caused his father, she knew, and he would blame himself all over again for them. But sitting next to him was the small tigress named Christina who would not let grief or guilt take him over. The girl Iris had learned to love would protect her most difficult child from everyone, including himself.

Iris's gaze moved on to Jimmy. Doctor that he was, he was trying to take comfort somehow from the fact that there had been little suffering, that his father's life had been extended after the first heart attack by good care. He wanted to be brave, this loving, accepting second son of hers, but he was holding his wife's hand so tightly that there was a danger that he might break the bones. That was all right, Janet was strong enough and she would keep him safe.

Phil did not have anyone to keep him safe, and that was a worry. But Phil didn't have the same needs that her other two sons did. Perhaps it was being the youngest, and always having been more on his own, or perhaps it was that he had already lost something precious and had learned to get through it. Phil would take care of himself.

That left Laura. Robby was coming back to New York to be with her. He was already on his way. That was as it should be, her husband would be at her side. The man she had married. The father of her child. Not that other one with his wild black hair. Perhaps now she would understand, this was what life was all about. When your father died, it was your husband who held you when you started to sway at the graveside, your husband who stayed with you at your mother's house on that horrible first night. He was the one you turned to with your aching, broken heart . . . And when you didn't have your husband, your Theo, with his compassion, and his humanity that had always been greater than yours . . . what did you do? Dear God . . .

No! I will not think about me. I will not let my mind drift to Theo. Because it will drive me mad. I will think about my children sitting here. I will smile at them, and reassure them.

But before she could do that, Laura started talking. "Mom, we have to make plans," she said ever so gently.

But there were no plans to be made. That had been made clear to Iris long ago. "There's nothing to be done," she told the faces surrounding her.

None of them understood. "You should call your synagogue, your rabbi will know how to advise you," Janet said.

"He'll help you with the service," said Jimmy.

"No," she told them.

"You shouldn't try to make the decisions by yourself, Mom," Steve said.

"It's the rabbi's job." That was Phil.

"There will be no service."

No one will say the beautiful words I

love, "Blessed are You, Lord, our God, King of the universe, the True Judge." No one will say the Kaddish for him. We will not sit shiva. Not for seven days, not for three days, not for one. His death will go unmarked—the man I loved for more than thirty years. I will not honor him because it was what he wanted. And suddenly, the scream in her throat had words. *And it will kill me!*

But she couldn't let the scream out. Because it would rake the roof of her house and echo up and down her quiet street and she would not be able to stop it.

"I'm going to my room," she told her children. She ran from the living room. But not to go to the bedroom she and Theo had been using for the last three years. No, not to the space they had furnished for a sick man who should not be climbing stairs every night. She ran up those stairs now, to their real room. She opened the door, and there it was—their bed.

She and Theo had bought it when they were first married, and they had never replaced it; not during their plush years when they lived in the big house they never could quite afford and not during the hard years when they had moved to this small house and had to squeeze it into the cramped master bedroom. She closed the door behind her and sat on the bed. This was where she had slept at Theo's side for more than a quarter of a century. It was where they had made love with joy and passion, and it was where they had had sex out of need and habit. They had comforted each other in this bed, they had ignored each other too, and quarreled and made up. They had conceived four children here.

There was a knock on the door. "Mom, it's Laura. I'm coming in."

Don't.

But Laura walked in and sat next to her on the bed. "What do you mean you're not going to have a service for Dad?" she asked.

Iris felt the scream starting to rise again. "Those were his wishes," she forced herself to say calmly.

"But what about you? Your faith is important to you."

Please, Laura, go away. Or keep your mouth shut.

"I'm going to honor your father's wishes."

"Dad would want you to have whatever you need. Mom, look at me, please. And listen to me. You have to do what's right for you now."

Don't say that.

"You have to do what feels good to you."

No!

"Give yourself what you need."

No!

"Dad is gone . . ."

And without warning the scream broke loose. But when it came out of Iris's mouth, it wasn't the wail of anguish she had feared, it was a cold hiss of fury. "I see," she heard herself spit at the daughter she loved. "Now I'm supposed to be like you, is that it? I'm supposed to do what pleases me, and to hell with everyone else."

Laura's face went white with surprise, and she pulled back as if she'd been hit. But Iris didn't care. It felt good to lash out, good to let all the anger go. "Now

you say I'm supposed to please myself.
I guess I should have done it all along. I
shouldn't have tried to be a good wife, I
should have slept around. Slept with
any man if it felt good to me. You know
all about that, don't you?" She watched
the realization dawn in Laura's eyes.

"Oh God," she whispered. "How did
you—?"

"What difference does it make how I
found out?" And finally Iris was screaming. "What goddamned difference? You
can't deny it."

"No. I can't."

"Get out of here."

"Mom, it isn't the way you think."

"You mean it isn't ugly and cheap?
Because that's what I think!"

"Did Daddy know?"

"Yes. I told him."

"You . . . How could you? You had no
right."

"I had every right, and he had every
right to know. He was your father. Of
course I told him."

Now Laura was crying. Well, let her.
She should cry. *Your father took your
side. But I am not going to tell you that.*

"It was none of your business," Laura sobbed.

"None of my business? You're my child. Robby has been in my family for more than ten years. He's Katie's father and she loves him. Do you think all of that just goes away because you decide that you're not in love with your husband anymore, or that he doesn't understand you, or any one of the hundreds of tawdry clichés people tell themselves when they want to justify having sex on the side?"

"It isn't like that—"

"No? What is it, Laura?"

"I don't have to answer that. Not to you, or anyone else."

"Fine, then I'll tell you what it is. It's the end of a marriage, and a home and a little girl's childhood. It's a betrayal of trust. It's cruel and it's selfish and it's cowardly. I'm ashamed of you." She was crying now too. The sobs were wrenching themselves out of some-place too deep inside to reach, and she was gulping for air. "I never thought I'd hear myself saying that, but I am. So ashamed."

"That's your problem, not mine."

"Get out of my room, Laura. Leave me alone."

The next thing she heard was the sound of the bedroom door closing behind her daughter.

Chapter Twenty-eight

In the end there was a service for Theo—a nondenominational memorial service held in the auditorium of the hospital where he had given lectures and taught several seminars. The room was big, but not nearly large enough for the crowd that spilled out into the hospital corridors. As she stood at the door greeting people it seemed to Laura as if everyone who had ever met her father had turned out to honor him. There were those he'd worked with: the nurses, doctors, technicians, secretaries and janitors at the hospital, some of them still wearing their uniforms so they could hurry back after the service to finish a shift. There were the patients he'd treated, and their families. His students came, as did many of Iris's students and colleagues. And then there were the friends and neighbors who had shared lemonade on the porch with Theo and Iris and had attended barbeques in their small backyard. On and on the people came to celebrate the life of a man who had arrived in this country knowing no one. Only in America.

There were flowers in vases—at the end of the service each woman would be handed a rose as she left the auditorium—but no music. Flowers were not a part of the Jewish tradition—but then, as Janet pointed out, this was not even close to being a traditional ceremony. In the days before the service so many friends had asked if they could say a few words that it became clear to the family that they would have to choose a list of speakers or they'd never be able to leave the auditorium. Steven gave the formal eulogy, stumbling a bit over the words he'd so carefully written, but it was Robby who had brought them all to laughter and tears with the stories he told. But then, Laura thought, Robby had always been good in front of an audience.

It felt unreal to Laura to watch how easily he slipped back into the role of a beloved son-in-law to Iris in the days that followed. He brought her cups of tea and little meals on small plates that she could nibble, and Laura could see how grateful Iris was to have him there. Laura couldn't begin to figure out how she felt about her husband's return. There was a comfort in the fact that he was a familiar presence, and he was eager to please in a way that he hadn't been for a long time. But in some ways he seemed alien, like someone she had known years ago when she was a totally different person. That didn't make any sense, she knew, but she wasn't thinking clearly. She was too raw from her father's death—and her confrontation with her mother.

That had been so ugly . . . She'd thought surely she and Iris would have to talk about it again when they were both cooler. But they hadn't, not until a week after the service. Then Iris had asked Laura to come upstairs to her bedroom—she'd taken to sleeping in the master bedroom again—when Robby and Katie were out on the porch.

"After your father died . . . that day when we came home from the hospital . . . I shouldn't have done what I did," Iris said. "I was too upset. I said things the wrong way. And it was the wrong time. I'd just lost my husband, and I was in pain, but you'd just lost your father. I forgot that. And for that I apologize."

But you're not apologizing for what you said. Laura thought. *You meant every word of it.*

"I'm sorry you found out," she said, keeping her voice cool.

"So am I. It's not something I wanted to know about you."

"I'm sure."

Laura started for the door, but Iris called her back. "When I told your father, he told me not to say anything to you. He said you'd work it out, and he had faith in you."

"But you don't."

"I'll wait and see what you do. And

you do have to do something. You can't
go on like this."

"I know that."

"Good."

———

Laura had told Iris the truth, she did realize she had to do something. She just
hadn't been able to face it. But with
Iris's words ringing in her ears, she knew
she had to go to Blair's Falls. So after
Robby had flown back to Ohio, she
booked a flight of her own, cleared her
schedule, and hired one of her workers
to stay in the house with Katie while she
was gone. Then she went into the city to
see Nick.

"I'm going to Ohio," she told him.

"Is this the scene in the movie where
you tell me that you're going to try to
make your marriage work?"

"I don't know what it is," she said and
the tears started to come. She couldn't
stop them.

"Laura, don't cry . . . Oh for Christ's
sake, what does that husband of yours
think he's doing? You've never talked
about him, and I don't want to start, but

does he have any idea what he's asking of you? Does he realize what you've accomplished here? And he's asking you to leave it all."

"I owe it to him to go out there."

"Why? What has he ever done to deserve that? Or you? And what about what you owe us?"

"Nick, I have to do this."

"Because you're married to him."

"And you said you understood."

"Well, I don't. Because he doesn't appreciate you and he damn sure doesn't love you, and . . . and I do."

"And I love you. I always will."

"But you're going out there to be with him. What happens if you stay, Laura? What the hell do I do?"

"I'm sorry . . . so sorry . . ." She was sobbing now. Suddenly the anger seemed to melt out of him and he put his arms around her and held her until the sobs stopped.

"No, I'm sorry," he said. "It's just . . . the thought of losing you . . ."

"You won't. Not ever. I promise."

"But you can't promise that, sweetheart. You never could."

He was right. She couldn't make any promises.

"It's all right." He stroked her hair the way she used to stroke Katie's when she was little and had had a nightmare. "Do what you have to do. I promised you I'd take what I could have for as long as I could have it, and that it would be worth it to me. It has been and it still is. Whatever happens."

But the pain was in his eyes.

Chapter Twenty-nine

The pretty part of Robby's hometown—
the actual downtown—had fallen on
hard times. It was the same story as that
being told throughout the country; there
was a charming Main Street, which had
been deserted by the shops and restaurants that had once lined its sidewalks.
Those businesses had relocated to the
nearby shopping mall, and the gracious old homes that surrounded the
town green had been chopped up into
rental units—usually with more people
crammed into them than they could
comfortably accommodate.

The house in which Robby had grown

up was on the outskirts of the town, in what had been a working-class neigh-borhood, but it too had gone down-hill, and Mother McAllister proudly an-nounced that she would be selling it and moving into what she referred to as a condo complex. Laura couldn't see any difference between the apartment her mother-in-law had picked out and the other two hundred and fifty units in the place, but Mother McAllister was ec-static about it. She was also pleased to see Laura, or at least she said she was, and she seemed very enthusiastic about showing her around town while Robby was working at the store. This was a new twist, since Mother McAllister had never tried to hide the fact that she wished Robby had chosen a different wife. Now, surprisingly, it seemed she wanted to be friends.

And that wasn't the only surprise for Laura. She soon discovered out that her mother-in-law wasn't the only one who had been shopping for real estate; Robby had been doing that too. And he was eager to show Laura what he'd found. On her second day in Blair's Falls he took her to see a house in a brand-new gated community built on a golf course.

"Now, this isn't going to be a historic old manse you've lovingly restored with your own hands," he teased. "But it's bright and airy . . . just wait until you see the way the sunshine pours in! Plus, buying in Windsor Estates is a great investment."

He drove past the security gate at the entrance—the real estate agent had given him a visitor's pass—and after a bit of searching, he found the house he was looking for. He led her inside, and immediately began a running commentary. "That bay window overlooks the golf course!" he cried. "All the appliances in the kitchen are brand-new."

He loved the place.

"This is just what we need, Laura. We're starting over and this house is modern and cheerful. I know Katie will love it too."

But I haven't agreed to move here.

Their next stop was Landon's Department Store—the family business. Once the store had been the anchor of the downtown, housed in a gray stone building that had been a Belle Epoque gem. Ten years earlier Uncle Dan had sold the gem, which had been bulldozed to make way for a parking lot. Now, according to Mother McAllister, gang members sold drugs there. Meanwhile, Uncle Dan had reopened the department store in a small shopping center. There was a bigger mall nearby, but it was home to several glitzy chain outlets and pricey restaurants. The shopping center was a much better spot for a family-run store that specialized in mid-priced goods and old-fashioned service. Uncle Dan knew his customers well.

Once Laura was inside the store, she realized that Uncle Dan was clever in other ways. In the back offices she was introduced to two people, both of whom held the title of senior manager. It was soon clear to Laura that their real job was to stay on top of the details—particularly in the area of finance—that would bore Robby. Her husband was the vice president of the company, but Uncle Dan had seen to it that he was supported by two professionals who knew what they were doing. Clearly, he was aware of his nephew's weaknesses.

But out on the floor, Robby was in his element. It was apparent that the staff adored him, and with reason. Not only did he know the name of every employee and the names of their family members, he had taken the time to learn something about their history as well. Laura soon had a demonstration of his main contribution to the smooth running of Landon's Department Store.

"Hi, Agnes," Robby hailed the gray-haired woman standing behind the lingerie counter. "I want you to meet my wife, Laura." He gave Agnes a big smile, which she happily returned. "Agnes has been with the store since nineteen fifty-six. Her husband, Johan, used to have a flower shop downtown; it was over on Third Street. Johan's shop was responsible for filling the planters outside the windows at our old building. Those were the days, weren't they, Agnes?"

Agnes's face was now pink with pleasure as she reminisced with the boss, and the lift she was getting from the exchange would carry her through her next encounter with a difficult customer who came in determined to buy a bra in the wrong size. It didn't matter that Robby's personal touch sprang from his own neediness, it was a definite asset to a small independent department store that was holding it's own by offering hometown friendliness.

Robby was even more charming with the customers than he was with the staff. When he stopped to chat with a Mrs. Granby—she told him her name in the first thirty seconds—who couldn't find a handbag in the color she wanted, he suggested that she come back in two weeks when they'd have a bigger selection. He also managed to learn that she had a dog named Buster and he told her about the new pet beds over in housewares. Laura was reminded of his days on the archaeological dig, when everyone had adored him. No wonder he was so happy working here.

Then suddenly everything changed.

They were walking through the shoe department when a girl called out to Laura, "Oh my land, you're the lady from *Good Day USA!*" Being recognized by total strangers was something that had been happening to Laura more and more frequently. Her wedding book had been a hit, and while she was waiting to negotiate her contract with *Good Day USA* she'd appeared on it three more times. With the result that there were now people in Ohio who knew her face. The power of television was amazing!

The girl and her companion had reached Robby and Laura. "It *is* you! I told Edna here that it was!"

Laura still wasn't completely comfortable with this kind of attention—although her publicist at the publishing house informed her that she would get used to it—but it touched her. People just wanted to be nice, she'd discovered. Plus, being polite to potential readers was good for book sales. So she began talking with the two girls— the more aggressive one was named Dottie—and within minutes there were five women surrounding her, telling her

how much they had enjoyed her TV interviews. And even though Robby was
smiling, she could feel that he was fad-
ing into the background and he wasn't
liking it.

"For heaven's sake, why is a star like
you in this little backwater town?" one
of the women asked Laura.

"I'm not a star—" Laura started to
say.

But another woman cut her off. "And
what are you doing in Landon's Department Store?" she demanded.

"Don't try to tell us you come to Ohio
to shop for your clothes." Dottie rolled
her eyes and everyone laughed.

"My husband works here," Laura
said, and knew immediately that she'd
made a mistake, as Robby stiffened at
her side. "This is his store . . . I mean,
his family . . . his uncle owns it . . ." she
stumbled, making things worse.

"I'm Robby McAllister." Robby
stepped forward with his most endear-
ing smile. "This store has been in my
family for four generations. My wife and
I are moving back here from New York,

and you know, I don't think this town is a backwater one at all."

The women nodded politely and smiled back at Robby, but it was clear that they didn't really care what he thought because it was Laura who had their interest. Two of them had read her wedding book and loved it. Then the inevitable question was asked: "Will you be writing any more books?"

"Oh yes," Laura assured them. "The next one will either be about gardening or restoring an old house."

A lively debate ensued about the merits of both topics while she felt Robby stiffen some more.

"I want to buy a copy of your book," said one of the women. "I'll run fast to the book department. Would you mind waiting here so you can sign it for me?"

"I have a better idea, I'll come with you," Laura said.

"I'm afraid we don't stock that book," Robby broke in. Then he took Laura's arm, gave the women another smile and said, "I'm sorry, but we do have to run. We're having lunch with the senior management from the store and we don't want to be late."

After the women had gone on their way, Laura said, "So why aren't you selling your wife's book?" She was only half joking.

Robby's face got bright red. "I . . . that is, everyone . . . thought . . . it would be a conflict of interest." But from his shamefaced look she knew that the decision to boycott her book was his.

—

Robby waited until they were getting ready for bed that night to bring up the subject of the move to Ohio. They were sleeping in his old room in his mother's house, and Laura couldn't help thinking that it was a pity the woman had chosen to keep it as a shrine to his promising youth. Robby had piled up academic awards throughout his grammar school and high school career, and the local newspaper had reported his triumphs. His mother had framed those articles and hung them on the walls next to his plaques and certificates of merit. Now the faded pictures of the bright-eyed boy contrasted sharply with the faded man standing in front of Laura. For in spite of his recent success at the department store, her husband's luster had indeed faded, there was no escaping that fact.

Suddenly Laura wanted her father. She hadn't felt the loss of Theo this intensely since the day he died, and it hit her like a physical blow.

But Daddy, you told Mom that you had faith in me; that I'd work everything out. I don't know if I can. I just don't know.

Robby moved to sit on the bed and gathered his thoughts. "Look, we both know what's going on here—" he began.

"We have some decisions to make."

He nodded. "Here's the way I see it. It would be a crime to let Landon's go out of family hands after all these years and there's no one else but me to run it. Besides, I like doing it. I'm good at it." He stopped and looked at her expectantly. Was he hoping she'd say that those few words had convinced her and she'd be leaving New York tomorrow? Did he think it would be that easy?

"I saw that." She carefully committed to nothing.

"I like living here."

"I know you do."

"And I'm going to be honest with you. If you wanted to stay home and take care of Katie and me, that's what I'd like best. And I think it would be good for you too. You get so involved in your work, I don't know if it's healthy . . ."

"Robby, let's not get into that."

"All right. I didn't mean to make you angry. I just wanted to say that I want you to be happy here. So even though I'd rather you didn't, if you prefer to work, I'll put up with it."

"That's big of you."

"You *are* angry. Damn it, I don't know how to talk to you anymore, Laura."

"I'm sorry. And I'm not angry. Go on."

"I've given this a lot of thought, and I know I'm asking you to give up a great deal by moving here and leaving your family and your business. But if you'll do it, then I'll live with the television interviews and the books and newspaper columns—and you can even start your business all over again and work seven days a week, as long as you don't do it in the house. I hated that so much. But I'll live with all the rest. I love you, Laura. I love you and I miss you. And I want you here with me." Then he flashed his old grin. "Hell, I'll even stock your books in my store. I'll have them put a display of them in the front window." He stopped grinning. "I'll do whatever you want if you'll just come here and live with me," he begged.

He stood in front of her, the pictures of his former self behind him on the wall. He wasn't a bad man, and she didn't want to hurt him. He'd scaled down his big dreams to small ones and now he wanted her to share them with him. He would "put up" with her dreams, and her career, and for him that was a big concession. And if all of this felt like a failure to her, all she had to do was lie and pretend she was fine with it, and he'd be happy to believe her. He just wanted her to be with him. Robby loved her as much as he was able to love anyone. It wasn't his fault that he had so little to give her. And it wasn't his fault that she'd come to know a man who did. The image of Nick's face flashed through her mind. Nick, who would never settle for second best and would always follow his dreams and make them work, just as she would. Nick, who had enough to give to last her a lifetime.

It was such a clichéd thought to be having at that moment. She was like the heroine of a hundred bad movies and plays, facing the choice between the man she loved and the man she'd married, between love and duty. And yet, like all clichés, this one was based in reality. And the potential for pain was real too. For so many people.

Daddy, I don't know how I'm going to work it out.

So she did what she'd been doing all along, she asked Robby to give her some more time.

"All right," he said. "You know I've been hoping you'd move after the first of the year, but I realize you have to get used to the idea of this, and I can be patient. Besides, your mother will need to have you around for a while after losing your dad. So take your time. I'll come back east in a month and we'll talk. And maybe, in the spring, if you're ready, we can decide when we want to put the house on the market."

He'd misunderstood her. He'd decided that she had asked for the time so she could adjust to the idea of moving. Hating herself for being a coward once again, she didn't tell him she still hadn't made up her mind what she was going to do. But there was one thing she could tell him with certainty.

"I'd never ask you to come back to New York, now that I've seen how happy you are here," she said.

———

On the last day of her visit, she had a final lunch with her mother-in-law. They went to one of Mother McAllister's favorite restaurants: a place with ruffled table mats and little salt cellars shaped like ducks. Or maybe it was swans. The food was made with lots of mayonnaise; there were gelatin salads and thick floury sauces.

Mother McAllister's affection for

Laura seemed to have waned during Laura's time in Blair's Falls. And now, as they faced each other over their sandwiches, it was obvious something was bothering her.

"I wish I understood you," she finally said.

"I'm sorry, I don't know what you mean," Laura responded. But she did. She would never understand Mother McAllister either. "I don't think I'm that complicated."

"I just don't know what you want. I know Robby thinks you've agreed to move here, but I don't. I think you're still trying to make up your own mind."

"It's a big decision to make," Laura said, noncommittal as ever. And a coward to the core.

"You could have everything here. A good home for Katie and for yourself. Nice friends. Robby has already joined the country club, and he'd take you to all the parties and the dances and show you off. He'd be so proud of you."

Laura remembered Robby telling her that his father had never taken his mother dancing and he'd never acted as if he was proud to have her on his arm. In her mind, Laura saw a young wife who knew she wasn't pretty, who was starved for affection and aching for kindness. Perhaps she could understand Mother McAllister a little after all.

"You'd have enough money to go back to New York anytime you wanted," her mother-in-law went on, "Robby knows how close you are to your family. He'd never begrudge you that. He'd never begrudge you anything."

"I know," Laura said.

If only it were enough!

The check came and Laura paid it. Then, assuming that lunch was over, she started to stand. But her mother-in-law stayed seated. "I won't make excuses for my son," she burst out. "Robby's not a strong man. He's made some poor choices, and he can't accept criticism. For years I hoped he would learn, or grow, or change . . . but now I see that he can't. He is who he is, and I love him. He seems to be content now, working at the store, and living among old friends." She paused, searching for the right words. "It's important to him to . . . to be the man, Laura. To be the breadwinner. I hope, if you move here, that will happen."

It was an honest statement from a woman who usually tried to hide her feelings. Honesty was required in kind.

"If you're asking me if I'd stop work-ing, I love what I do," Laura said. "I don't think you realize what it would mean to me to have to give that up."

"No, I don't. At your age I would have been thrilled to have a husband who was kind and loving to his child, and wanted to support me. I would have been grateful to help behind the scenes and let him be the one who was impor-tant."

You'd send me back to the Dark Ages, if you could! But Laura tried to be gen-tle. "Times have changed."

Her mother-in-law nodded. She looked down at her hands, which were folded on the ruffled table mat. When she looked up again, there were tears in her eyes. "There's never been a divorce in our family. We believe in honoring the vows we make and I don't want my son to be the first one to break his. I don't want..." she faltered, and trailed off. She stood up. She'd hung her handbag over the back of her chair. She retrieved it, opened it, looked around in it for something she did not find, then she closed it again with a snap. "I want him to be happy, damn it!" she said fiercely. Then, without waiting for Laura, she turned and walked out of the restaurant.

———

On the drive to the Cincinnatti airport and then again on the plane trip home, Laura tried to list in her mind the reasons why she should make the move. It would be a simple life, and wasn't that a good thing? Katie would go to a nice All-American school in the middle of the country, where the kids were less sophisticated than they were in a town that was close to a big city like New York. That would be good too—wouldn't it? Katie would have both her mother and her father full time. There was no doubt that that would be good. And Laura could still work, she could open another catering business and she could still write her books. Her collaborator lived in New York, so it wouldn't be easy, but it could be done. It could.

She would miss her family, but she'd only be a plane ride away from all of them. And even though Iris would miss Laura and Katie, she would support anything that kept Laura's marriage intact. And Robby would be happy at last. Laura could be a good wife, and a good daughter, and a good mother, and still do at least some of the work she loved. She couldn't have it all, but she could come close. What she couldn't have was Nick. Unbidden, a memory flooded her tired brain.

It was the day before she was scheduled for her first television interview, and she was with Nick, in his private living room behind the loft.

"I'm not sure I can do this," she'd said. "I don't know anything about television . . . or television cameras . . ."

"Don't worry about the camera, it will love you."

"I know you say I'm beautiful, but—"

He'd stopped her mid-sentence. "Let me show you something," he'd said. He led her to a wall where he'd hung a collage he'd put together of the pictures he'd taken of her sitting at her kitchen table talking about her family. "Look at this," he commanded. "Your face doesn't have a bad angle." He paused. "That's not your problem."

"What is?"

"You're too damn perfect."

"Oh for heaven's sakes, that's not true!"

"That's the way you're going to come off. You've built a successful business, you can cook and sew and do just about anything in a home, including re-store one. You write advice columns and features in magazines and you've written a book. And on top of all of that, you're gorgeous. My advice, darling? Tomorrow, be very, very funny."

"What?"

"In real life, you tell jokes about yourself all the time. Do it when you're on television tomorrow morning. Tell them about every mistake you've ever made, every disaster. Undercut the Perfect Laura image before it alienates all those women in television land who need to lose ten pounds and feel guilty about thawing out frozen dinners three nights a week."

She'd tried to argue that there was no Perfect Laura image—or at least there shouldn't be—but in the end, when she went into the interview the next morning she'd done what he'd suggested.

"And it worked, didn't it?" he'd crowed a couple of days later.

"I gather I'm getting fan mail. Thank you."

"You were the one who did it. Don't thank me."

"But you gave me the pep talk. You helped me. You always do."

Suddenly he got serious. "I feel like . . . we're in this together, Laura. It's you and me. And I like that. I like not being alone." Then he'd grinned. "And besides, you're a very sexy lady."

Now as she sat on the plane flying home, she thought once again that she was living the old weepy movie cliché about the woman trying to decide between the man she'd married and the man she loved. She despised those movies. Then she started to weep.

Chapter Thirty

Nick was out of town working on an assignment, and for the first time Laura was glad she couldn't see him. She was still trying to decide if she could actually do what Robby wanted. Or would she disappoint her mother and her husband—and herself? Would she break the promises she'd made, and give up on the marriage she'd tried to save for so long? And what about Katie? What would a divorce do to her little girl? Katie loved her dad. What would she do with Robby in Ohio and Laura in New York? How torn would she be bouncing between two houses? And two states?

When Laura thought about Katie, she'd decide that she could go to Ohio, and make the best of it, because that was the only way to keep her family together. The term "broken home" was a real one if there was a child involved; children needed two parents, and no amount of legal jargon about visitation rights or joint custody could change that simple reality. For a whole day Laura would be strong and determined. She'd remember that she was her Nana's granddaughter. But then eventually the night would come, and Nick would fill her thoughts and her dreams and her longings.

Nick seemed to realize that she needed time to herself, because he'd only phoned her twice, and the calls had been brief. Robby, on the other hand, was calling every day full of news; the house he loved so much hadn't sold yet and he'd been talking with Uncle Dan about getting a loan for a down payment until they could sell the place in New York. He'd checked into a school for Katie. With each of his phone calls she felt more trapped.

There didn't seem to be any lightness anywhere in her life. She missed her father and so did her brothers. Conversations with them often ended in tears or bittersweet reminiscing. And Iris was keeping her distance. Laura knew she was mourning for Theo with all her heart but she wasn't sharing that with her daughter. She had said she would wait to see what Laura was going to do, and she was sticking to it. If it hadn't been for Katie, and her work, Laura thought she might have climbed into bed and stayed there.

But life did go on. Katie begged for her own telephone and Laura reluctantly gave in. Steven was teaching a course at a university in White Plains, and he and Christina often stayed with Laura on the weekends. At work, Laura catered a second reception for the classical pianist she had introduced to Phil.

"Guess what?" she said to Steven and Christina as they lingered over Sunday morning coffee. "Phil has been handling Mai Ling's financial affairs, and he's done such a good job at it that she's recommended him to several of her friends. Now he's got so many of them wanting to be his clients that he's decided to quit his job at the brokerage house and set up shop as a business manager for musicians and other artists. I think he'll be happier—he loves music, and even though he says he doesn't miss it, you can tell that he does. This is a way for him to be involved with it again."

"It sounds like a great fit for him," Steve said.

"What about this Mai Ling, is she pretty? Do you think he's attracted to her?" Christina demanded.

"My wife, the romantic, wants everyone to find a mate," Steve said fondly.

"And then I want them to get married," Christina added. "As far as I'm concerned the whole world should be married. Or at least, all the people I love should be. Well, you know what I mean, Laura."

The bagel Laura was eating seemed to stick in her throat. She had to work hard to swallow it. "If you're married to the right person, it can be wonderful," she finally managed.

"That goes without saying," Christina said as she gave Steven a sweet little kiss. "You have to find the right one."

The two of them looked so happy—and so smug—sitting there together, secure in their shiny new love and marriage. *It's not so damn simple,* Laura wanted to tell them. Instead, she stood up and started to wash the dishes. *You're being an idiot,* she told herself. But it didn't help.

—

She had thought Katie was in her room while the adults were chatting that morning. But after her brother and his wife had driven away, she sat on her front porch to look out at her gardens, and Katie came outside and plopped down next to her. They sat together in silence for a moment, then Katie said, "I'm never getting married."

"What brought that on?" Laura asked, amused.

"You don't like it. Being married makes you unhappy."

Now the amusement was gone.

"Katie, what on earth would make you say a thing like that?"

"When Aunt Christina talks about Uncle Steven, she gets all lovey-dovey. You never do that with Daddy."

Oh God, she picks up on everything.

"Different people have different ways of expressing themselves," Laura said.

"Oh, I know that. But I can tell when you're not happy about something. It's different for someone like Aunt Christina. She doesn't mind living where Uncle Steve needs to live and she doesn't really have a life of her own like you do. All she wants to do is have children. That's another thing, I'm never going to have a baby."

"Now you're talking nonsense."

"No, I'm not. You had me too soon, before Daddy had a chance to get all of his education. He had too much responsibility and it set him back."

"Where did you get that idea?"

"The last time I was visiting Grandmother Mac I heard her say it on the phone to one of her friends. It hurt my feelings at first. But it does make sense.

I can see where children could get in the way."

"You never got in the way for one second! And I will never leave you alone with that woman again."

"Mom, don't blame her, she was just telling the truth."

"No, she wasn't. You have been my pride and joy, and—"

"I know all of that. But you didn't go to college because you had me. And what about Grandma Iris? She had to wait until all of her children were grown up and out of the house before Grandpa Theo would let her go back to school and have a career. That wasn't fair."

"It's true that when my parents got married, Grandpa Theo didn't want Grandma Iris to work—that was a part of the culture he came from. But she understood that and she never thought it was unfair. Besides, that was a different time. Women don't have to make sacrifices like that today."

But Katie was staring at her with clear, steady eyes. "They do if they're married. We're going to move to Ohio, Daddy told me on the phone."

"I'm not at all sure about that."

"You'll do it. And you don't want to. You're going to have to give up your business too."

"I can start over with a new business—"

"But that's not right when you worked so hard. And how can you be on television two times a week if you live out there?"

"I'll work it out. You can always work things out—"

But the big beautiful eyes wouldn't let her finish. "You can't be on television, Mom. The show starts at six in the morning and you'd have to be in New York the day before. You're not going to spend that much time away from home each week."

And that was when Laura faced it, that she wasn't going to be able to write her books either. Not if Lil was in New York and she was in Blair's Falls. And if she didn't have a beautiful old Victorian home, what would she use as a background for her photographs? And . . . without Nick, who would shoot them?

"I think marriage is okay for a woman

like Aunt Christina," Katie went on. "I love her, but she's not very smart. The thing is, you are. So it's awful for you. And I think I'm like you." She stood up. "I'm going inside," she said. "I still have some math homework to do."

Perhaps another mother with another child would have dismissed the discussion as idle chat. But Laura knew her daughter. Katie didn't just say things like this on impulse. She'd been thinking about it for a while.

What kind of lesson am I teaching my little girl? That being a wife is a trap for smart women? Is that what I want her to think? But, God help me, isn't that the way I've been feeling myself lately?

A man didn't have to make his wife choose between her work and her family. He could admire her talents and accomplishments. Nick admired hers; she remembered all the times during the spring when he would take a picture of her doing something and he'd try to get it just right because he wanted to show off her skill and talent. A man didn't have to be threatened by a woman's strength. But Robby was threatened.

How many times had she downplayed her achievements so Robby wouldn't feel inferior? How many times had she put herself down to build his ego? Was that what she wanted her daughter to see? And did she want her daughter to watch her give up everything to keep the family together?

But I have to be honest. This isn't just about Katie, or my mother, or even Robby. It isn't about living in Ohio or New York, or who does what work or brings in more money—although those things are all part of it. I made a mistake when I was nineteen years old. I was just a girl and I married the wrong boy. I didn't mean to hurt anyone, and I've tried to live with that mistake as well as I could. But I'm not going to pay for it for the rest of my life. Robby and I are wrong for each other and I'm not going to try to deny it anymore. I have a right to be happy too. If that's selfish, then I'll live with it.

So she would get a divorce. It wasn't going to be easy. Robby would probably be angry and hurt and she had never wanted to cause him pain. She herself would mourn for the past and the hopeful youngsters she and Robby had been. He had been her first love after all. But in the end she would be free.

That night she slept soundly for the first time since she'd come back from her visit to Ohio. The next day she drove to her mother's house.

———

"I wanted to tell you this in person," Laura said to Iris. "Because you're not going to like it." Her voice wasn't wavering, the way she had been afraid it might. That was good. "This is a bad time for me to be doing this, I know. It's so soon after Daddy's death. But it really can't wait. You were the one who taught me that it's best to pull the Band-Aid off all at once. It hurts, but then it's over." Now her voice was wavering after all. She couldn't bring herself to say what she'd come for, so her mother did it for her.

"You're leaving Robby," Iris said.

"Yes."

"For that man. The photographer."

"No. For me. I made the decision for myself."

"Stop it! At least be honest with yourself!"

"I am, Mom. For the first time."

"You had an affair. It was new and exciting . . ."

"It wasn't like that."

"It was more fun than being faithful to the same man . . ."

"Mom, don't do this. I'm not Daddy!"

"How dare you say that to me?"

"It's what you're afraid of, isn't it? That I'm like him?"

For a moment she was afraid her mother was going to slap her. She could feel how much Iris wanted to and braced herself for the blow. But instead Iris screamed, "Your father is dead!"

"I know that. And I miss him every day. But I also know he hurt you. And that's why you can't see that my marriage was already over when I met Nick—"

"This is disgusting! That you would use your father's memory like this."

"Someday you're going to have to forgive Daddy."

"Shut up, Laura. Just shut up. You want to divorce Robby? Go ahead. Do it. But stop telling yourself it has nothing to do with the fact that you're sleeping with someone else."

"This is hopeless." Laura was screaming now too. "I can't talk to you. How the hell could anyone talk to you?"

"Don't. Get out!"

Laura started for the door, but some last hope of making this better or easier stopped her. She turned back to Iris, and took a deep breath, then she said quietly, "I just wanted you to know what is going to happen. Robby is flying in this weekend from Cincinnati. And I'm going to tell him."

Chapter Thirty-one

Under most circumstances the TV anchorman for the six o'clock news had a calm demeanor that nothing seemed to touch. But even he seemed shaken when he looked at the cameras and delivered the breaking news of the evening: *Dr. Lester Peterson was an excellent private pilot with many hours in the air,* he informed Americans across the country. *His Cessna 172 was only two years old and it was beautifully maintained. No one knows why the doctor was trying to make an emergency landing at the Cincinnati airport when Midwestern Airlines flight 5533 was lift-*

ing off. The commercial plane was bound for LaGuardia Airport in New York, and a full federal investigation of the incident will begin immediately. At this time, all that is known is that air traffic controllers tried to warn the pilot of flight 5533 that the Cessna was in his path, but the pilot, a twenty-year veteran with Midwestern Airlines with an impeccable record, was either unable to maneuver his aircraft out of the way fast enough, or he thought the smaller plane had veered off and managed to clear his. Either way, the collision that followed was one of the worst seen in that part of the country in years. Tragically, there were no survivors from either the Cessna or the commercial plane.

As the visibly rattled anchorman was delivering this news, Laura was on her way to LaGuardia Airport to pick up Robby, who had boarded Midwestern Airlines flight 5533 an hour and a half earlier in Cincinnati.

———

When Laura tried to look back on that evening in April, one thought was clear in all the horror: *Thank God, I didn't bring Katie to the airport with me to get her father.* The rest was a nightmarish blur.

She'd left the house to drive to La-Guardia with time to spare. She'd been trying to gather her thoughts because she knew she'd be asking Robby for a divorce, so she hadn't turned on the car radio. She hadn't heard the news coming out of Cincinnati.

At the airport she checked the Arrivals board and saw that Robby's flight was delayed. That was what it said, at first. Then the listing was withdrawn and there was an announcement on the loudspeaker asking that anyone who was meeting a passenger traveling on flight 5533 from Cincinnati to report to the Midwestern Airlines ticket counter.

After that, the blur began. The soothing tones of airline officials melded with the shrill voices of loved ones demanding information. The loved ones were then rounded up and ushered into a room that was away from the rest of the airport, and—Laura realized later—away from the airport televisions, which were now reporting the accident. There were fluorescent lights and folding chairs in the room, as well as a phalanx of clergymen, policemen, a doctor, a nurse and other professionals whose job it was to help in a crisis. The white-faced families and friends stared with big panicked eyes at a man from Midwestern Airline's customer relations department as he stood in front of them and delivered the message they had already figured out but had not yet comprehended; that Flight 5533 had crashed. Cries and screams filled the room, but no one left it. The customer relations man didn't yet have any information about fatalities. So they all waited, each one hoping that somehow, some way, there had been one survivor after all. Or that one passenger on the list hadn't made it to the airport on time and had missed the flight, or that they themselves had gotten the time and date and flight number wrong. They rocked back and forth in grief, they cursed and wept and prayed, but no one left—at least not right away. Because to leave was to accept the horror; to admit that there was no mistake, no miracle and no hope.

Laura would never remember when she finally accepted it. She didn't remember calling Phil and telling him she couldn't drive home, but she must have, because he came for her. She didn't remember the trip back to her house, walking in the door, or telling Katie what had happened. She knew she'd done all of these things but she didn't remember them. She never knew how Phil got her car back from the airport. Jimmy and Janet came to spend the night, and Iris was there in the morning. But she didn't remember calling any of them. All she knew was, there were no survivors, and Robby was gone. And she thanked God that she hadn't taken Katie to the airport.

Chapter Thirty-two

After Robby's death, it was as if everything went black. The blackness was
deep and it crashed over Laura in
waves. She felt as if she might drown
in it.

*I wanted to be rid of Robby. I wanted
to be free.* And even though she knew
she hadn't wanted this or willed it, another wave would crash over her.

Mother McAllister wanted to bury
Robby in Ohio, and the minister of the
church he'd been attending had called
Laura to ask if she would give her con-
sent. *I didn't even know Robby had
started going to church again,* she

thought. *I didn't know.* But she had agreed to the Ohio burial. That was where Robby had been happy. And besides, she realized with a shock, in the whole time he'd lived in New York, he hadn't made one real friend. Nor had he felt close to anyone in her family but her mother.

All those years with no one but Katie and Mom and me. Robby, who loved a crowd and a party. He must have been so lonely. Why didn't I see that? But I know why. I was where I wanted to be and I was doing what I wanted to do. I didn't want to know if he was lonely.

She flew to Ohio with her mother and Katie, who cried together—but she stayed dry-eyed.

I can't seem to cry. But that's as it should be. I wanted to be free of him. It would be hypocritical if I cried.

Her mother-in-law had already started making the funeral arrangements when Laura arrived.

"How can she do that?" Christina demanded. Laura's brothers and their wives had driven out to Ohio for the funeral. "You should be the one planning this. You were his wife!"

But she wasn't planning to walk away from him and I was.

So the funeral was held in the church Robby had recently rejoined. Hymns Laura didn't know were sung. Words she didn't recognize were said for the soul of the man who had slept at her side for more than a decade. And after the ceremony was over, strangers who were friends of her mother-in-law provided salads made of mayonnaise and Jell-O and casseroles made with cream of chicken soup. And Laura sat in a chair in her mother-in-law's house like a guest.

"How could she treat you like that?" Janet fumed when they were driving back to the motel.

Because I didn't love him. I cared about him, but I didn't love him. And she did.

———

After she was back home in New York, she waited for the reality of what had happened to sink in. Somehow she had to comprehend that Robby's life was over, but she didn't seem to be able to do it. She remembered how he had loved Paris and couldn't make herself understand that he would not go back to see it again someday. He would not see Katie graduate and he would not walk her down the aisle on her wedding day. He'd never live in that new house he'd loved so much. And he would never know that Laura had decided that she wouldn't be living in it with him. The boy who had married her under the pear trees in her grandmother's garden when the phlox filled the air with the scents of cinnamon and vanilla would not know that she was going to desert him.

For richer or for poorer, in sickness and in health, she had promised him, but then she had wanted to be free. And now she was. The black wave crashed over her.

———

"I can't, Nick. I can't see you anymore." She was in the doorway of his loft. She wouldn't go inside. She would not stay.

"You're upset, give yourself some time."

"No!" Laura was shouting. But she wasn't crying. She seemed to have lost the ability to do that. "Don't you see? It would be like dancing on his grave."

"It feels that way now, but in a few months—"

"You want me to benefit from his death? Is that what I'm supposed to do?"

"Of course not!"

"He wasn't even forty years old!"

"I know. But for God's sake, the accident wasn't your fault."

"I cheated on him. I was going to tell him I wanted a divorce."

"It wasn't a good marriage. Stop punishing yourself."

"Guess what, Nick? Sometimes punishment is what we deserve."

"I don't think I deserve it. So stop punishing me."

"I'll do better than that. I'll get the hell out of here."

And she left him.

He called her over and over, until she changed her phone number. He must have accepted the fact that she was serious, because he didn't try to find out what her new one was.

One morning when the dry brown leaves were swirling in the wind outside her kitchen window, she called her mother on the phone.

"You'll be happy to hear that I ended it with Nick," she said, and hung up. And then, at last, she cried for a long time.

———

There was plenty to do, thank God. Katie was the first concern. She was grieving for her father, and while sometimes she needed to talk, most of the time she just seemed to need Laura's company. They went to movies and out for pizza. They watched television together and walked around their property with old Molly. And Laura went back to work. She started writing her second book with Lillian, who, thankfully, didn't ask any questions when Laura said they would have to find a different photographer. Laura signed the contract to do the homemaking segment of the morning television show. Everyone was very kind to her—she was a widow after all. Accepting their sympathy made her feel like a fraud. She felt she should confess that she had not been the loving wife they thought her to be. She should say that she was sorry for Robby because he had died much too soon, but she should admit that she had wanted to be free. And there was another man she was mourning. That was the real loss.

There was only one person who knew about that loss—her mother. And Iris would never understand it. So Laura read the warm little notes that came in the mail and she listened to the offers of sympathy and help that were left on her answering machine, and if she wished she could talk to Iris, she pushed the wish away. She couldn't afford to think about it. And she couldn't afford to think about green-blue eyes, or the man who had laughed at her jokes. And smiled at her . . . for a while.

BEGINNINGS

The past is but the beginning
of a beginning and all that is
and has been is but the twilight
of the dawn.

H. G. WELLS
1866–1946

Chapter Thirty-three

There is a saying that time heals every-thing. It doesn't. After a loss, the pass-ing of time allows you to absorb the pain, and make it a part of yourself. But after that, you can never expect to go back to being what you were before. You'll find new ways to laugh, and even to enjoy life, but you'll never do it the same way you did when you were a wife, and not a widow. As a widow you are a new person. All of this, Iris had learned; she had been a widow for a lit-tle more than a year.

It had been a year full of loss; her son-in-law's death in a random accident had been shocking and tragic. Iris had grieved and still did grieve for a life ended much too quickly. But it was the loss of Theo that had changed her into a new person, that was what had made her a widow instead of a wife. And a year after the fact she was still waiting to find out who the new Iris Stern was going to be. And how she was going to live.

Which was not to say that she was sitting in her home with the blinds drawn. She was functioning quite well. She prepared three meals a day for herself, and since she'd learned about cholesterol and salt content during the last three years of Theo's life, she was actually eating more healthily than she had when she was younger. She slept the requisite eight hours a night, and taught her classes at the college with the same focus and dedication she'd shown before she became Iris Stern the widow. She had even gone to the opera twice with Janet and Jimmy. Once they'd seen a modern thing she couldn't remember ten minutes after they left Lincoln Center, and the other time it had been *La Bohème*, which she had liked as a girl. Janet, she knew, had been worried about that choice, fearing that a tragic love story might be too painful for the recently bereaved Iris.

Don't be ridiculous! Iris had wanted to say to her daughter-in-law and, indeed, to all of her sons, who were still tiptoeing around her. *If I try to avoid everything that reminds me of Theo, I'll have to kill myself.* And after the first moments of searing pain following his death, she'd known that she would never even think about doing that. It would be an insult to Theo, and a betrayal of the love they had shared. No, she was more than willing to go on living; she just needed to know how to do it. And who she was now. Those were the big questions. She wasn't sure where the answers would come from, she just knew that she couldn't get on with her life until she had them.

The problem with this waiting period was, her senses seemed to have shut down. She didn't see colors anymore, she couldn't really hear music—*La Bohème* to the contrary—and the sensible food she was eating didn't have any taste. It was only at night in her dreams that her senses came to life—a kaleidoscope of brightly colored images tumbled through her brain, vivid reds following vibrant blues and greens and yellows. And Theo was there, pain free, and smiling tenderly at her. She knew he was talking to her, although she couldn't make out the words, but she understood, as one does in dreams, what the message was. *Make it up with Laura.* And she couldn't.

She and Laura were cordial enough, mostly for Katie's sake, although they'd made sure that Laura's brothers didn't know about the breach either. But they hadn't spoken in any meaningful way in a year. Iris didn't know how her daughter was coping with the cruel joke that had been Robby's death. She didn't know how much Laura was hurting over the man she'd given up. And she wasn't going to ask.

The last—and only—time any of that had been mentioned had been on the phone. Laura had said, "I know you'll be happy to hear that I've ended it with

Nick," and she'd hung up. And the truth was, Iris had been happy to hear it. And in the months since, she had been glad that Laura hadn't changed her mind. Perhaps a better mother would have said, *My darling, Robby is gone and your life must go on. If you have found someone to love, you have my blessing.* Well, she couldn't do that. The man—Nick—had been Laura's lover. She had cheated on her husband because of him. If poor Robby hadn't died so tragically, she would have broken up her marriage for him.

I know Laura is mourning for Robby—for the boy she married and for the father of her child. She's not a heartless witch running from Robby's graveside to her lover's arms. But I still don't want her to go to that man—not ever.

I'm not a judgmental woman. Theo always said I was too willing to see the other person's side in a fight. When the kids were young, I was the soft one. So what is it that makes me so harsh about this one human failing? Infidelity. Cheating. Having a fling. Or the uglier words people throw around these days. Why can't I understand this as I understand so much else? It's been going on since the beginning of human history, good people have succumbed to the power of sex, and it doesn't make them monsters.

I know all of this intellectually. But I don't feel it. In my gut and in my heart—and, yes, damn it, in my soul—I feel that committing adultery is vile. It causes pain, destroys trust and breaks up homes. It damages children unless they are unbelievably strong.

It damages adults too. It can turn a woman who prides herself on her open mind and gift for compassion into a woman who cannot forgive. God help me, has it done that to me?

Laura said I couldn't hear what she was trying to say about her marriage because I was afraid she's like her father. She said I still hadn't forgiven him. I tried to. And I thought I had. But maybe I haven't. Maybe that's what I'm waiting for. To forgive.

Chapter Thirty-four

The date on the train ticket stub was a year old. Iris sat at her kitchen table, studying the stub, trying to understand what it meant. She'd found it in the jacket Theo had been wearing on the day he died. Normally Laura would have been with her when she started emptying the pockets, but since she and Laura weren't talking about things that mattered, Iris hadn't told her daughter that she had finally decided that it was time to go through Theo's clothes.

She had resisted doing it for a year and she still hadn't touched his dress shirts with the monogrammed cuffs, or the good English blazers he had worn when he was working at the hospital every day. They were still in the bedroom, because Theo had arranged them in his drawers and in his closet himself, and she couldn't make herself disturb his handiwork. But her sons had started insisting that she must disturb it—and sift and sort and discard and donate. Steve had threatened to send Christina to help her if she didn't.

So she had started small, not with the bedroom closet or the bureau drawers, but with the old jacket Theo had been wearing when she'd found him unconscious at the head of the stairs leading to the cellar. The paramedics had taken the jacket off him and given it to her, and she had stuffed it in the back of the coat closet. It had stayed there, until today when she had taken it out. She had laid it on the kitchen table, and smoothed it out carefully. Then she had gone through the pockets. She'd been hoping for a stray coin, or a glove, anything he might have left. Maybe something with a lingering scent. What she had found was the train ticket stub. When she pulled it out, her first impulse had been to phone Laura. But she didn't do that anymore.

The train ticket had been used on the day Theo died. For three years after his heart attack, he hadn't gone into the city unless she was driving him because the trip was too stressful for him. He'd known he was sick, and he'd been very careful not to strain himself. But that day he had gone into New York to do . . . what? And then he'd come home and he'd gone into the cellar, knowing he'd have to climb back up the steps when he was already exhausted.

Theo had gone into the cellar from time to time, but always when she was home and could stand at the top of the stairs to be sure he was all right. He used the cellar as a storage place for the old patient files he'd kept, because every once in a while the young doctor who had taken over for him would have a question about something that wasn't in the office records. Then Theo would make his way down to the basement—slowly and carefully—to look up the information. That was what Iris had assumed had happened on the day that he'd had his heart attack. But now it seemed that might not have been the case. Theo had gone to New York earlier in the day. And he hadn't told her he was going. Iris stood up, walked to the cellar door, and opened it.

A waft of dank air came at her, and she recoiled instinctively. The cellar was unfinished, and while it was dry enough, it was dirty and dark and full of cobwebs. Theo hadn't minded it, but she'd always found it creepy and had avoided it.

Someone had closed the cellar door after they took Theo away in the ambulance on that terrible day. She had always assumed it was one of her boys, but she didn't know for sure. There was a chance that she might have looked down into the gloom of the cellar to try to see what Theo had been doing down there if the door had been open, but because it was closed it had been easy to put the mystery out of her mind. Until now. She started making her way down the staircase that led into the cellar.

The staircase had been built along

one wall, and there were railings on both sides of it. There was a good-sized ledge on the wall above the railing, where the kids used to stack their ice skates in the wintertime. Above the ledge was a light switch. In the darkness Iris fumbled along the wall and found the ledge. She moved her hand up to find the light switch. There was something blocking it. It was flat and rectangular and it felt as if it had been wrapped in the kind of heavy brown paper one used for packing things. It had been placed on the ledge and it was leaning against the wall, covering the switch. Iris was sure it hadn't been there the last time she'd turned on the light.

Taking the package off the ledge wasn't easy. It wasn't heavy but it was large and she was slightly off balance because she had to lean back to lift it. When she finally managed to get it down she had to hold it with one hand and try to hang on to the stair rail with the other. Thankfully, she only had a couple of steps to climb.

In the light of the living room she took a look at her treasure. It had indeed been wrapped in brown paper and there was an address label from a thrift shop in Manhattan stuck to one corner of it.

Bells went off in Iris's head. There had been a family dinner . . . she had been so angry at Laura, she remembered . . . and Katie had been talking about a photograph . . . no, it was a painting . . . that looked exactly like Iris. The child had mentioned that she and her mother had seen it in a thrift shop, and Iris had said she must go there and see it for herself. But then Theo had had the heart attack, and she'd forgotten all about it. The thrift shop was on Madison Avenue, she remembered that. Iris looked at the address label on the package she was holding. Madison Avenue. She began tearing off the paper.

When the picture was free of the wrapping she turned it over so she could see it. And almost dropped it in astonishment. She had expected to see a vague likeness of herself—something an imaginative little girl would make into a spooky story. But this was like looking into a mirror! The woman in the picture was elegantly dressed in

turn-of-the-century fashion, and her expression was haughty, but there could
be no mistaking that nose and mouth,
that neck—or most of all, those eyes.

*It's me. I don't know how or why, but
this is a picture of me. Or someone related to me . . . Mama didn't have any
relatives in this country, so could it have
been someone on the Friedman side?
But it must have been very expensive to
have your portrait painted . . . none of
Papa's people could have afforded it.
And none of them would have spent
their money that way, even if they could.*

*Theo put it in the basement . . . he
had to be the one who did it, that's the
only way it could have gotten there. He
went all the way into the city to get this
picture because he knew Katie was
right, it did look like me. But how did he
know it would? And then he tried to hide
it. That's the only explanation—he put it
in the cellar to hide it. From me? He
risked his life to do that . . . he lost his
life . . . but why? What did my husband
know?*

A memory floated into Iris's mind of
one of those chance meetings she and

her mother had with Paul Werner when she was a child. This time when they ran into him, his mother had been with him. The mother had been very sick and they heard that she had died soon after. Anna had been so nervous that day. But then, whenever Paul Werner showed up she was nervous . . . and different. Afterward, she had lied to Joseph and denied meeting Paul and his mother. Iris had hated Paul for turning her mother into a liar.

Later in her life Iris would come to know Paul as the benefactor who had rescued her family. Her proud husband had been willing to allow Paul to help them . . . and she had never understood why. She had never known why Theo and Paul had been fond of each other either. Before Paul died, they had been friends . . . The kind of friends who might tell each other things? Intimate things? Secrets that had been buried deep.

Iris was grasping the picture so tightly that the canvas was buckling. She looked again at the face that was exactly like her own and she thought she might be sick. Every instinct said to throw the damn thing in the trash and never think of it again. But it was too late for that, there was no way to stop thinking about this now. Besides, she had been trying not to think certain things, and blaming herself for certain thoughts, since she was a child. It was time to know the truth.

There was something else Katie had said about the portrait . . . something about the woman who had donated it to the thrift shop. She had owned a store on Madison Avenue, a high-end boutique . . . yes, it was where Anna used to buy her clothes. Iris had bought there too. Chez Lea, that was the name of the place. But what was the name of the woman? Iris remembered addressing her as Lea . . . , but what was her last name? Iris had never known it; she'd been the woman's customer, not her friend.

But they would know a donor's full name at the thrift shop. They'd know if she was still alive—she must be in her late seventies by now, if she was—or if the picture had been given to them by an executor of her estate. If she was still alive, they might even know where she lived. It was a place to start anyway. Iris put the picture down and went to the phone to dial Manhattan information.

Chapter Thirty-five

Leah Sherman—the manager of the thrift shop *had* known her last name— had sold her home on the Upper East Side of Manhattan and moved to Riverdale. To a "retirement facility" called The Colony, according to the rather grand person who had answered the phone when Iris called and asked for directions to the place.

The Colony, which was perched high on a hill in the priciest section of Riverdale, resembled Versailles. There was no other way to put it. To reach it, Iris had to drive through a stone gate, which looked like something one would find at a château in the Loire Valley, and wind her way through an acre of formal gardens that were dotted with fountains and statues before she finally reached the main building.

She stopped the car and sat still, hoping that her heart would stop pounding against her rib cage—which it had been doing for the last hour. But if anything, sitting still made the pounding worse. Before she'd left her house, Iris had had a moment of craziness, and decided to take the portrait with her. But then sanity had returned, and she'd realized that Leah Sherman would not need to see it. The woman had owned it once. And she knew the story behind it. She had told Iris she did when they had talked on the phone. That was why Iris was here—to hear Leah Sherman's story.

But now Iris was thinking maybe she wouldn't get out of the car. Maybe she would just turn on the ignition and drive back through the endless garden down to the Henry Hudson Parkway and then head back to her home, where she would be safe. Where she wouldn't have to hear whatever it was that Leah Sherman had to tell her. Iris's heart would probably stop pounding then. But she didn't turn on the ignition and she didn't drive away.

A doorman stuck his head in her window and asked her for her car keys. She heard him say something about valet parking, but she wasn't really paying attention. In a daze, she handed over her keys and he opened her car door, and there was nothing to it, she had to go into Versailles. She entered the lobby and had a vague impression of high ceilings, and walls painted in mellow shades of gold and cream. She forced herself to look more closely and saw elaborate crown moldings, crystal wall sconces and a matching chandelier. There was a velvety carpet beneath her feet, the windows were swagged with gold silk, and scattered everywhere were comfortable-looking sofas and chairs, accompanied by end tables, coffee tables and lamps. Iris started to shiver, even though it was warm in the lobby.

Leah Sherman was waiting for her, standing next to the front desk. Iris recognized her immediately; Ms. Sherman hadn't changed much since the days when Anna and Iris had shopped at Chez Lea.

She hasn't seen me yet, Iris thought. *There's still time to run.*

But she stayed rooted to the floor. Now she was shivering *and* her heart was pounding. Suddenly, Leah Sherman spotted her, and gave a little wave. It was too late to escape now. If she had really wanted to. Leah Sherman was headed her way.

The woman had never been a great beauty, Iris remembered. One of Anna's friends had said once that the proprietress of Chez Lea, with her snub nose and dark round eyes, had a monkey face. But Leah's figure had been superb, and she'd carried herself like a queen. She'd also known fashion and had been able to predict trends months before they came into being. And of course, she'd always been exquisitely turned out. She still was, Iris noted as the woman came toward her. Ms. Sherman had let her hair go completely white and was wearing it in a flattering bob that curved forward to brush her jawline. Her hands were beautifully manicured, and her makeup had been expertly, but discreetly, applied, as was appropriate for a woman her age. She was wearing gold jewelry—a wide bracelet and a matching chain around her neck—and a lilac-colored suit that set off her white hair and dark eyes and was cut to showcase the fact that her legs were still very good indeed.

As she approached Iris, the ebullient smile Iris remembered from the old days was missing. But that was to be expected. She knew from their phone conversation what Iris wanted to discuss.

"Mrs. Stern," Leah Sherman said. "I'd have known you anywhere. You haven't changed."

"It's Iris, please. And neither have you."

"Thank you. And I'm Leah." They stood facing each other, not knowing what to say next for what seemed like a very long time. Finally Leah led the way to the elevator.

"This is a beautiful place," Iris said—to

say something—as they were whisked up to the sixteenth floor.

"I think so. I moved here a couple of years ago, after my husband died. I had a large house in town and it was too much for one person. This is what they call a progressive care facility—right now I have my own apartment and total independence, but if I should start to need help as I get older, I can move to another area where there's more assistance. The people here will decide when or if that's necessary for me, which is why I chose this place. I want to spare my stepdaughters from having to make that choice for me. I've seen what that can do to families."

"That's very thoughtful of you." Talking seemed to help stop the shivering, Iris had discovered. Nothing could stop her pounding heart.

"Well, as you said, it is a lovely place and I enjoy being with other people. I was so isolated in my house, I'm finding I like apartment living."

Leah had a penthouse suite—there were two of them. Each had two bedrooms and two baths, Leah told Iris, and a terrace that wrapped around three sides of the apartment.

"We residents furnish our apartments ourselves," she added as she ushered Iris into a living room that somehow managed to be both grand and cozy. And very feminine. "So even though this is a much smaller space than my home, I was able to bring most of my favorite things with me." She gestured to a painting on the wall that Iris was pretty sure was an original Matisse.

Leah didn't offer the usual polite tour of her home and Iris didn't ask for one. The business ahead of them was serious. They sat on the comfortable sofa in the bright living room, and Leah drew in a deep breath. "So you want to know about that portrait you found."

I'll always remember this moment, Iris thought. *For the rest of my life, I'll remember sitting here on this sofa with the sunshine streaming in those windows, and the tree branches framing the Hudson River in the background.*

"I'm sure you've figured out by now that the story behind the picture has something to do with Paul Werner," Leah said.

Iris nodded. She couldn't answer out loud because her lips were too stiff to form words.

"I knew Paul all of my life," Leah began. "His aunt adopted me when I lost my own mother as a child, so I was almost like family. Paul was a good man, he was kind and generous—well, you know all of that. But when he was young, he was too afraid of disappointing people. It was his big failing. In his twenties he was engaged to be married to a girl he'd known all of his life. But he fell in love with someone else. She was a maid in his mother's house. She was beautiful and smart and full of life and curiosity—as Paul was. As his fiancée was not."

"I see," Iris managed to say through her stiff lips.

"Paul didn't have the courage to end his engagement and he married his fiancée. The girl he loved married someone else too. I know that Paul was never really happy in his marriage. I can't tell you what the girl's marriage was like.

But I do know that the feelings she and Paul had for each other were the kind that last a lifetime."

Iris nodded.

"Paul and the girl went their separate ways for a few years. But of course he never forgot her. Not ever. One day she came back into his life—she literally showed up on his doorstep. She had an appointment to see Paul's mother, but she'd gotten the date wrong and Paul's mother was out of town. Paul and the woman he had never forgotten were in the house alone together." Leah paused.

The hard part is coming. She's trying to find the best way to say it, Iris thought. "What happened?" she asked in a voice that seemed to have gotten steadier for some reason.

"Paul and . . . the woman . . . they made love that afternoon. There's no other way to say it. It was love and it was inevitable. For those two people it had to happen. I know that may be hard to accept." She stopped. She was looking at Iris, waiting for permission to continue.

Iris gave it. "Go on."

"A baby was born as result of that afternoon. Paul was never acknowledged as the father and he and the mother kept their secret for the rest of their lives. For Paul it was a heartbreaking decision, but they both believed it was in the best interest of the child. Years later, when that child and her husband were in trouble, Paul told the husband who he was and offered to help them. Which he then did."

"Paul's child was a girl," Iris said softly.

"Yes."

"And her husband knew the secret."

And protected her from it for all those years. Oh my darling.

"Paul's wife died, and so did the husband of the woman he loved. But even though they were both free, they stayed apart."

"Because the child . . . their daughter . . . might have figured out the truth."

"They were afraid it would hurt her too much if she knew."

Of course they were. I wonder if they

were right. I can't tell right now, I'm too numb.

Leah had finished her tale. Iris stood up. But then she didn't know what to do next. There was no etiquette, no code of manners that would cover this. She sat back down again.

"Is there anything else you want to ask me?" Leah asked gently.

"I don't think so."

"Would you like me to tell you the woman's name?"

That would be an afterthought at this point. But so many sacrifices had been made to keep this story secret. A man had gone to his grave without ever revealing that he had a child and grandchildren. Another man had risked his life. And a woman . . . a beloved mother and wife and grandmother . . . had given up the man she loved.

"No. I don't need to hear you say the name," Iris said. She stood up again. "Thank you. You've been very kind."

Leah walked her to the door. But instead of opening it, she said, "There's just one more thing. Paul and this woman were special. They had the kind of connection that is very rare, they truly were soul mates. I knew them both so I can say that. I'll always wish they could have had a few years together. As far as I'm concerned, love like that shouldn't go to waste. But they were honorable in ways that I'm not. And it was very important to them to feel that they'd done the right thing."

"I understand," Iris said.

She drove back home slowly. She felt as if she'd been in an accident, or was recovering from a serious illness and needed to be careful because she was still wobbly. When she was home, she made herself a cup of tea and ate a slice of toast, and noticed again that it was food for a convalescent.

She sat in her living room and waited for the emotions to come. She waited to feel the rage and the pain sweep over her and drown her. Her whole life had been a lie: she should feel crushed by that. She should be destroyed.

Instead she felt lighter. Because she realized that nothing important had changed. Joseph Friedman had been her father and she still loved him with all her heart. She still had the same history, the same family, the same heartaches and joys. None of it had been taken away from her. All that had happened was, the doubts and suspicions that had haunted her since she was a child had been validated. She had been validated. And she finally understood her mother.

She thought of the girl Leah had described, the beautiful, smart maid who was so curious and eager for life. That girl had been so young—little more than a child—when she'd fallen in love with a rich boy she couldn't have. But the child had made a life for herself anyway. She'd made her choices, and she'd lived the consequences of those choices without complaint. Brave child. Brave woman. *My mother.*

I'm so glad I found out now and not earlier. Everyone was right, there was a time when this would have devastated me. But now, I'm just grateful to know. Now, at last I can empathize. Empathy is the secret of survival. Because life is not fair and love is almost impossible unless you can put yourself in another's shoes.

As she thought these things, suddenly Iris knew her time of waiting was over. She knew now who the new Iris Stern was and how she would live. The portrait was where she'd left it, leaning against the couch. She rewrapped it and took it back to the cellar, down to the filing cabinets full of Theo's old medical records. She placed it there, sandwiched between two of the cabinets so it wouldn't get warped. She couldn't hang it anywhere in the house, but she didn't want to destroy it either. This seemed to be a safe place for it.

Having disposed of the portrait she went up to her bedroom. She walked to the closet, and looked at the clothes hanging on Theo's side. She opened his bureau drawers and looked in them too. Then she began emptying them. She pulled the shirts out gently, marveling at the silky cotton her husband had so loved, running her fingers over the monograms, which had always seemed a little vain to her but they had pleased him so. Oh he had been a peacock in his way, her Theo.

She took blazers and suits and ties

and sweaters and pants off racks and shelves and hangers. She breathed in the scent of their owner, and then she packed the clothes in boxes—some for her sons, some for dear friends, the rest for a homeless shelter Theo had supported. She had thought once that she would need help in making these decisions, and perhaps the old Iris would have. The new Iris did not hesitate as she put a cashmere vest in a box for Phil and a blazer in another box for Jimmy.

She opened a drawer and found cuff links and tie clips and wristwatches—Theo hadn't been a man to wear jewelry, so there were only a few pieces, but they were all made of eighteen karat gold. These treasures she would not give out right away. She would wrap them as gifts and over the years she would hand them out on special occasions, thereby keeping Theo's memory alive, and giving herself pleasure.

The bed was covered with the boxes she had filled. She would have to move them to the floor so she could sleep tonight. In the morning she would tell the recipients the boxes were coming and send them on their way. But now as she looked at the bed, she said out loud what she had been thinking for the past hours.

"I forgive you, Theo. I thought I had before this, my darling, but I hadn't. Not truly. People love, and they betray love, and then they love again. No one understands love and only a fool would claim to. All we can do is accept each other as we are. And forgive each other."

—

It was lunchtime, and she was very hungry. She made herself a sandwich with some cheese she found in the refrigerator and ate it quickly, because her day's work wasn't done yet. There was a wrong she needed to make right. She had to do it for her mother's memory. She had to do it because she was a mother herself.

Anna had loved a man for almost sixty years and had never known the simple happiness of going to sleep in his arms at night and waking up next to him in the morning. She'd had a few desperate moments of joy, and many more of guilt and regret. Perhaps that had been the only way for her, coming from the time and place she did. But the world had grown gentler since then. For the second time in as many weeks, Iris called Manhattan information, and then drove into the city.

———

The photographer's studio—Nicolas Sargent was his name—was in a trendy part of town, on the West Side. Iris took her chances that he might be there and he was. He recognized her as soon as he opened the door. And he was shocked.

"Mrs. Stern! What . . ." Then shock gave way to fear. "Laura! My God, is she all right?"

"She's fine," Iris said. "Physically, she is. But she's miserable."

The fear vanished. She watched his eyes—they were greenish-blue and quite expressive—go blank. "There's nothing I can do about that."

"Don't be ridiculous. Of course you can."

"She told me she didn't want to see me again. We're finished."

"She didn't know what she wanted. She'd just lost her father and then her husband died. On top of all that she felt guilty because she'd wanted a divorce. There was no way she could think clearly."

Hope sprang in his eyes and the life came back into them. They really were very expressive. "Are you saying she's changed her mind?"

"I'm saying that next Friday morning she'll be appearing on that show, *Good Day USA*. When she's going to do one of her segments, she hires a sitter for Katie and comes into the city the night before. The show puts her up in the Hotel Mayfair. It's next door to the studio, on 66th Street. She usually checks in at about five in the afternoon, so you can probably find her in her room by five-thirty."

"Mrs. Stern, Laura told me she didn't want to see me again."

"So? Are you going to let her get away with that? Your generation is so strange. I can't imagine my husband allowing me to push him aside like that."

"Excuse me, I'm not allowing her to do anything. I am simply respecting her wishes."

"Oh right. Because you are both equals and sweeping her off her feet would not be politically correct. Forgive me for saying so, but that sounds as romantic as a tub of wet laundry. I know it's not fashionable today but there was something to be said for the man who took charge. And for the man who did what he felt and not what he thought."

The green-blue eyes were sparkling with laughter now. He had a sense of humor. Good, he was going to need one.

"You think I'm being too cerebral, do you? I should try the caveman approach?"

"I would have said Prince Charming, but that's my generation's fantasy. However, you seem like a resourceful young man, so I'm sure you'll figure it out. Remember, Laura comes into town next Thursday night."

Next, she drove out of the city, past her own exit on the highway. She kept going until she had reached the old Victorian house that had become so well known to the readers of Laura McAllister's book on the do-it-yourself wedding.

"Mom!" Laura said. It was the second time that day that someone had been shocked to see her. "I wasn't expecting you."

"I know. But I have something to say to you."

So they sat in Laura's kitchen and wrapped their hands around thick mugs of the excellent coffee her daughter had made. Her perfect daughter who always did everything so well. Laura had a look Iris remembered. It was the one she'd seen in the mirror when she and Theo were estranged. Of course, there was a difference—Iris had let herself go during those times, neglecting her clothes and sometimes even basic grooming. Laura was far more disciplined. Her shiny hair was brushed and tied off her face with a ribbon, her makeup was in place and she was wearing one of her signature brightly colored coveralls. But her eyes were the giveaway. The light that had always glowed in them had been extinguished. She looked weary and pale beneath the carefully applied cosmetics. Iris remembered what Leah Sherman had said about the beautiful young girl who had fallen in love with Paul Werner.

"There's something I want you to see," Iris said. And from the side pocket of her purse she drew out a letter. The envelope was worn, and it had never been sealed. There was a name on the front. *Iris* had been written in old-fashioned spidery script.

"Your grandmother left this for me to find after she died," Iris said, and she handed the letter to Laura, who opened it silently and started to read. As Iris knew, the first page of the letter was tender but it was not that important, Anna had simply written it to express her care and devotion for her daughter and grandchildren. It was the last paragraph of the second page that Iris had read so many times she'd memorized it.

Loving is all there is, her mother had

written, *when you look back and count up. Treasure it, for God's sake, because it's all there is. Everyone isn't lucky enough to take it when it's offered or to hold on to it when one has it. Things get in the way, circumstances that can't be helped, or sometimes our pride and resentments, our absorption in self or a mistaken sense of duty. Dear Iris, don't let that happen.*

Laura finished reading and looked up at Iris. "Why did you give me this?"

"Because it could have been written to you. But I'd add one thing. Guilt can get in the way too if you let it. If you wallow in it."

"I have reason to feel guilty. I've made some big mistakes."

"As long as we're alive we're all going to make them. It's about the only guarantee we get. I know I've made some that were terrible. I wanted things from you that weren't fair to ask. I forgot what's important. You're a beautiful woman, Laura, you're strong and honorable. You have a right to be loved. That's what your grandmother was saying to me, and that's what I'm saying to you."

That was when her daughter started to cry. "Sometimes it's too late, Mom," she said.

"And sometimes it's not. Now, I want you to do two things: keep that letter and never forget what it says . . . and next Thursday night when you hear a knock on your door at the hotel . . . open it."

———

After her mother was gone, Laura looked down at her grandmother's handwriting on the well-worn pages she was still holding. For so much of her life she'd thought Nana was the perfect wife, and the pleasant, tranquil relationship she'd seen in her grandparents' home was the only kind of marriage worth having. *Nana was so content, she never seemed to be depressed or angry. I thought she had all the answers, I wanted to be just like her. But this letter . . .* Laura looked down again at the last paragraph. *Every sentence is full of regret. The paper almost aches with it. Cheerful, cool Nana regretted . . . what? A passion she never had . . . or did she have it and lose it? Or am I reading all of that into her words because now I know I don't want to be like her anymore.*

I want passion. I want a love that touches my mind and body and soul. My parents had it at their best, but they could be destructive too. Now I know it doesn't have to be like that. I can have my own way of loving and it will grow and change as I do. I can find a man I can laugh with, my lover can be my best friend. I don't have to be my mother. And I don't have to be Nana. Not anymore. It's my turn now.

Chapter Thirty-six

The rich buttery smell of roasting chicken was in the air. The cup for Elijah was in the center of the table, the matzo was under the embroidered cover that had been newly purchased for this day. The china on the table was new too, as was the Seder plate. Janet had offered to lend Iris one, but Iris had wanted her own. What was the point of having your very first Seder in your own home if you weren't going to use your own Seder plate?

"Grandma, isn't the gefilte fish supposed to hold together?" Katie called from the kitchen. Katie had been staying with Iris for two days to assist with the cooking of tonight's feast. She'd volunteered for the job, saying, "You've never done this before, Grandma, and neither have I, so we won't feel bad when we mess up something. If we had Mom around, she's so good at all of that cooking stuff, we'd be scared to try things." Besides, Laura hadn't volunteered to help.

And as it turned out, Katie had been right, she was the perfect assistant for Iris, because she had as little natural aptitude for "that cooking stuff" as Iris did. So they'd giggled at themselves for two days as they baked and boiled and fried and sautéed.

"I think maybe doing domestic things well skips a generation, Grandma," Katie had sighed after they'd both forgotten to take the hard-boiled eggs off the burner, and the water had cooked down to nothing in the pot. "You and I are kind of alike."

"I'm sorry about that," Iris said with a grin. "I wish you'd inherited one of my other traits."

"I'm just going to have to be very

good at something else, because I don't think I'm going to get much better at cooking."

She is like me, Iris thought. And that made her smile. *She has an unusual mind, and so did I. But she's not afraid like I was. She has a remarkable mother.*

Iris hurried into the kitchen to check on the gefilte fish, which indeed had disintegrated into a disgusting-looking mass. "All right, one less course to serve," she said as she threw it into the garbage. "Thank God for the chicken. I think we did well with that, at least."

"And the potatoes," Katie added. "We are excellent at roasting potatoes."

And if the rest of the dishes turned out to be a disaster when the family sat down at the table, Iris had the name of a deli on hand and she was ready to order in. She was making her own traditions today.

She pulled the chicken out of the oven, and found a place for it on the countertop laden with food. She looked around the kitchen happily. This was what she'd been wanting for years. She'd cleaned the house until it sparkled, she'd run around the grocery store picking up all the special holiday foods and she'd been cooking steadily for the last two days. Now, at last, everything was ready.

I'm going to have the Seder in our house, Theo. I'm very happy about it.

"We should go upstairs and change our clothes, Katie. Do you want to run over the questions first?" As the youngest child present, Katie would be asking the four questions that night.

"No, thanks. I know them by heart."

Katie was using Laura's old room, but after a few seconds she knocked on Iris's door.

"Could you help me with my buttons, Grandma?" she asked. She was wearing a rose-colored dress with a lacy jacket that buttoned at the neck. It was a little old-fashioned—not enough to be dowdy, but it was unique. Like the small person wearing it. It had been chosen by a mother with an unerring eye.

Iris tended to the buttons. "There you go," she said. But Katie didn't move.

There was a troubled look on her face. Clearly, she hadn't come in just because she wanted help fastening her jacket.

"Is something wrong, sweetheart?" Iris asked. "You can tell me anything."

"Yes, I know. But this is a little hard." The troubled look intensified.

Dear God, what can it be?

"Don't be afraid, Katie. It's always better to say it."

Katie nodded, then she blurted out what was bothering her. "When I heard that Daddy had died, I felt bad, Grandma. And I still miss him every day."

"Of course you do, sweetheart."

"But at the same time, I was so glad we weren't going to have to move to Ohio! That was one of the first things I thought about."

"That's natural. You didn't want to leave your home and your friends. Just because you thought of it at that moment, that doesn't mean you didn't love your father. Or that you wouldn't have brought him back if you could."

Katie thought about that for a moment. "Yes, I would have moved to Ohio if it would have brought him back. But I like it here. I like being a part of days like today."

Iris leaned down to hug her. In a few years Katie would have her own life and she might not want to be a part of a day like today. But now . . . now her grand-mother could still hug her. "I'll tell you a secret," Iris whispered into Katie's ear. "I was glad for a second when I heard that you weren't going to Ohio too."

"I'll be spending a lot of my vacations with Grandmother Mac in Blair's Falls, though. I already went there for half of last summer. Mom says she doesn't ever want me to lose touch with my fa-ther's family."

"Your mother is a good person."

"Yes, I think I'm very lucky."

—

When they had finished changing into their party clothes, they went back downstairs.

"This feels funny," Katie said. "There's nothing left to do until everyone gets here."

"Everyone" meant the family, of

course. Jimmy and Janet would be coming with Rebecca Ruth. Jimmy would sit at the head of the table and act as leader. Iris could have done it herself, but she felt shy about it. Phil would be bringing his client Mai Ling, who was as lovely as she was talented. Iris had hoped that something more than friendship might start blooming there but so far her son hadn't lost his heart. However, he was a happy man these days because he loved his work. Being a business manager to several of the more exciting young classical musicians on the scene suited him perfectly. Steve and Christina would be coming up from Washington, and they had told her they had an announcement to make. Iris was almost positive she was going to be a grandmother again.

"I'm getting a little nervous," Katie whispered.

"Me too," said Iris.

"Maybe we should check the soup again."

But the doorbell rang. "This is it!" Iris said to Katie, and she moved quickly to open the door.

"*Zissen Pesach,* Mom," Laura said. "Happy Passover."

"*Zissen Pesach,* darling."

Laura stepped inside and looked around. Iris followed her gaze from the vases of fresh flowers to the sofa, which had been reupholstered in honor of the day. The air was as fragrant with cooking smells as Iris's mother's kitchen had been. Laura's eyes sparkled—it could have been tears or happiness or both. "Dad would be proud of you, Mom."

"I hope so." Iris had to blink away tears of her own. She leaned in to kiss her daughter on the cheek. She was so beautiful, this child of hers. The sad look was gone from her eyes, and she was glowing again.

Iris turned to Laura's companion. "Nick," she said. "Welcome. Come on in."

ABOUT THE AUTHOR

BELVA PLAIN is the *New York Times* bestselling author of *Evergreen, Random Winds, Eden Burning, Crescent City, The Golden Cup, Tapestry, Blessings, Harvest, Treasures, Whispers, Daybreak, The Carousel, Promises, Secrecy, Homecoming, Legacy of Silence, Fortune's Hand, After the Fire, Looking Back, Her Father's House, The Sight of the Stars,* and *Crossroads.* A Barnard College graduate who majored in history, Belva Plain lived in Millburn, New Jersey, where she and her husband raised three children. She died in 2010.